YES, YOUR EXCELLENCY

V. E. O. Stevenson-Hamilton

YES, YOUR EXCELLENCY

V. E. O. STEVENSON-HAMILTON

Thomas Harmsworth Publishing
London

© 1985 V. E. O. Stevenson-Hamilton

First published 1985

Stevenson-Hamilton, V.E.O.
  Yes, Your Excellency.
  1. India—Politics and government—1919-1947
  I. Title
  325'.341'0954   JQ224
  ISBN 0-9506012-9-2

ISBN 0 9506012 9 2

Printed in Great Britain at
The Pitman Press, Bath

for Valerie

Photographs are included in this book
which are reproduced by kind
permission of The British Library
(India Office Library and Records).
Thanks are particularly extended
to Mrs. Patricia Kattenhorn for
her help.

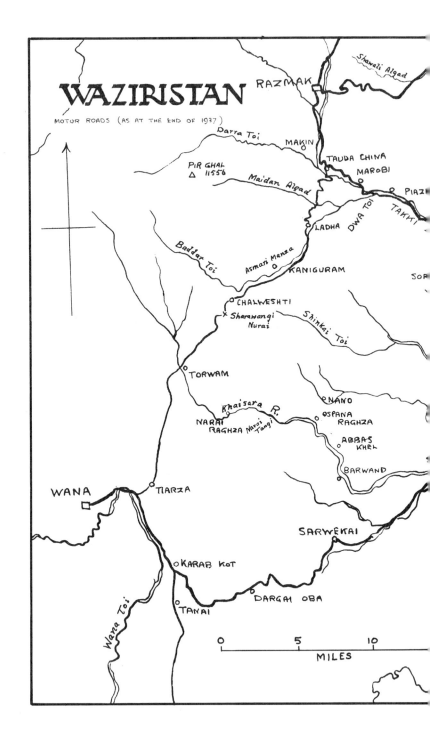

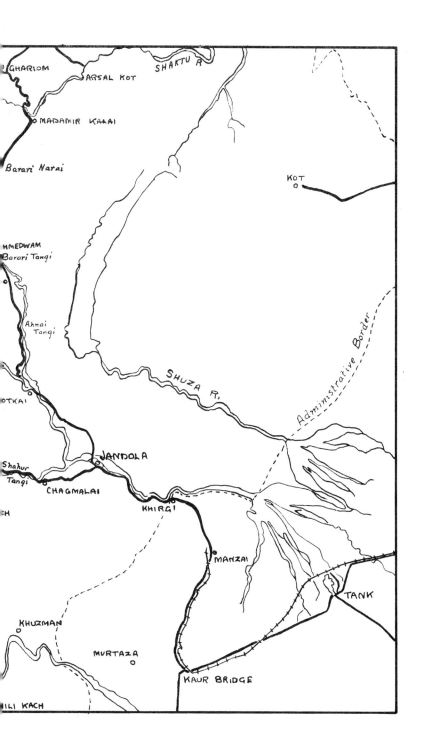

I

To travel hopefully is a better thing than to arrive

'But darling, everyone else went on deck hours ago; I've already locked that difficult one, why did you have to open it again?'

'You'll 'ave to 'urry ma'am,' interjected the cabin steward.

'Jaldi, mem-sahib' chorused a trio of slightly odiferous official baggage coolies, poking their dusky faces around the lintel of the door. My mother had her own interpretation of military discipline as it applied to her, based on being a very pretty woman.

It was the last voyage of that particular trooping season, and the ship lay heaving in the monsoon swell in Karachi roads. The troops were on deck waiting their turn to descend the swaying companion ladders to the tenders waiting below.

Everyone was glad to disembark; once Port Said with its vendors of dirty photographs, its conjurers who produced eggs from unexpected places in the clothing of their audiences, The Golden Horn etc, etc, had been passed, boredom had set in.

The ship's bell struck on the appointed hour for the officers' families to assemble and my father made yet another of a series of attempts to organise my mother.

'All right, I suppose I can trust you to carry him down into the boat on your own. I'll be on your heels,' she said.

My father was the last to board the tender, already filled with officers and their wives; friendly feminine arms reached out for *me*. Looking around he realised that mother was not with him. He gazed agonisedly up at the deck but all he could see was a line of diced Glengarries above the grinning faces of his own particular Jocks.

'I can't wait any longer, sir!' bellowed the cox'un, 'Ill 'ave to cast off; your missus can come with the next party' – and cast off he did, for what sensible young subaltern risks courting the unfavourable notice of senior wives whose paths are bound to cross his again sometime? He saw some eyeing him disapprovingly, sitting grim and green faced round the gills, striving desperately to retain their dignity and charm for just those few more essential minutes.

Once on terra firma, I was as swiftly handed back.

'Sorry, must go, you'll only have to hold him for a few minutes and it's time you learnt anyway. No! That way up! See you at Indian Cavalry Week in Lahore! Bye-Bye! Be good!'

All his female acquaintances were making a bee line for the railway station, with the obvious intent of bullying the unfortunate Railway Transport Officer.

Well, thought father, the helpless male pose had served its purpose for as long as could be expected; but he now had a foreboding, nature being what it is, of the next likely event and his complete and total incapacity to deal with it.

He cast a desperate glance across the muddy yellowish coloured sea towards the ship, only a cable's length away. Surely the tender was taking a long time to come back. Where was it? Good God! It had not even started. Here it was, empty, tied up to the quay below him. What an infernally inconvenient time for a tea break. He walked over to an officer who was wearing the brassard of the embarkation staff and who was strolling away. 'Tender? You're out of luck, that was the last trip today, look at the sea rising, the Port Authority says it's getting far too rough and they won't risk it. Don't worry, we're arranging onward rail transmission tomorrow for everyone left on board, come back about 7.30am.'

'But dammit, this bloody brat is only two months old, my wife is still on board and I don't know a soul in Karachi, you've got to do something.' 'There's a transit camp where you could probably get a bed, but they certainly would not stand for a baby. I'd help you myself but I am a bachelor.' Backing further away from father he seemed to be making some serious resolution.

My father's immediate reaction was to consider the pros and cons of throwing his son and heir into the sea, with the pros definitely uppermost. What probably annoyed him most was the certainty that mother would be on deck, watching him and laughing her head off.

As he paced up and down a desperate hope was born of despair. India was proverbial both for the unfailing warmth of her hospitality and for her marked preference for improvisation; let her now prove herself, unfair a test though it might be.

Hailing a tonga, he directed the driver to proceed with all speed to that magnificent edifice, that symbol of the Raj, that Eastern bastion of male segregation, the great and glorious Scinde Club itself. It was the only place in Karachi of which he knew the name. He half hoped it might reciprocate with the Punjab Club of which he was a member.

Luckily, it was a hot mid-afternoon on a week day. As they left the sandy street with its strings of plodding baggage camels and rattled up the Club drive between the beds of cannas, no military band was blaring brassily on the lawn, no flannelled figure was wandering to or from the tennis courts, no Qu'hais sat in little circles of cane chairs on the grass sipping their gimlets, only an old gardener was plugging breaches in his maze-like canal system which conducted the dirty bath water from the back of the building to each of his flower beds.

The lazy silence was broken only by the universally accustomed shrieks of one of the Indian cuckoos, the brain fever bird, mingled with the locally unaccustomed shrieks of myself.

Tucking me under his arm, rugby football fashion, father hurried through the dim smoking room peering nervously left and right, fearful of some lurking denizen, perhaps one of the

3

Club Committee, who might be changing a library book.

The comparative safety of the bar once gained he felt safer, no one would come in at this time of day. By not the flicker of an eyelid did the grave Punjabi Mussulman barman betray any surprise at the sudden entry of a strange Highland officer in full uniform with a baby under his arm. He would no doubt be enlightened in due course. One must never hurry the West.

Not a shadow clouded the tranquility of his grey eyes as father poured out his story. Unfortunately, the Secretary Sahib was on leave; would the sahib-bahadur forgive him for a moment while he thought?

Both attracted and no doubt repelled by my continued screams a couple of startled khidtmagars now appeared, their accustomed siesta rudely ruined. A short conference ensued in muted Punjabi; the honour of the Club was at stake! continued whispering; their faces lit up; the barman actually smiled; I was suddenly whisked with a quickness that deceived the eye over the bar and out of sight and sound. My father goggled, one moment I was there and the next I was not, it was like the Indian rope trick.

'If the sahib-bahadur would care to come back to the Club in the morning at any time of his convenience, before the bar opened might be best, the baba-sahib would have been fed, rested, and in a condition to be received back into the bosom of his family.'

My early memories are mostly equine, of my father's polo ponies kicking some retainer and of falling off my own little steed.

My mother kept a pet lion at one period but I don't think we were encouraged to meet; I don't recollect meeting my mother much either. All was fine until I was nearing four when it was essential to send children home because of the Indian climate. This posed a problem as my only relations – my elderly and unenthusiastic maternal grandparents living in England, an odd bachelor uncle living alone in a mud hut in Africa, a very odd

4

aunt breeding horses in the Argentine and a paternal grandfather aged seventy-three living alone in a barely modernised mediaeval Scottish tower in which, incidentally, I had been born – none of them evinced the slightest wish to have me. There was absolutely nowhere for me to go.

My parents could hardly realize their luck when the brother-in-law of an officer in the regiment had a most opportune nervous breakdown in the course of which he jumped out of his nursing home window. Cables sped and with unanimous approval I was sent off to Scotland to console the sorrowing and childless widow.

My new honorary Aunt Margaret, with a heart of pure gold but the unfortunate characteristics of some of the Saints spared no effort to make a happy home for me, helped by plenty of money. I remember a pair of beautifully groomed chestnut cobs, high stepping in unison, drawing in fine weather a smart Victoria, and in wet a Brougham smelling of musty leather. An elderly cob was responsible for more menial jobs. A couple of retired hunters broken to harness completed the stable.

Of servants there were legion. All the female staff were Highlanders, for Aunt Margaret had, like everyone else, quickly realised that in the Highlands the women do all the work. Plump old Jessie from Fort William was the cook with, under her, a scullery maid; Louisa, the parlour maid, had a double usefulness, as parlour maids wore cuff links which could be borrowed by guests in an emergency; Janet, the head house maid from the Islands with a girl under her; MacLeod, the ladies maid from Fort Augustus (ladies maids were never addressed by anything but their surnames): she shuffled about upstairs too old and blind to do any useful work. Their combined ages, together with those of the kitchen cats, must have been close on 500 years.

French was spoken at table if anything cropped up that the servants were not meant to hear; although I waited long years in vain for anything spicey it did make me eager to progress in that language.

Superimposed upon the staff was my current governess; I got through seven in four years but rather doubt if it was entirely myself who was to blame. It seems that their duties were varied for among other talents they were expected to drive horses. I remember being hurtled into the stable yard with all the harness coming off and a hysterical Miss MacKay complaining to the groom that Flirt, one of the hunters, did not take her corners nearly as carefully as Dan, the old cob.

Of the outside staff Mr Anderson from Aberdeenshire, together with a groom, did all five horses and the car, first a 1907 Renault which had to be routed to avoid anything in the nature of a hill and later a Baby Rolls which while not exactly speedy could at least take one where one wanted. The gardener was a lanky Borderer with a boy under him. To complete the picture was Mr. Birkett, the keeper. But one must not forget an important member of the household, an Aberdeen terrier who was old, smelly and of uncertain temper; he attacked the gundogs of whom there was a kennel full.

Before marriage Aunt Margaret had been a Johnstone-Stewart of Physgill brought up to the solid county family virtues. Poor dear, she was not exactly clever and despite an elder brother who became an Admiral had some ideas which it was rather difficult to shake. As an example one of the farm boys, aged about fourteen, had a cheerful turned up red nose, it therefore logically followed that he must be a confirmed alcoholic. As a young officer on leave I was resolutely forbidden to give a small sherry party which apparently betokened the most dreadful depravity. Sex could not be mentioned and death was always referred to in a hushed voice. As for bad language . . . She had an innocent little story of some husband who shocked her by his rather mild swearing. 'And when his first baby was born and started to talk the first thing it said was 'damn' and do you know that man never smiled again.'

With her unfortunate combination of a kind heart, faith in human nature and ample money she was, of course, imposed upon by one and all. Every summer the house filled up, chiefly with old school friends. On one occasion there were twelve women staying there, mostly of unparalleled hideosity. Not only did she herself have some very strange ideas about bringing up small boys, but nearly all these females and some of her own sisters, of whom she had started off with ten, had very advanced ideas too, culled presumably from women's magazines. I suffered every annoyance and indignity. I particularly remember one woman who was permitted to wake me up every morning at 6am and stand over me while I drank a large glass of cold water. Winter was far more restful.

Her elder sister, Poll Hume-Gore was a real tonic. With her late husband and sons in the Highland Brigade she knew all about the male of the species as poor Aunt Margaret did not. Taking advantage of this house full of servants to enjoy ill health, she would bid one to her darkened bedroom after breakfast where one would find her propped up with pillows in a huge canopied bed, reading *The Times* and chain smoking Turkish cigarettes.

'Come and kiss your old Aunt good morning;' she would command and were any boy so ill advised as to do so she would usually reward him by seizing him by the back of the neck and soundly boxing first one ear and then the other before leaning back cackling with laughter.

Every Sunday morning before breakfast the entire household would be subjected to early morning prayers. Filing into the dining room with reverent expressions, family and guests through one door, servants through another, we would sit, stand and at intervals kneel at the chairs arranged for us round the walls. Something funny could usually be counted upon to happen by accident or design. The Collect for the Day would be rudely interrupted by a dog fight under the table, or one of the ill favoured women would step on a strategically dropped marble with most rewarding results.

Church on Sunday was pure purgatory. We sat in the very front pew. After about an hour of supreme boredom I would hear all the village children being permitted to escape before the sermon. But not I. Even after the service there was no quick release since Aunt Margaret could not be restrained from chatting outside the porch with all the congregation, mostly acidulated spinsters; it seems that God gets the women that men don't want.

Weekdays made up for it. With horses to ride and the woods full of pheasants and rabbits, I continued my sporting education under Mr. Anderson and Mr. Birkett.

When Aunt Margaret went abroad for two months every year I was sent away to stay with a family friend where the pattern was exactly the same: a vast house, servants, dogs, a car. She too was an angel but a sensible one. From there we sometimes went to stay with her brother the Earl of Home at Douglas Castle. I seem to remember footmen in white breeches and powdered wigs and actually enjoyed going to pray in the tiny ancient church. For here the Douglas's had once murdered the entire English occupying garrison of the castle while at their devotions.

The castle had a large oak studded park in which roamed two herds of Highland cattle who fought each other on sight. I still distinctly remember sitting out in a boat in the middle of the little loch and watching Lady Home coming down towards us presumably to call us in for tea. Unfortunately, someone had left a gate open and belligerent bellows suddenly brought to her notice the undoubted probability that she was about to occupy the very centre of the stage in a battle royal.

Pulling up her skirts, and in those days there was plenty of skirt to pull up, she legged it up the slope and cleared the nearest fence in a style that would have done credit to her nephew, that famous Olympic hurdler, Lord Burghley.

At school age during the holidays I sometimes used to go and stay with my paternal grandfathers, a retired 12th Lancer Colonel with a huge white moustache, at one of our two family seats, Kirkton in Lanarkshire. He spent most of his time in a dark, damp and dismal dungeon which he had converted into a study. I hugely enjoyed Kirkton as there were no old ladies continually wanting something, no fetching and carrying, no prohibition of the gramophone on Sundays, no restrictions about anything. The housekeeper-cook Maggie Wharrie was a tough, practical Lowland Scot who remained my loyal friend throughout her life.

The house itself, a most forbidding looking pile, consisted of a dark square tower, the foundations of which dated from the 12th century. It had at one time served as a monastery and had also been the home of the notorious Major Weir, burnt for witchcraft in Edinburgh on the 12 April 1670. His sister, who confessed to having dealings with the Queen of the Fairies, was burnt at the same time. Their spirits still roamed; no one from the village would come near the place at night and the servants sometimes gave notice very suddenly.

My grandfather, who never drank, actually saw Major Weir in his bedroom. I myself at prep-school age heard what could only be his footsteps coming down the corkscrew stair just outside my bedroom door, and slept with an open Boy Scout knife under my pillow for a long time afterwards.

Few of the rooms at Kirkton were used. My grandfather slept at the top of the tower in the Kings Room, reached by the corkscrew stone newel stair; the King was Charles I. Below was the dining room, again with five foot thick walls, pierced by tiny windows. At the bottom were two barrel vaults which supported the house, one of which had been converted into the study. Kirkton may have been cold, it may have been pitch dark, there were no other boys to go round with, there were no children's parties or dances, but I felt part of the scene. The old man and I were of the same flesh and blood. I was aware that I resembled some of the ancestors who gazed rather uncompromisingly down from the dining room walls. There was a sense of continuity. As a boy I knew I was the legal Heir of Entail of my bachelor uncle who hated this place and had made his home in the hut in Africa. All being well I would inherit both these big houses and estates and the money that went with them. I would be the 17th Laird and a Scottish Feudal Baron. I hoped to go into the 12th Lancers and then come back from the wars and retire here and become a DL and a JP like my grandfather. In short — this was where I really belonged. I had been born here and would presumably die here.

Poor Kirkton. Later on when I was in India my uncle sold it to someone who pulled it down and built a 'ranch type' house on the site. Both Kirkton and Fairholm, the other house a few miles away and too big to live in, were packed from floor to ceiling with huge gloomy Victorian furniture, over, under and between which very moth eaten stuffed animals peered at one reproachfully. Fairholm had a stuffed lion in the hall, Kirkton a full sized stuffed crocodile hanging upside down from the ceiling. I used to go over to Fairholm on my cycle, trout rod or gun slung over my shoulders, over the Clyde, on through the Duke of Hamilton's land and eventually through our own lodge gates and over our bridge across the Avon which surrounded the house on three sides. At the very end of the bridge was the stump of a tree the branches of which my father had grabbed when his run-away horse could not quite take the corner and had jumped the parapet to its death in the river far below.

On the right was the ford used before the bridge was built and through which Mary Queen of Scots and her small retinue had splashed, chased by enemy cavalry, on her wild ride South on the 13th May 1568, to captivity in England after the Battle of Langside, leaving 300 Hamiltons, including one of the family, dead on the battlefield behind her.

In front was the park, in which were the ruins of the old house, destroyed by enemy action in 1570 and again in 1579, in company with all the other Hamilton houses and castles in the country, in the struggle for power. Not far from it rose the new house, built in the eighteenth century when there was less chance of having it burnt over one's head. At the bend in the avenue were traces of a prehistoric mound.

The fee duty payable to the Duke, a kind of ground rent to remind us of our feudal duties, was a red rose and a Scottish groat, on demand.

The fishing was bad, the trout too few and far between and the grayling too cunning, but the scenery superb as the river cascaded over the shelves of red sandstone, the opposite bank rising steeply up wooded braes to the rim of what was more a cup than a saucer.

The shooting was badly poached but a few pheasants still lurked in the depths of the 'Captain's Wood,' so called because my great-great-grandfather is reputed to have lost it to the Duke in a wager, my rich grandmother having to buy it back again. The old man was the only relation that I ever really knew. Although, no doubt, a tedious little boy I don't think he disliked me, all his loathing was reserved for his elder son in Africa. My uncle had removed to the disused laundry all the huge oil paintings which formerly hung on the stairs, replacing them by the heads and horns of various animals he had shot. Since the laundry leaked and was used by the local pigeons as a latrine, all that remained were some shreds of canvas in some exceedingly dirty frames.

Fairhom had its ghosts too, a melancholy young man who had been jilted by a young lady staying in the house.

This old grandfather had seen happier days. Inheriting Braidwood, the Stevenson estate, later sold to Lord Clydesmuir, he had married three heiresses starting with my grandmother. On the death of the latter the two Hamilton estates thus went by Entail to my father's elder brother when he was eight, who now lived in his mud hut in bachelor solitude.

Although the village maintained that my grandmother had died of a broken heart owing to his behaviour, actually it was in producing my father. Four years later he married the rich Miss Leyland, a name well-known in Shipping and Car circles, after disinheriting my father of Braidwood in favour of any issue of Miss Leyland on the insistance of his future father-in-law who stipulated that without this provision there would be no dowry.

Killing off Miss Leyland in exactly one year but after she had produced an heir, he married his third, the daughter of a very rich Australian wool magnate who devoted much money to presenting new sets of bells to various churches in the Hastings area, causing her offspring to wince every time they hear a carillon. For their subsequent divorce one briefed the famous Carson, the other Rufus Isaacs. She then retired to No 1 Queen's Gate, which smelt of cats.

Now the old boy had only his memories. He had been ADC to Queen Victoria, Edward VII and George V (incidentally marching beside each of their coffins). His stories of Court Life were fascinating but usually ended gloomily with 'All dead, all dead!'

One memory was when at Windsor Castle taking a forbidden short cut through the royal apartments to get back to his own room after a dance, he ran into Queen Victoria face to face, in her nightie, scurrying to the loo. She showed no signs of amusement.

The only piece of advice he ever gave me before I went out into the world was:- 'Never get into a railway carriage alone with a strange woman!'

Christened in the Church of Scotland, as were we all, he attached so little importance to worship as never to permit a parson of any denomination whatsoever to enter the house, with the exception of the Catholic priest, a witty Irishman who made him laugh. He did stretch a point in permitting the C of S Minister from Hamilton to cross the threshhold to marry him to my grandmother in the Fairholm drawing room, a family custom.

Shortly after I went to Aunt Margaret the Kaiser's war broke out from which my father only came home once. He must have had a premonition, as during his 10 days leave he kept on reiterating rather desperately 'If anything happens to me I am sure your uncle will look after your future.' What a hope!

My mother, not the sort of woman to be stuck in India with a European war on, appeared in France wearing uniform where she drove some General about in a staff car. She came home too when I was in my teens and I met her for tea in her charming flat in London. She was very pretty, she was amusing, we understood each other's jokes and I adored her. And that was the last time I saw her for a dozen years, during which time my father had died on active service.

Turning serious for a moment she told me never, never to forget that my uncle had warned her that if she ever tried to exercise her maternal obligations over me he would break the Entail on the estates, which one apparently can do after 200 years, and make it his business to see that I was penniless. Why? In God's name, why?

It was difficult to find out much about my uncle. I recollect meeting him once when a very small boy and remember him being very nasty to me quite unnecessarily. To me he always remained an utter enigma. Commissioned in the Inniskilling Dragoons he had resigned his commission directly he got his majority. Hating Scotland, not caring a fig for the estates, he had gone to South Africa and from then on had hardly left his brain child and life's work, the Kruger National Park.

The first blow soon fell. On entering Sandhurst one had to declare the arm of the service in which one expected to serve. On asking my grandfather's advice on whether I should be happiest in the 12th Lancers or the Black Watch he broke the news that there was no question of my going into either, not indeed into any crack regiment as they all demanded a private income of between £200 and £400 a year from their officers and my uncle had decreed that I should live on my pay with no allowance at all. Why?

Two of the three gentlemen cadets with whom I went round at Sandhurst were future Lancers. Every living male member of my family, and there were then six of them, had entered the cavalry or the Highland Brigade. Why not I?

A close neighbour, Lord Belhaven and Stenton, brought consolation and advice. As Major Hamilton he had been a Fourth Gurkha and assured me that all their officers were of good family forced to live on their pay and thought of little but fishing and shooting and, of course, polo. I decided to plump for them which he said he could arrange as his brother-in-law was

Lord Birdwood, the Commander-in-Chief in India.

The next surprise came when I was commissioned. On this momentous occasion most of my friends got a present of a gun, or a saddle, or the promise of a polo pony when they joined their regiments. I myself got a nasty letter saying I was out on my own in the world now and could sink or swim as I thought best.

My maternal grandfather, an 18th Hussar, had when Equerry to the Duke of Connaught met his young bride to be, my grandmother, then Lady in Waiting to the Duchess. As may be imagined they were furious about this Indian Army business, and told me so, but since they were not on speaking terms with my uncle their fulminations were rather wasted, nor had they any spare cash themselves, with which to help me along.

So off I went to India once more. It being obligatory to spend a year with a British regiment before posting to the Indian Army I had applied for and got an attachment to that magnificent regiment, the Royal Scots Fusiliers, stationed in the Khyber Pass.

People were very kind in lending me horses to ride about although I had not learnt to play polo nor could I afford it. There was, however, one little snag: one could not go outside the little ring of blockhouses encircling the camp without an excellent chance of being murdered by the locals; two officers of the Seaforth Highlanders, Majors Orr and Anderson, had gone for a walk round the corner about two years previously and been shot dead.

The medical orders were incredible. I have a photograph of myself wearing a huge helmet during a heavy snowstorm. Spine pads were still worn, those fantastic relics of a bye-gone age, large triangles of quilted cotton which hung from the back of the neck down to the waist.

When my turn came along I went down to Peshawar with an escort of Jocks to draw the week's pay, going down the Khyber by train one day and returning the next. In front of the engine were two long trucks on which travel was free. When they were black with people clinging onto them, all was well; when they were empty, it was sure indication that there was a mined bridge somewhere along the line.

On joining my regiment, the 4th Prince of Wales's Own Gurkha Rifles, in Bakloh, I found life as different as chalk from cheese: no traditions, such as having to wear long trousers in civilian clothes in a temperature of 120° because shorts were 'not done' except in uniform; no longer the feeling that one was in some sort of military crêche.

After an initial six weeks of instruction I was given my own company, followed shortly by a second, despite my total inability to speak Gurkhali. The clerks luckily spoke English and the Gurkha officers and old soldiers somehow understood my Urdu.

Within months the battalion was posted to Razmak in Waziristan, the real pick of the Frontier stations, with a decent climate, where the Mahsuds and Wazirs, the best and most tireless of umpires rewarded any slackness or tactical error with at the best a bullet or two, at the worst a whirlwind attack in overwhelming numbers.

Here among the Indian troops whom I had been encouraged to despise, were three absolutely crack regiments whose smartness far surpasses any regiment except perhaps the Guards and whose speed across country was fantastic.

Their men were all of good yeoman stock, Sikhs, Pathans from friendly tribes, Punjabi Mussulmen and the like with a natural dignity and courteous charm unfortunately lacking in European troops. Their martial bearing immediately proclaimed them for what they were and what their families had been for centuries; they regarded the denizens of the bazaar and non-martial classes as pure dirt. There was very little liaison between them and British troops owing both to the language barrier and an entirely different outlook.

I got no leave at all for two years. In my third year I did, however, get leave and went straight to Kashmir with a great friend in the Gordon Highlanders partly to fish but really to try and get hold of a couple of girls of our own age group, the odds being about twenty to one against, in view of the severe competition.

We were both lucky, however, and were all four invited to the Maharajah of Kashmir's annual ball. This was the first big dance, not counting the Sandhurst Ball, to which I had ever been and I was absolutely thrilled. The palace stood on the edge of a lake which reflected the coloured illuminations hung in all the trees. A huge moon shone down on us as we strolled about the warm scented gardens or sat on the tactfully situated sofas between the bushes. Champagne flowed all night and he had a most excellent dance band, possibly imported for the night from Calcutta. He had even produced a cabaret in the shape of his newest and prettiest dancing girl Zahura who gyrated about looking absolutely divine and smiling like an angel. Although obviously not having a word of English she wound up by singing 'Tipperary' which brought the house down.

As I waltzed round the magnificent ballroom in a happy alcoholic haze, my already pretty partner getting more and more attractive as the evening wore on, my attention was suddenly rivetted by a strikingly good looking middle aged woman sitting on a sofa with her partner watching the dancing. Where had I seen her before? In the pages of some glossy magazine? I became aware of my partner reiterating 'What's the matter, have you seen a ghost, you might at least pay some attention to me.' Well, I thought I had seen something far more devastating than any pale ghost, but was I right? I would look a pretty average idiot if I walked up to her and said 'Hello Mother' and it turned out to be a perfect stranger.

We all four held a rapid council of war, in which mine was the only dissenting vote, I was terrified. I knew my mother was in India, she had married a Brigadier Campbell-Ross, late of the 13th Lancers IA and now commanding an Indian Cavalry Brigade. "Of course you must risk it. What if she thinks you are mad or tight? You have been writing to her and trying to meet her all your adult life, now it may be your only chance. Buck up, she may leave the dance early.' So said the girls and the Gordon.

Petrified, I crossed the floor towards her, 'Hello Vivian, fancy meeting you here! Come and sit down for a moment and keep me company, I know Alan wants to go to the bar!'

From beginning to end she behaved with the utmost composure, accepting my invitation to a dance later on which she insisted on sitting out. I felt like a newly joined subaltern being greeted by the General's wife exerting all her charm safe in the knowledge that she would never have to speak to me again. And so it proved. I wrote from time to time for years but went on getting the horrible answers to which I was so used. It was better when there was no answer at all, so I eventually gave up.

When I was 23 a citrus farmer called Graham and his wife asked me to visit them in the Transvaal for part of my furlough from India. They in turn passed me on to a Hollander, one Olivier and his wife in Mozambique which contained the very best shooting. I stayed with them for several days while they clued me up, lent me the camp equipment I needed, produced one Kafir who knew the route to the Lembombo Hills, a second who cooked and talked his own version of English and virtually did everything to enable me to go big game hunting. Olivier himself came down with me to Lorenço Marques, the capital, where he knew the Portuguese Governor who gave me a shooting permit.

I am afraid they all regarded a young man of 23, ignorant of either Kafir or Portuguese, coming out on a one-man safari on a no-cost basis, as the most tremendous joke but thanks entirely to their efforts I was very successful.

While in South Africa I thought it politic to look up my rich uncle, whose heir I was, in his mud hut, with grave misgivings as he had a bad reputation with the entire family for sheer venom. Added to this, three old unconnected gentlemen whom I met had had trouble with him and refused ever to speak to him again. Also, he had apparently proposed to my mother who turned him down flat in favour of his penniless younger brother, which may have piqued him a bit.

I found a not very attractive bald-headed man little more than 5ft high, living miles from civilisation off a diet consisting almost exclusively of mealie meal porridge, various forms of venison from lion kills, and oranges.

He had a lovely sense of humour and was absolutely charming.

I stayed with him, riding a pony about the Kruger National Park armed only with a camera and fly whisk, as he did himself. He told me there was no danger unless I got between an alarmed hippopotamus and its water hole. Of this I should be careful. I was. I earned my keep by drilling the Police guard in preparation for a visit by the Governor General.

Why that reputation and why was he living like this? A few months after, I left him on the best of terms (he even tried to help me with my fare to Cape Town); he married, and in due course his marriage was blessed.

From that date, quite unaccountably, although he had been my legal guardian and a trustee of my father's will, perhaps unfortunately, he would never write to me except through a lawyer; he would never meet me – while sitting in a car in Edinburgh he hid his head in a rug on seeing me walking down the street, being watched by a delighted crowd of my friends looking through a window. In fact he disowned me completely and I came into no family money at all.

The explanation or reason for this extraordinary behaviour, all my friends including Maggie Wharrie have tried to find out, remains unanswered to this day.

II

Dargai Fort is not a lovesome thing, God wot

At the time of which I am now about to write I was no longer a two month old baby, nor even a rosy cheeked young Second Lieutenant with eyes shining with enthusiasm and innocence. I was a jaundiced officer with nine years service mostly in North West Frontier outposts. The Khyber Pass, Waziristan, Bannu, The Khajuri Plain, I knew them all and now it was to be the Malakand – the most boring of the lot. The year was 1934.

I was just returning from leave in the United Kingdom, madly in love, of course, as was the case with all normal young officers in that situation.

The train, every carriage full of blown sand, was now slowing down as it neared the buffers of its final destination on this totally uneconomic strategic line built solely to rush up troops and supplies in the event of war with Afghanistan or invasion from beyond; Napoleon, Queen Catherine of Russia and even Hitler had seriously considered the latter project. War or any chance of excitement seemed remote. The Kaiser's war was over; the Russians had, it was hoped, their own troubles; Hitler had not yet been heard of outside Germany.

I screwed up my eyes and peered through the white dust adhering to the carriage window; all there was to see was a shimmering waste backed by bare unfriendly hills. Looking through the opposite window the nothingness was relieved by the brick walls of Dargai Fort.

19

'If there be paradise on earth, it is this! it is this!' has never been said to describe Dargai.

It really is a dump and must contrast most unfavourably with any prison which it looks not unlike. The latter at least must provide modern sanitation, food cooked by a changing quota of excellent chefs and the certainty of novel and interesting acquaintanceships?

I should have nothing more up to date than a night commode, known colloquially as a 'thunder box,' be living on Gurkha food which required the digestion of an ox, an asbestos throat, and a well controlled imagination and for entertainment would be listening to the Gurkha soldiers discussing the rival merits of the platoon football teams.

Here, or in one of the other two forts further up the pass, I was condemned to live for just under two years. It was too much of a change from my cosy little service flat at 28 Half Moon Street, Mayfair.

Emerging through the gate, with a broad grin on his face, was the Officer I was to relieve, Geoffrey D' Oyly-Lowsley, waiting only for me to take over B Company and the fort to go to England on furlough himself.

Tomorrow would see me sitting in a sweltering little office full of flies, checking and signing my name for a cupboard full of musty but very secret files which I could bet required amending, counting all sorts of military stores which would never be used, looking through a training programme in which there would be nothing new.

My luggage was hauled out of the train and put into a little two-wheeled mule cart drawn by two very independent looking mules and we started walking towards my new command. Dargai Fort, a company outpost of the Malakand Garrison, was exactly what I had expected from the descriptions from my brother officers. A very high brick wall surmounted by battlements relieved only by a steel gate in the exact centre and by two loopholed steel sentry posts stuck high up on the corners, squarely and uncompromisingly comfronted us. As we walked through the gaps in the belts of barbed wire entanglement the pungent, acrid smell of incinerators caught me by the throat, rudely assailing nostrils which had taken months to grow sensitive to more subtle scents.

Inside the gate the sentry, his belt and boots shining like black patent leather, his tunic, shorts and felt hat all starched to the consistency of cardboard, sprang to attention and shouldered arms. Passing him we picked our way round and through a maze of small single storied barrack buildings, cookhouses, washhouses, stores, magazines and odd quarters all packed into a space carefully designed to be just, but only just big enough for our accommodation.

Here were all the every-day scenes of Gurkha barrack room life; polishing of boots, cleaning of rifles, three youths lying on their stomachs watching a couple of beetles fight; laughter, snatches of Gurkhali song and whistling; the squealing of mules shackled fore and aft, craning out their seemingly telescopic necks towards each other and baring their huge teeth in rough mule play.

We arrived at the British Officer's quarter, a couple of tiny rooms built up against the opposite wall of the fort, where Geoffrey left me to change out of my dusty travel-stained clothes. I gingerly put one foot into the bath, the usual small galvanized iron tub into which one alternately tips highly chlorinated cold and boiling water from a couple of old cut-down paraffin tins. While dressing I found myself once again tapping out my shoes before putting them on, just in case they might harbour a lurking scorpion. I have never been stung by a scorpion but I can never forget the experience of a very choleric and alarming Mountain Artillery Colonel, Martin was his name.

One night he arrived for dinner looking even more empurpled and awe inspiring than ever and as usual we lesser fry scurried off to the dimmer corners of the room until a couple of gins should have reduced his temperature. Addressing us, which he hardly ever did conversationally, he exploded, 'D'ye know

21

what's just happened? I gave my damned mess trousers an extra good shake before putting 'em on and the biggest bloody scorpion I have ever seen fell out of the fork!'

As I finished dressing the orderly bugler and piper sounded 'retreat,' knife rests were pulled across the gaps in the barbed wire, the iron gate was shut with a clang, the Union Jack run down from the top of the fort and files of men, their rifles loaded and swords fixed, silently filed up on to the battlements to take up their alarm positions. There they remained crouched motionless behind the sandbagged head cover, for bullets knock lethal fragments off brick, their fingers on their triggers, staring out on to the quickly darkening landscape now given over to prowling gangs of armed raiders, while the Gurkha Officer of the Day, gym-shoe shod like everyone else on duty at night, went silently from sentry post to sentry post closely shadowed by his Orderly.

After the usual half-hour of 'stand-to' during which time every man in the little fort was silent and all activity ceased, a whistle blew and my newly appointed orderly, whose position was inside and just behind my open door, unloaded his rifle and unfixed his sword. Then, as the various posts were 'stood-down' the troops climbed down the ladders from the wooden galleries running round inside the wall, cigarettes were lit up and a murmur of voices rose from all sides as the whole place came to life once more.

Geoffrey, returning to find me dressed, my uniform smelling of mothballs but at least clean and presentable, suggested that we should go down to that hub of social activity, the Coffee Shop, our archaic term for the canteen.

In the long hut dimly lit by swinging hurrican lamps a queue had formed leading up to the trestle table from which the Coffee Shop NCO was dispensing rum from a steel barrel. It really had no right to be called rum, it was merely juice from the sugar cane crushed out and processed in various distilleries in the Punjab; it had, however, a good powerful kick and no injurious after-effects, and it was very cheap. We, sitting behind the table with

GO of the Day, knew that the only way of drinking it without blistering our mouths was to drown it in sweet fizzy lemonade, but it still tasted of nothing much but rusty iron barrel; the effect, however, was satisfying. This Fort was not going to suit me.

The unfortunate British Officer had no one to whom to talk, there was no cinema, radio programmes were in their infancy in India, there was as yet no TV, the Fort library seemed composed entirely of trash and there was nowhere to go. One could occupy oneself by working until late afternoon seven days a week but, as an alternative to football, the only recreation was to walk round and round the outside of the Fort, varied by the occasional stroll down to the irrigation canal across which Geoffrey had not yet succeeded in throwing a stone lefthanded. Then there were the long evenings.

I started assuming my responsibilities next morning before breakfast first of all going to the Company Office where the Gurkha clerk greeted me in what is, I believe, referred to as a 'Sandhurst accent,' picked up from us.

We gradually waded our way through the Mobilisation Scheme, the internal Security Scheme, the Railway Security Scheme, the Secret Ciphers, the Confidential Rolls, the Fort Defence Scheme, the Malakand Mobile Column Scheme, the Secret Intelligence Summaries – as fast as I scanned through and signed for one pile of files another was pushed towards me. By lunch time the secret documents were finished with, the key of the cupboard was handed over to me and the responsibility for that little lot was now mine.

Next, we had to go to the Guard Room and count the cash, contained in a square wooden kit box padlocked to the floor. With the Guard Commander breathing down our necks we counted parcels of dirty notes and arranged coins of all donominations over the table; once more I signed my name. Breathing sighs of relief, we now passed on to the Post Stores where I was confronted by rolls of barbed wire, machine guns and their numerous spare components, heliographs, drums of

23

field telephone cable, piles of mule saddlery, picks, shovels and crowbars, lift and force pumps, fire buckets, tentage, hundreds of empty sandbags, boxes of ammunition, grenades, armourers' tools, spare cooking utensils and heavy pieces of engineering equipment of which I knew neither the names nor the functions. I signed and signed until I had writer's cramp.

All was not yet over; there still remained the reserve rations, a store full of sacks of flour and rice, sugar, tea and salt, and tinned milk; I felt more like the new manager of a grocer's shop than a soldier. At long last all was handed over, all the papers signed and countersigned, everything explained and it was now my turn to order the mule cart to take Geoffrey's luggage down to the station.

After some months in this wearisome place it was B Coy's turn to be relieved and go off up the pass to Chakdarra, a Fort on a rock in a loop of the Swat River and obviously the inspiration for all those Frontier screen sets.

Romantic as one might wish from the outside, there was little else to recommend it. It had indeed in 1895 been the scene of a historic attack by the tribes who, worked up into a religious frenzy by the oratory of the mullahs, the beating of drums and the waving of green flags, had hurled themselves sword in hand upon the defences in a series of ferocious charges, climbing on each others shoulders to surmount the wall until all the approaches were covered with a vast pile of dead. The unfortunate Punjabi battalion inside were having rather a bad time too, as, heavily outnumbered, there were fewer and fewer to man the walls and more and more wounded in rows on the floor of every building as the siege grew longer. What was worse, they ran out of water; this was where Gunga Din, a genuine water carrier, crept through the lines of enemy every night with his goat skin, down to the river; had the enemy caught him they would, as he well knew, first of all have removed portions of his anatomy on which he presumably set great store, as is their happy custom, before getting down to more refined torture.

The Author—as he
had to dress up on
important occasions.

His Excellency the Governor entertains his guests at a garden party

There was, however, one other little interlude which could have proved rather too exciting.

Archie Best, the Political Agent, responsible to the Governor of the Province for the good behaviour of the local tribes and for our relations with the rather wilder ones in unadministered territory, was having trouble with the Mohmands. Knowing that a showdown was inevitable and thinking that when this came about he would like quick communication with the Governor, he concocted the fantastic idea of laying a telephone line to where he thought the battle would be fought, this being before the days of field radio sets.

My CO on being asked if he could provide someone who knew about laying telephone lines and being for some reason in awe of the young PA, offered me as a kind of propitiatory sacrifice. To give him his due he was too new to the regiment and to the Frontier to realise the implications, but I was told to take half-a-dozen Gurkha signallers, unarmed because the prospect of obtaining our rifles would be the greatest inducement to attack, in an ordinary rattletrap bazaar lorry, with a tribal escort, to a hostile area miles and miles away from any form of assistance.

Off we went in the lorry, spluttering and rattling, on its threadbare tyres up the stony track, out of range of our comforting machine guns in the Fort, round a hill behind which we had never glimpsed, past villages we knew only from the map, past groups of tall surprised looking tribesmen each with his rifle slung over his shoulders, past black-clothed hard-eyed women who drew their cloaks across the lower halves of their faces when they saw us, on and on for miles until we were stopped by a minion of the PA.

The work took us three or four days, feeling rather like slaves, working in the hot sun being stared at by all and sundry while our armed guards lounged in the shade. We did not like the looks of the hostile tribesmen, indistinguishable from our escorts except that the latter wore dirty cotton brassards, who had come to find out what was going on, and did not seem too pleased when they had learnt.

Every morning on arrival I fully expected to find that our cable had already been stolen to string native beds, but Best had seemingly passed round the word that there were high tension cables, and that anyone who touched them would shrivel up!

The work completed, we sighed great sighs of relief when Best thanked us and told us that we should not be required again. Poor Archie Best, the tribes took a few days to decide what to do, for the next time he went up, some weeks later, they shot him dead.

Apart from this, the place was dull, for as in Dargai there was nothing to do except work; one could not wander away out of sight of the sentries on the Fort wall without the very real danger of being knifed, shot or kidnapped for ransom and there was no one to whom to talk, except the troops whose topics of conversation were slightly limited.

One might wonder why I did not try and establish friendly relations with the local villages, so that I might at least go out for rides. The answer was knowledge of the Pathan character.

They are extremely brave, they have a tremendous sense of humour, they are perhaps the most virile race in the world, they can be diabolically cruel and they are very very treacherous.

For me, the final straw came when a column came marching over the pass on their way to spend a few weeks out in the hills to deal with the Mohmands who were giving trouble, all highly elated at the prospect of seeing action. One of my friends got an MC in this little affair. With them came Brigadiers Alexander and Auchinleck, both to become Field Marshals and the latter rated by the Germans as being our best British General in the 1939 war. They all spent the night bivouaced under my Fort walls and their departure early next morning did nothing to reconcile me to being a lines-of-communication soldier.

It was time for me to seek pastures new. If I did not already know all there was to know about commanding a Gurkha company, then I never would.

There were a number of extra-regimental postings, known as

'jobs,' open to Indian Army Officers such as myself. I was too young to qualify to take the staff college examination but there were other things.

Three years with the Assam Rifles was very popular with those from Gurkha Regiments. They enjoyed the very best of shooting but it was very very lonely, they seldom saw other white men, and white women never.

Then there were attachments to the various units of the Frontier Corps, irregulars manned by Pushtu-speaking British officers and thus popular with Frontier Force Officers who already spoke the language. These Officers lived alone with their troops in tiny forts.

Lower down the scale of jobs one could always become a Station Staff Officer, sitting in an office controlling the allotment of married quarters, issuing dog licences and so forth. Not for me.

The only employment that seemed to be of any interest of which the Adjutant had received information was the post of Commander-in-Chief and Financial Adviser to the Sultan of Muskat. It was incredible that they should be seeking a humble Lieutenant for this high sounding post. It could only be surmised that Muskat had a minimal army and no finances, not enough to pay even a Captain; I applied immediately but luckily, as it turned out, my application was turned down. This, of course, was before Muskat became important.

What I was looking for was not three years tucked away in a far corner of some impenetrable jungle, desert, or desolate gloomy valley into which the sun never shone, surrounded on all sides by the perpetual snow and ice of the inner Himalayas; I wanted to learn something about an India which I had read about in Kipling but which I had never seen.

What could one learn of educated Indians from the barrack room? Whom did we meet outside the Army? Minor railway officials on station platforms, the denizens of the bazaar, coolies, peasantry, our own servants.

No British Officer of my acquaintance had ever sat next to an

Indian woman at dinner, much less danced with one.

This was all very limiting, bad for us and bad for the army. Since through force of circumstances I had made the Indian Army my career I really must find out at least a little about the middle and upper classes.

Must all Indian lawyers or accountants of necessity be inefficient or scoundrels? One read of some pretty staggering cases in the press but were they not paralleled by things which occurred at home? Indian politicians? A vague memory stirred of my grandfather fulminating against 'that blackguard Lloyd George' and 'all those confounded radicals.' I must learn more but here the conditions were wrong.

It was now that my previous CO wrote to tell me that there was an ADC job to a Governor coming up for which he was prepared to recommend me. Since these jobs were never advertised and extremely hard to get, I accepted his offer immediately. In due course I was, to my jubilation, accepted.

III

Not a whited sepulchre

A few weeks later found me alighting at Lahore station where a magnificent bemedalled figure clothed from head to foot in scarlet and gold met me on the platform and announced that a car awaited me outside. I followed the chuprassi to the station entrance where I found myself skirting an area cordoned off by police in the centre of which was drawn up a vast car with the number P2, presumably waiting for someone of great importance. With a gracious wave of the hand my resplendent escort invited me forward and told me that this was indeed for me; the police all saluted and from the driving seat stepped a portly Indian chauffeur clad in the regulation blue serge uniform topped by a shimmering white waving turban; this was the redoubtable Ganpat, one of the best known and, incidentally, one of the best informed figures in the Punjab.

He saluted, asked me in English whether I had enjoyed a good journey and bowed me into the back which was already occupied by a middle aged lady of comfortable contours who immediately started putting me at my ease with a flow of motherly chat. I had no clue as to her identity but was profoundly grateful for her presence as my morale was receiving a severe shaking; it transpired that she was the housekeeper who had taken the opportunity to do a little shopping.

Leaving the station where the other passengers were as yet being driven crazy by the mob of yelling coolies squabbling over their baggage, the car threaded its way through the tangle of interlocked taxis and tongas each striving to secure a fare, and gained the comparative quiet of the side streets beyond, past the bazaar quarter, on between large bungalows with neat compounds surrounded by hedges.

The car swung off the main road and through some tall wrought-iron gates in a high wall; a scarlet-turbanned policeman and a Punjabi military sentry coming to attention and saluting as we passed; the headlights now lit up a broad drive flanked by beds of eight foot cannas leading up to a huge white palace surmounted by a dome on which was a flagstaff; I had arrived.

Pat le Marchant, my fellow ADC to be, met me at the porch and straight away conducted me to the kind of room in which, if this had been London, one might expect some captain of industry to sit while negotiating his take-over bids; it turned out to be the ADCs' office and here was another scarlet-coated figure who salaamed and asked me what I would like to drink. Much as I needed a little something, I was dubious as to whether it was advisable to be introduced to His Excellency while reeking of alcohol but was reassured when told that both he and Lady Emerson were out at some official dinner with the other ADC.

My suite of rooms not only contained a bathroom with bath and pull-the-plug, modern sanitation being unknown elsewhere in Northern India, but another novelty, one of those long mirrors with sides in which one can see not only one's front but one's profile and, with a little dexterity, one's back as well.

My rough Pathan bearer, whom I had picked up on the frontier, looked as out of place as I felt but twirled his moustache as he shook the Malakand sand out of my clothes onto the Persian carpet. Scion of a long line of Mohmand raiders, murderers and rifle thieves, it would take more than red coats and long mirrors to disconcert him.

Pat came to collect me at exactly twenty-five past eight, for here it soon became second nature to time everything to the exact minute; leading me along a pillared verandah, up a marble staircase, along a wide passage, and through a doorway set in a very thick wall, we finally came into a completely square dining room of most unusual architecture and decor.

While toying with my sherry, I begun to look around; the walls were hand painted with delicate oriental designs in pale gold and subdued crimson on an ivory background; apart from there being no pictures, there appeared to be no windows; craning my neck back and still further back, my gaze was rewarded by a distant painted dome, far, far above me, and at the very tops of the walls I could just see some of those narrow pointed windows typical of Mussulman architecture.

Course followed course and wine succeeded wine, brought in by no less than three khidtmagars in the Government House livery. These three wore long scarlet coats whose stand-up collars hooked tightly under the chin and which reached down to well below the knee; round their waists were wide gold embroidered black cloth belts and standing straight up from their heads were stiff foot-high scarlet caps, of the type associated with gnomes, bound round the base with white muslin turbans.

After the constant crash and bang of ammunition boots on the stone floors of little Frontier forts, I was quite startled by these huge six foot figures topped by another foot of turban gliding about behind one, while from nowhere would suddenly materialize the end of a fiercely upturned moustache and a white gloved hand, like the goings-on at a spiritualistic seance, except that these hands did not emanate ectoplasm but held decanters or plates.

Lord Kensington, the ADC whom I was to relieve, appeared after the Emersons had gone to bed. I knew that he would be leaving directly my various new uniforms were ready, without which I could not perform the bulk of my duties; but I now received the shattering news that Pat too would be going back to his regiment in a few weeks, before we went up to Simla!

Everyone seemed to have a touching faith in my ability to pick things up quickly.

The job as they explained it did not sound too difficult but had its snags.

The social side could at times be both physically and mentally tiring; on one's best behaviour all day and for half the night talking and listening with apparent interest to what seemed an unusually large percentage of crashing bores, pompous asses and social climbers; never saying too much nor appearing to say too little.

Just to reassure me and ensure my enjoying a good night's rest they stressed that much of my time would be spent in gorgeous raiment, leading processions in and out of rooms, standing on platforms and so forth; since I was there chiefly to be stared at, stared at I would be, and any little mistake spotted and discussed with glee by a hyper-critical audience. And so to bed.

While dressing next morning I walked over to the window. The garden was indeed lovely, acres and acres of it; beyond the broad sweep of the tarmac drive was a closely cut lawn stretching away into the far distance where grew tall trees giving here and there between their trunks a glimpse of the white walls surrounding the grounds; in the middle distance, surrounded by lawn, was a fifty foot seemingly artificial mound the sides of which were ablaze with flowers; a whole army of gardeners was working on the slopes, squatting down on their heels tending the flowers; flocks of little green parakeets sped shrieking with swift wing beats from tree to tree, their narrow pointed tails seemingly too long for their bodies.

We breakfasted on the wide semi-circular verandah above the front porch; here I was introduced to HE and Lady Emerson. Conversation was general and the meal went off pleasantly enough; I did not hold the table enthralled but to the best of my knowledge succeeded in avoiding any major gaffe and on one occasion actually raised a smile on the face of HE. I would, however, have been happier had I been quite sure at what he was smiling. Some kind military friend, apprehensive that I might get a swelled head, had impressed on me that the whole raison d'être of an ADC was to give his employer, weighed down by cares of state, something at which to laugh; well, apparently I had, and might with a little luck survive for the single week which the same kind friend had prophesied as being my length of stay.

There was, however, one very important person by whom to be vetted before I was finally accepted. This was Major Dick Lawrence, of Hodson's Horse, Military Secretary to the Governor and my immediate boss; an international polo player and grandson of one of the Lawrence brothers who made themselves so famous in the early days of British rule in Northern India, he was known by, and knew the life and background of every important Indian in the province.

After breakfast and my interview with Dick the first item on the programme was a tour of the house and grounds. The dining room in which about fifty people could sit down to meals was the oldest part of the building, dating from the middle seventeenth century, and was the tomb of a Mohammed Kasim Khan a cousin of Akbar the Great. Mohammed Kasim was a great patron of wrestlers and the place had become known as 'The Wrestlers' Dome.'

He probably used the place during his life time, as was the custom, and a very practical one too, for they all built themselves tombs while still in good health and the big central rooms were ideal for a party. Whether or not he was buried under it was quite a different matter and one which the Punjab Government did not want to know anything about at all. For any Christian, above all the Governor, to take up residence in an occupied Mussulman tomb was political dynamite and had the presence of his sarcophagus been admitted the whole province would have been in a ferment. In due course I penetrated the warren of tiny passages and storerooms below, each a different shape and size and all very dark, but despite taking all the obvious measurements I could not for the life of me say whether or not there was a sealed-up room somewhere in the middle.

When the Sikhs under old Ranjit Singh took over Lahore as capital in the early part of the nineteenth century the Wrestlers Dome was acquired by a Sikh General of the name of Ran Singh as a residence. Disenchanted with just one huge room, he built a room on each side of the square plinth and then linked up their corners, giving himself an octagonal house with four completely triangular rooms. These latter had no appeal for the wife of the first British occupant, Sir John Lawrence, who altered them, after which practically every Lieutenant Governor, and there were about fifteen of them, pulled down this and built that, until there was a hotch-potch of ball rooms, smoking rooms, billiard rooms, bedrooms and offices, all at different levels round the original Dome which was mercifully left untouched.

At the top of the social scale of those living in the grounds were the Superintendent, together with his staff of clerks, the Post Master and staff of our private Post and Telegraph Office and the stenographers of HE. The Military Secretary and the ADCs, together with their assistants. Now came the indoor servants, of whom there were no less than 29, and over 120 outside, such as grooms, gardeners, washermen and carpenters. I have no doubt that there were other retainers as well but Heaven and the Superintendent alone knew who they were. Nearly all these people were married and would at a conservative estimate have had at least three children each, for India is a land of large families. There must have been seven hundred people living on the premises. No one could accuse Government House of not providing employment for people. There were also, of course, a company of infantry and about a hundred police who lived in the grounds as well and furnished the guards.

After dinner on my second night it took me some time to get back to sleep and I lay awake ruminating. One could not have sat silent throughout the meal but had I been a bit incautious in volunteering the information that I knew the principal figure in an incident about which a version had just appeared in the papers, and about which the whole of Northern India was commenting, amusedly (most civilians) or disapprovingly (the army)?

I had I hoped sufficiently stressed that I had hardly met him; I had seen him about the place when I was in Peshawar about a year or so ago.

34

He was an Irishman who had risen from the ranks and like many whose basic wants had been entirely looked after by the army, his food, clothes and accommodation having been provided free, he had no idea of money.

It seemed that this particular young man had got badly into debt, which is silly, but then borrowed from the bazaar money lenders, which is lunacy; being, however, an individual of resource he had thought out a simple and foolproof method of restoring his financial status quo.

He happened to be Treasure Chest Officer, whose tedious but necessary clerical task was passed on to all last-joined officers in turn in Indian regiments. So what could be simpler than to remove the required sum on some pretext or another from the Quarter Guard to his own bungalow?

Counting out the money in little piles on his table he despatched his bearer to the bazaar to summon the various money lenders to come and collect.

It seemed that they had good reason to suspect that there would be only enough for the first arrivals, for in no time at all the sound of wild yells and galloping hooves heralded what might have been mistaken for a chariot race careering up the silent, hallowed, tree lined, very European Mall.

This hard fought race proved, however, quite unnecessary for each creditor as he entered the room saw his money in a pile labelled with his name. They eyed one another. 'Where on earth has he collected it from?' 'Allah alone knows but now we will, el ham dal Illah, never need to set eyes on the Banchhut again!'

But as trembling fingers reached out to pocket the notes, a sudden movement made them glance up into the muzzle of a large .45 Service revolver pointed at their heads.

Almost speechless, appalled at this perfidiousness, they were then forced to watch this most un-Sahib like Sahib take a match box out of the pocket and set fire to their I.O.U.'s before their very eyes.

'Khuda de wakhla' they murmured, eyeing him venomously;

and unversed in Pushtu as he was, one doubts if he can have mistaken the epithet for praise.

Little remained to do, so it seemed to our friend, but bid them farewell before returning the money to the treasure chest and then popping along to the club for a drink in which to celebrate his ingenuity. He had no doubts but that he would go far. He soon had to.

The money lenders must have sneered at the clumsy effort of this 'besharif' officer to outwit them, they whose trade it was to lend and collect money in one of the toughest cities in the world, where the reward of duplicity was the dagger thrust.

That very evening a deputation could have been observed waiting respectfully for the Commanding Officer Sahib on the roadway outside his bungalow, on their grim bearded faces smiles, in their hands photostat copies of their I.O.U.'s all witnessed, signed and sealed by a notary public. The deputation was indeed observed, with the result that by the time the Adjutant had been summoned and told to produce the officer, the latter was nowhere to be found. It soon transpired that he had been seen catching the Frontier Mail, presumably with the intention of boarding a ship upon whose deck he would be out of the reach of the Indian Courts.

Early next morning the Station Staff Officer down in Lahore was changing into drill order, with polished leather leggings, spurs, medals and sword, and hiring a taxi to take him to the station to carry out the first arrest of his life, and this on the very platform.

Arriving in plenty of time he paced up and down wondering how he would recognise the chap, although there should be no difficulty as of the half-dozen other officers likely to be travelling some would surely know him.

Reaching the end of the platform he heard the train coming in from behind him, so was in an excellent position to start at the engine and work his way along. In the very first carriage was an obvious officer, dressed in the universal attire of grey flannel trousers and khaki drill riding coat. '. . . of the . . .'s? Yes I do know him, he got in at Peshawar and is back beside the guards van.'

Anxious not to lose time the SSO elbowed his way through the frenzied mobs at the doors of the third class carriages, dodging the corners of tin trunks that the porters were carrying on their heads at about his eye level, stepping over baskets, bundles and crawling babies, avoiding old ladies sitting in bunches all over the platform, being obstructed by coolies fighting for possession of the luggage of protesting travellers, slipping on melon rinds.

Eventually, reaching the rear portion of the train he was lucky to recognise someone he knew. '... of the ...'s? Yes I do know him, he got in at Peshawar and is up beside the engine but why on earth are you dressed up like that?'

Looking round in fury, he happened to glance up at the footbridge and there, sprinting across and just about to descend the steps leading to the station entrance, was his quarry clutching by the hand what looked like a dusky mate, a slim long legged girl who was now bounding down the stairs like a chamois.

Casting dignity to the winds the poor SSO gave chase, discovering what he had always suspected, that a sword and spurs are not well designed for the fast negotiation of stairs.

Arriving empurpled and gasping at the ticket office, his medals askew, his helmet in his hand, a glove somewhere on the platform, he just had time to see a taxi whisking off and was lucky in having his own ready to pursue it. The quarry, after dodging about in the suburbs, took the road roughly parallel to the Karachi line presumably with the intention of getting onto a train at some small station and, in due course, catching a boat at Karachi.

Both cars were of roughly the same elderly vintage, both running on the canvases of their tyres and both seemingly liable to immediate disintegration as, with flapping mudguards and horrible squeaks, they swerved in clouds of dust round the strings of totally uninterested camels and donkeys bearing merchandise to market and over luckless scraggy squawking village chickens.

Indian taxi drivers, however, are a sporting lot and this their normal mode of progression, so it was not long before the leading vehicle had run out of petrol somewhere in the desert and the chase was over.

The subsequent court was not feeling lenient and, in due course, our hero found himself in Dharmsala jail for a couple of years. The rest of the story could be apocryphal but may as easily be true. The SSO put in a claim to the Creditor of Military Accounts for quite a large sum of money in taxi hire, only to be told that he had been given authority to take a taxi to and from the station only and that since he was a mounted officer in receipt of charger allowance he should have used his horse for any further duties. His claim was disallowed.

Commendably keeping his temper he politely wrote back pointing out that since the other officer was using a car his charger would have been useless for the mission with which he had been entrusted but was not altogether surprised to receive an answer to the effect that no authority had been given to a 2/Lt to use a taxi!

IV

I don the gilt

Having seen the residence required by the Governor of the mighty Punjab, and the staff necessary to run it, it was time for me to start taking my own place in the machinery and Pat and Bill were both insistent that I must get measured for some of my necessary uniforms that very day; their solicitude over my sartorial completeness, although very kind, did not seem altogether altruistic and, on reflection, it was at once self-evident that without the correct clothes I could not take over any of the public duties. Not only did I lack all the special uniforms worn by the Personal Staff but I was very low in civilian clothes.

We, therefore, went down to the shop of Messrs Ranken & Co, Civil and Military Tailors, with a large uniform case of Bill's clothes in the back of the car; some had originally belonged to Robin Drummond-Wolfe of the Black Watch.

First of all came a 'Staff Coat.' This was an evening tail coat made of dark blue cloth with primrose coloured silk facings; down the front, at the cuffs and in the small of the back were gilt buttons wearing the lion crest; it was worn with normal evening dress trousers, white waistcoat and white tie and was used for all official evening functions; it looked very smart indeed.

Next came 'Undress Blue,' the term 'Undress' being used in a purely relative sense as it was formal in the extreme. To get into this I was first of all made to don a pair of very very tight dark blue overall trousers with a broad red stripe down the outside of each leg, already strapped over black patent leather Wellington boots; to the heel of each boot was fixed a long swan-necked spur; these spurs made a very pleasant and martial jingling noise when I walked.

Having got into the boots and trousers all at the same time, I was handed a dark blue full length frock coat which reached below the knee; it looked quite obvious that the garment would never meet in front; obvious, however, only to myself, as Mr Ranken's British cutter, groping about in its recesses found a row of stout hooks and eyes which he fastened from across my Adam's apple down to my waist; unable to breathe or to bend my neck, I now found him pulling forward a row of buttonholes in an inner flap attached to the right side, which he pushed over a number of large flat bone buttons sewn into the inside of the very thick material forming the front of the left; I was now doubly secured, but this was not all. Seizing the left lapel he pulled it over disclosing two long rows of huge winking lion-embossed brass buttons, the right row of which he fastened into buttonholes inclining from my right shoulder down to my belt. 'Undress' conjures up visions of at least moderate comfort but this was little less than a straight jacket. Next a new gold sword belt was produced, fastened in front with a big square gilt buckle; from the left side hung gold sword slings ending in gilt hooks designed to fasten to my sword by smaller buckles, also gilt; my own sword found favour with nobody, the hilt and steel scabbard must both be silver-plated: Mr. Ranken would attend to it.

We had yet to come to the hat or rather hats. For ceremonial out in the sun when wearing 'Undress blue' I would need a large white Wolseley helmet surmounted by a long gilt spike and kept on my head by a heavy gilt chain when, however, wearing 'Full Dress' my gilt chain must be replaced by one of gun-metal; for occasions when the sun was not strong I must have a black patent leather peaked blue cap with a broad red band round it and the lion crest in front, woven as usual in gilt thread.

The final glory was the aiguillette; this was a broad band of fine and closely intertwined gold and crimson threads forming a thick cord which encircled the right shoulder, came down over the right breast in a graceful loop and fastened onto a little concealed hook below the chin whence it hung down to finish in two gilt peg-shaped objects about four inches long which dangled on the chest and always got in the way at meal times. This originated in a heel rope and peg for tethering a horse but why it should have become a hallmark of the Monarch and his or her Personal Staff, Governors and their Personal Staffs and Officers of the Household Cavalry remains to me one of those military mysteries.

I was now asked by Messrs Ranken's cutter to produce my own Regimental Full Dress which had to be worn on the very grandest occasions. The cutter looked at it rather disparagingly; nevertheless, he would see what he could do with it. As ADC, I needed, however, something else to wear with it: a bunch of red swan's feathers in the form of a plume, screwed into the top of my Wolseley helmet in place of the gilt spike; also a pair of straight spurs to push into the heels of my Wellingtons in place of the swan necked variety.

I began to think that I had spent enough, although a few items were secondhand from Bill, but this was not to be. Mr. Ranken's manager tactfully pointed out that I might require a few suits – perhaps he might make suggestions?

I should need a normal suit or two for everyday use when there was nothing much doing and, of course, a black formal pin-stripe for luncheon parties and a light formal suit for tea parties, then there would be a morning coat and striped trousers with, of course, a grey top hat and also a black top hat. What about my present overcoat? I would require a dark overcoat for going out at nights and a light overcoat for a cold day. Before the summer I should, of course, need a couple of light gaberdine suits; were my tennis clothes really presentable? It was, of course, most essential that I should have a large stock of white doeskin gloves, hard shirts, hard collars both for day and for evening, coloured shirts, yellow gloves, socks, handkerchiefs and all the rest of the minor paraphernalia. A most important item would be sent up to Government House this very evening without fail, a white 'Bombay Bowler' with a single narrow gold stripe in the paggri, for wearing in civilian clothes when on duty.

During the period when I was constantly revisiting Ranken's to have my clothes fitted and refitted I started taking over the more domestic tasks.

As ADC(2) I was first required to make myself acquainted with the arrangements for food and drink, as upon me would rest the final responsibility that they were acceptable both as regards quality and quantity. To assist me in my duties was Mrs Farmer, the housekeeper. Mrs Farmer issued all the groceries. In an excess of enthusiasm I decided to go through Mrs Farmer's vast store cupboard with her ledger, a suggestion to be met with very little enthusiasm on her part; she certainly had a ledger but I could not make out where I started, there were no dates at all and many crossings out; it seemed that she had her own way of doing things, with never a complaint for fifteen years; no ADC had ever gone into this before, nor even suggested it, she had never been shown how to keep a tally of her issues and so on and so forth. She started to snuffle and finally weep quite openly. I felt most embarrassed: it would be dreadful were she to give notice. I acknowledged defeat and retired mopping my brow.

Running the wines was simple; it was the duty of Khizzar, the butler, to report to me every two or three days when the stock in his pantry was getting low, when I would retire to my bedroom to search in the pockets of my various suits, for the key of the wine cellar; accompanying him to the gloomy caverns below the tomb, I would present him with a few bottles of this and that and a few tins of cigarettes which I would hastily enter up in my own ledger.

After my inglorious defeat by Mrs Farmer, I decided to see how Khizzar Mohommed ran his department.

Entering his pantry, I was horrified at what I would have to check were I to do the thing properly; not only were there three or four opened bottles of whisky and gin to be measured out peg by peg but, since at the big dinners we started serving wines from eight points simultaneously, there were eight decanters half full of port, ditto of Madeira and Sherry, together with opened and partially expended bottles of every kind of liqueur under the sun, some of which were hardly ever tasted but had to be quickly available in case anyone asked for them. The upshot of my grand stock-taking was that his stock agreed with his books to the last peg, which was more than I could say of my own as, however scrupulously I entered them up, there was invariably at the end of the month one bottle too many in the cellar or one tin of cigarettes too few.

Another responsibility of ADC(2) was cars but since we had a highly efficient British garage superintendent in the person of Mr. Rowson, to whom I passed on all orders, all I had to do was to ensure that he knew when cars were wanted. Mr. Rowson himself drove P1, the biggest and best of the fleet; slim of figure and erect of carriage, with a keen blue eye and carefully trimmed grey moustache, he looked far more like a retired Colonel than does the genuine article and was constantly, when in mufti, acknowledging salutes from polite young officers.

While taking over these various duties I had also to learn and take part in the daily routine. The first task on going into our office was after breakfast. One ADC had to ring up the private houses of all the Ministers and the Secretaries of Departments and various other officials according to the day of the week to ask whether they had any business which they wished to discuss personally with HE.

Exactly five minutes before the time of departure for the secretariat a little procession would drive up to the porch. First there would be a British or, more often, Anglo-Indian police sergeant mounted on a motor cycle on the front mudguard of which there was a blue pennon with the word 'Pilot' on it; he was armed with a pistol. Next came the big Humber P1 driven by Mr Rowson; in the front seat beside him sat an Indian Police gunman dressed in a smart long blue coat, also armed with a pistol concealed in his clothing. Behind P1 came an open Police escort car containing five uniformed Indian armed police.

The arrival of this cortège was the signal for the ADC in waiting to take his automatic pistol out of a drawer in his desk and start looking at his watch. At the exact minute he would collect HE from his office further along the passage, raise his hat as he opened the door of the car for HE to enter, run round to the other side of the car and get into the left-hand back seat beside him. The shutting of the car door was the signal for the procession to move off towards the Secretariat at the other end of Lahore. As we swung out of Government House gate and down the Mall at a good brisk pace all traffic from the side roads would be halted by the constables on point duty and the motor cycle pilot would wave all other vehicles well into the sides of the road to ensure us a safe and swift journey.

It may well be asked whether *all* these pistols and the armed escort were really necessary, to which the answer is that there was very little likelihood of their being required provided that they were there. Viceroys and Governors have, however, been attacked; Lord Hardinge was the target of a bomb which killed two servants beside him and Sir Geoffrey de Montmorency, the previous Governor of the Punjab, was shot in the back at close range when attending some function at the Punjab University; they can, of course, be replaced, but an incident of this nature is not conducive to the maintenance of public confidence. Religious fanatics and the mentally unbalanced behave unreasonably and unpredictably and the danger lies where they have not got previous police records and are not under surveillance or even known.

As an instance of one of many strange acts of violence which have been done in the name of religion, the story may be interpolated of Mahmud the Donkey. Mahmud was a stallion donkey who lived at one of the Government mule breeding establishments in the Eastern portion of the Punjab where his duties, which we may assume he carried out with the zeal and enthusiasm befitting a Government employee, were essential for the breeding of mules. The Officer-in-Charge of this farm was a Senior Officer of the Veterinary Department who happened to be a Hindu. Mahmud the Donkey had been employed for several years when an entirely unknown Mohammedan resident of Sialkot, at the other end of the Province, heard about him and was incensed at his name which happens to be one of the thousand-and-one names of the Prophet. Without writing any letter of protest or even informing anyone, this Mohammedan undertook the long and expensive journey from Sialkot, murdered the unfortunate Hindu Veterinary Officer and as quietly returned to Sialkot. He was caught and hanged, Mahmud was renamed Bahadur and the incident closed; the lesson, however, remained to be read and remembered.

On arrival at the Secretariat HE would ceremoniously be ushered into his office and the ADC would retire to his own little office next door.

On returning from the Secretariat just before lunch there might be a lunch party awaiting us, the final arrangements for which were being checked over by the other ADC after which the afternoon was devoted to a series of interviews which had been arranged days ahead by the Military Secretary. Those granted interviews would be a series of officials from out-lying places; businessmen, politicians, nawabs, rajahs and all sorts of public men; the ADC-in-Waiting greeted them on arrival, put them in the waiting room, ushered them in and in due course ushered them out again.

After tea HE might play a round of golf or go for a walk, always with a discreetly armed ADC and gunman in attendance, before again returning to his office to wrestle with files which were received from the Secretariat and carried into his office in huge piles as they arrived.

The ADC-in-Waiting could usually expect to get a night's undisturbed rest but this was not always the case; part of his duties was the encoding and decoding of all cipher telegrams and these had a habit of arriving from midnight onwards. Having just achieved a deep sleep, there would be a knock on the bedroom door and a chuprassi would enter bearing a telegram with three large blue crosses on the envelope denoting that it was 'immediate.' Hastily donning a dressing gown and searching about for keys, he would pad along to the office and extract the cipher books from the safe.

There were two sorts of immediate telegram, the confidential code one and the secret cipher. The former was comparatively simple and arrived in a series of blocks of letters, the only action necessary for its interpretation being to hunt backwards and forwards through a volume the size of a London telephone directory; it usually dealt with matters that could as easily have come in clear by post and have been dealt with next day or, for that matter, next week.

The second type, however, called for considerable concentration, as it was all in blocks of figures. Wearily grasping a second huge volume, this time full of nothing but pages and pages of figures, and having discovered on what page, block, line and figure to start by, a process which was sufficiently difficult in itself, one placed one row of figures below another row of figures and by a complicated system of adding and subtracting, produced a third set of figures. One then looked up the answers to these figures in yet a third volume and if one had been both very accurate and very lucky, the message would generally come to life before one's eyes. More often, however, one would have missed out a figure somewhere or made a silly mistake in addition and subtraction, with the result that the outcome would be complete gibberish and one was forced to start all over again from the beginning. With a message of perhaps four or five hundred words an excerpt from some important political speech as yet to be made, starting again was no light matter and the longer one went on the more tired one became and the more one made fresh mistakes.

Since one mistake of only one figure could and did throw the whole thing out, it was essential to keep calm and not be thrown into a frenzy by an incautious glance at the steadily rising sun. Sometimes, of course, the mistake would lie at the door of the transmitter and one would break off for coffee while everything was being checked through by the telegraph offices; it was more annoying still when the message had to be referred back to the originator, causing a few more hours delay and positively ensuring the disruption of any further attempt at sleep.

One of our complaints against these messages was that they were couched not in journalese but in the rounded periods and long-winded phraseology commonly encountered in departmental directives.

Some of the longest messages that we had to decipher were those in connection with the abdication of King Edward VIII. These required the combined efforts of both ADCs and lasted over a period of several nights. We naturally had to keep our mouths very tightly closed about the contents of all secret correspondence but this world shaking information was so uppermost in our minds that we hardly dared speak to anyone at all for fear of unwittingly giving something away. The danger in India was that since no one saw the American magazines, the general public, both British and Indian, were completely in the dark regarding any kind of crisis: should they suddenly find themselves choosing between their loyalty to their King or to a politician and a prelate of whom no one had ever heard anything either good or bad, there was every chance of the emergence of an overwhelming 'King's Party' which would seriously embarrass the government in Whitehall.

Another class of telegram that could not be taken lightly and that had to be dealt with immediately upon receipt was any appeal from a member of the public to stay the execution of a convicted criminal. We, of course, had never heard their names before and did not know the dates or times of their executions, as violence, including murder, was too prevalant among all our fighting races to be of news value. These telegrams although addressed to the Governor were not shown to him but were transmitted by the fastest means to the Home Secretary who, if he thought that any fresh evidence was forthcoming would, of course, postpone the execution. There had, indeed, been an incident in the dim past which served as a warning that any slackness in delivery anywhere along the line might have an unfortunate result.

An ADC had been handed one of these things very late at night; it happened to be a Sunday, when on tour with the Governor somewhere in the wastes of the Nili-Bar desert. This was before the days of local wireless communication and they were in camp about fifty miles from the nearest telegraph office; they had gone through a hard day's work in intense heat and the ADC was very tired; fighting off the inclination to risk it till the morning, he woke up an equally tired chauffeur and off they drove over the dumpy, sandy roads to retransmit the telegram to the Home Secretary. A few hours later in the grey light of dawn a grisly little scene was enacted in the prison and it was not until all was over that the Prison Governor, anxious to think about something else as quickly as possible, walked over to his office to see what the early post had brought. Propped up against the inkwell in the centre of his desk was an envelope marked with three large blue crosses. It had been there an hour or two and was from the Home Secretary.

V

The tocsin of the soul – the dinner-bell

Shortly after Bill Kensington departed to rejoin his regiment I found myself at my first dinner party; I have, I suppose, been to many big dinners but never in my life have I seen anything quite so formal or quite so picturesque as these Government House affairs. There were usually one or two a week and they required the efforts of the whole personal staff to run and their mechanics are not devoid of interest.

The first obstacle, that of whom to ask, having been surmounted it was necessary to issue invitations in ample time; it was 'not done' to refuse and we had to give people every opportunity of organizing their own social activities to conform to ours.

Having got the list of acceptances, which would number exactly thirty-eight people and show a slight preponderance of men over women, we got down to classifying everyone according to Precedence. Precedence was all important; that odd couple of pages in the front of Debrett was as nothing compared with what we had to contend; The Warrant of Precedence of India was a whole volume and a very thumbed one too. It was of merely academic interest to us whether or not the elder son of a Marquis was senior to the younger son of a Duke; what did concern us was that the vast majority of our guests were officials and we took steps to have them as well assorted as possible, which did not make Precedence easy.

A few instances such as the following show that one could not get far without reference to the book. Was the Roman Catholic Metropolitan senior to a Financial Commissioner? Was the Director of Public Instruction senior to a Secretary of Government (PWD)? Where did the Vice-Chancellor of the University stand with regard to a Judge of the High Court with less than thirty years' service? How did the Chief Engineer of the North Western Railway compare with the GOC of a Military District outside his own District? There was even worse to follow: there were about forty-five categories in the warrant, all devoted to such senior people that no soldier of rank junior to Colonel was recognised at all. Since numerous officials of equal standing shared a number, it became necessary to discover in some unobtrusive way whether, say, Dr Smith, a Professor of Medical Jurisprudence in one college, was senior or junior to Dr Mohammed Khan, a Professor of Ophthalmology in another. One never dared to take a risk as most of these officials had been meeting each other at various functions for years and knew, or at any rate their wives knew, their relative seniorities to a day.

Having sorted out these precedences, one grabbed a large sheet of paper, drew a rough plan of the table, took a deep breath and started off. Writing down the name of Lady Emerson opposite the centre of one side of the table, we put the most senior male guest on her left to take her in and the next senior on her right, then crossing over to the other side of the table, we wrote down HE with the most senior lady on his right and the second senior lady on his left; so far so good. Now we crossed the table again and put the third most senior lady on the right of the second most senior man and the fourth senior lady on the left of the most senior man, with, on the other side again, the fourth senior man on the right of the first woman and the third man on the left of the second woman. Now doing a little bracketing of partners and checking up that the third man was not and never had been married to the second woman, one found the fourth woman and the fourth man both without partners, so put the fifth lady on the right of the fourth man and the fifth man on the left of the fourth lady, with the sixth lady on the left of the third man, herself being taken in by the seventh man on her left; having thus got into the swing of the thing, one then went without pause for the remaining three quarters of the table.

Should it so happen that there was no senior single man at the party, with the result that all the senior couples found themselves taking each others' husbands and wives in to dinner, we had a simple variation. Leaving the original six places, which could under no circumstances be changed, we put the fourth man on the left of the second lady and the third man on the right of the second lady, the latter man taking the fifth lady; this had the effect of making husbands and wives sit as far from each other as possible and ruled out any straight swaps among families.

The whole thing was really simple unless someone distracted one by peering over one's shoulder and saying they thought one might be wrong; there were, however, occasions when one got to the ends of the table, where the ADCs sat, to find that one of them had an empty chair beside him; then one called for a drink and started all over again from the beginning. These, happily, were not the days when women could further confuse one by assuming military ranks and there was no question of Colonel A Jones and Colonel B Jones mucking up the whole thing by turning out to be husband and wife. We did, however, have some Jokers in the pack; the heads of firms of which there were several important ones, had no official precedence at all, so we could slip them into the table plan where we thought suitable, besides being useful to us for this reason their wives were usually prettier and more expensively dressed.

This rough table plan was usually completed by lunch time and then sent down to the Government Printing Office, which in due course returned fifty copies on beautiful stiff paper with the Lion Crest in gold at the top. The government printers were wonderful men, for, as often as not, at sometime during the afternoon or evening one of our guests would telephone to say that he or she was ill and could not come, for India is a country with diseases that can suddenly make one quite ill without warning; we had then to cancel the first plan and start again but, no matter how late we sent it down, we always got it back in time, even if its arrival synchronized with that of the guests.

A good half-hour before the first guests might be expected to arrive (and since no one dared arrive late some arrived very early), ADC(2) would arrive all dressed up for the fray and start checking up on the khidtmagars. We found it best to have one khidtmagar to every two guests, the kitchen being some way from the dining room, but since we did not have a full-sized dinner party every night it was obviously uneconomical to employ all these men permanently, so we imported about fifteen from outside when required and also brought in our own personal servants. It sounds a tall order suddenly to produce fifteen trained waiters but there was always a small pool of excellent servants in Lahore whose masters, all senior officials, had given them retaining fees while on leave in Britain, for when one had served in India for a few years and collected a staff of servants whom one liked, one kept them for life.

On arrival they were issued out with Government House livery and then lined up and inspected. For some reason the smallest men would always choose the biggest clothes, for which a psychiatrist would, no doubt, produce a scientific reason, leaving the smaller sizes for the bigger men whose great muscular wrists would show between gold cuff and white gloves, so off they had to be sent to change; belts would be crooked, paggris not straight and sometimes, worst crime of all, a lock of hair visible on the forehead below the paggri.

The ADC then went round checking the guests' name cards with the table plan, for every place must be labelled so as to obviate any possible confusion. A stroll round to see that the rooms were warm and that none of the lights had fused, that the cigarette boxes were full and the ashtrays empty and he would take up his position at the door of the big drawing room to receive guests, to introduce the earlier arrivals to one another and to make up his mind as to the identity of those people he had never clapped eyes on before.

Meanwhile, the other ADC who could afford to appear a little later, quickly checked over the cloakrooms to see that the soap was unused and the towels clean and that, in addition, that of the ladies contained innumerable little dishes, trays and bottles holding safetypins and cotton wool, needles and cotton, scissors, nail files, powder and heaven alone knows what else. A very important item, which we kept outside in the porch, was a box containing several pairs of women's long white evening gloves without which they were not allowed to appear; there was hardly a dinner party when one, if not two ladies, had not left theirs behind and had to be comforted and re-equipped. Another article of dress which was obligatory was stockings but these we did not provide; we telephoned the nearest male relative in the morning and gave him the onus of passing on the raspberry.

The ADC on the door then chatted to the Sub-Inspector of Police in charge of parking arrangements until the headlights of approaching cars warned him to assume a welcoming smile and take up his position in the porch. While handing ladies out of their cars, stopping flustered people from darting into the wrong cloakrooms and, of course, giving out those long white gloves, he was very busy noticing which woman came with which men, not in any nasty spirit, but to find out who was married to whom.

After counting in our thirty-eight guests, ADC (1) would follow the last couple upstairs and assist his colleague in making introductions and handing round cigarettes and sherry and then go into a quick huddle to check up on everyone's identity. When the fingers on the clock pointed to exactly twenty-eight minutes past eight we would line up the guests while one of us departed to return again in exactly two minutes, fling open the door at the far end of the room and announce in stentorian tones, 'His Excellency and Lady Emerson.'

Leading HE to the end of the line, one of us would walk slowly down in front of him reeling off the names without pause as he shook hands, a pace or two behind him the other ADC would introduce Lady Emerson in like manner. This would have been quite simple had one known all the guests but there was always a large proportion, especially in Simla, whom one had never seen before they entered the room, and it was against all the rules to ask them who they were or even to be seen consulting the list of names in one's pocket.

To the uninitiated, and we took good care that everyone did remain uninitiated, these introductions seemed nothing short of miraculous. They had probably seen us at official ceremonies but knew full well that we had never seen them, so how could we have sorted them out and got all their names right without ever asking who they were? The solution was simple enough. We had spent a long time in compiling dinner lists, issuing invitations, checking off acceptances, working out precedence and compiling the table plan so as we could hardly help but have learnt all the names parrot-wise a day or two before the dinner; having then learnt this list of names forwards, backwards and all jumbled up so that one could announce every name in any order without pause, we sat down to scrutinize it more closely. Disregarding those whom we knew by sight, we concentrated on the strangers who might number as many as twenty, this twenty comprising, say, eight married couples and four single men. Forgetting about the eight ladies for the moment, we turned our attention to the twelve men.

Four of these might be soldiers, who are the simplest; soldiers have been defined by some wit as 'men who fight for their pay,' and even when wearing civilian clothes this constant struggle is usually betrayed by their stern and uncompromising expressions; when dining at Government House, however, soldiers wear Mess Dress and can immediately be picked out, by their decorations and, of course, their ranks; so much for the soldiers. The next people to find were those with distinctive evening dresses, such as Political Officers, foreign diplomats, Police Officers or the clergy; it was most unlikely that there would be more than one of each, so they presented no problems. Of the remainder, two or three would certainly be Indian Civil Servants, distinguishable from each other by their decorations.

This left a few men wearing ordinary civilian tail coats, who might be any of the many varieties of engineer, gazetted Railway Officers, or business men; failing identification of any sort, one could ring up one's friends and ask for a description. A further simplification occurred by some of the list being Indians; particulars of all these men having been memorised before their arrival, it merely remained for the ADC in the porch to keep a careful eye on who got out of what car, no matter how pretty the lady for whom he was producing a pair of gloves.

Mistakes over introductions hardly ever occurred and when they did they went unnoticed, as the people being introduced were at this stage too flurried to listen to what one was saying. George Still, of the Corps of Guides IA, a Viceregal ADC, found himself introducing no less than twelve members of a Japanese Military Mission, all looking exactly alike, all having names that were hard to memorize and all of whom wore decorations such as the Order of the Rising Sun or the Flowering Chrysanthemum, together with badges of rank that he had never seen before; he is credited with having gone through the lot without a mistake. I once found myself having to introduce a gentleman from Madras with the rather difficult name of Vijagaravaicharya; having first discovered the number of syllables, I spent quite a considerable period rehearsing it aloud and had just reached the stage of being able to reel it off to my satisfaction when the telephone rang to convey his regrets for having been taking ill and being unable to attend.

After dinner we started work in earnest. Our first action was to present a man to Lady Emerson and a Lady to HE; then, going round the room, we presented men to all the ladies and made them sit down in chairs which had carefully been arranged in couples round the room; the four or five men left over were then shepherded back to the 'pen', which was the small drawing room where there were drinks.

Returning to the big room, we move round with cigarettes and planned the first 'switch,' these switches being governed by the rules that no lady might have any man presented to her twice, including her dinner companions, nor might she have a vacant chair beside her for even the space of time that it took us to cross the floor with a man. Allowing about seven minutes, we produced two men from the 'pen,' one of whom we introduced to Lady Emerson whose first partner we took to some other lady, whose first partner we removed and took to a second lady, whose first partner we escorted back to the 'pen;' the second man had momentarily been left by a pair of empty chairs and while one ADC took up HE's second partner and introduced her to him, for HE was the only man in the room who stayed in the same chair and had partners brought to him, the other ADC removed his first partner and brought her over to sit and talk with this man from the 'pen,' while the first ADC took the man who had previously been talking to HE's second partner over to some other lady, removing her first partner back to the 'pen.' Returning to the 'pen' we would then collect two more men whom we introduced to two ladies, taking off their partners whom we introduced to two other ladies whose first partners we then took back to the 'pen' where we would now find the single original inhabitant; taking him off to the large room, we would introduce him to a lady, take her partner to a second lady and take the latter's partner back to the 'pen.' Simple!

Having completed the first 'switch' to our satisfaction, we returned to the big drawing room to work out the next. Consulting our lists on which HE and Lady Emerson had placed ticks against those to whom they wished to talk, we might find that the latter's next choice was already in the room; this, however, presented no difficulty and, studying our watches for the precise minutes, we started in again; bringing a man from the 'pen', we presented him to the lady to whose partner Lady Emerson wished to talk, thus releasing the latter to be taken up and presented to Lady Emerson, whose partner having started off the evening in the 'pen' could now be introduced to another lady; this now completed three changes in the second 'switch,' so bringing out two of the earlier arrivals in the 'pen,' we took one up to the empty pair of chairs and then, taking up HE's

His Excellency the Viceroy arrives at Government House for a week's stay.

The Mall, Simla, which housed the European shops and restaurants

partner, brought back his second to talk to this man; the other arrival and HE's present partner's last partner were then introduced to two more ladies, whose partners were introduced to two others, whose previous partners were led away. This completed nine changes in the second 'switch' so that every lady in the room had by now had at least one change of partner and there were half-a-dozen men who had not yet been allowed to escape to the 'pen' for a drink and a breather. Each 'switch' now became increasingly difficult, as already so early in the evening of the twenty men or so present there were five or six whom each lady could not have presented to her agin, so that by the end of the party our brains were reeling!

There were other little complications with which we had to contend. Some of the guests had wives who spoke only French, or perhaps Persian; the quite lovely little Rani of Mandi could never be induced to utter in any language at all but so pretty was she and so charming her smile that there was never any lack of volunteers eager to just sit beside her and surreptitiously gaze at her; a good friend of mine the Nepalese Ambassador, who had a sense of humour, was not permitted to partake of food, at any rate publicly, with any but other very high-caste Hindus, so, therefore, had to be timed to arrive with the port. We had to know who were vegetarians, who had religious taboos, who were on a special diet for medical reasons and what the diet was.

Eventually the evening would draw to an end and all that remained for us to do was to see our guests into their cars before ourselves retiring or, alternatively, joining a party at a dance at one of the big hotels, in either case hoping against hope that we would not be waylaid by an office orderly with a broad grin and a cipher wire, nor next morning be called up by some delighted friend anxious to be first with the tidings that we had at some period introduced a husband and wife to each other.

VI

Primrose, the elephant

About the first of my non-routine duties was to accompany HE on a visit to the Borstal Institution, wearing one of my new lounge suits and my white hat. HE was taken round by the Inspector General of Prisons, Colonel Puri, an Indian, while I followed with the Officer-in-Charge.

I then had to represent HE at a funeral, dressed in my undress blue, my sword on gold slings. The grave proved too narrow for the coffin, the grave digger could not be found, and after some abortive spade work by men in morning coats we all went home leaving the late lamented still above ground. I had met him and could imagine his comments from on high.

More cheerful duties were those involving taking HE and Lady Emerson to the finals of various tournaments. We watched them all; tennis, which drew British and Indian competitors from all over India; hockey, which has really become India's national game and at which they were all supreme (for the all conquering Olympic team which never had a single goal scored against it failed to win a single practice match before leaving India) and football.

We had also one military engagement. This was the King's Birthday Parade at which HE took the salute of the garrison. Motoring down to the big brigade parade ground at Mian Mir, the ground where Ranjit Singh, the Lion of the Punjab, used to review his Sikh army, we mounted our horses to watch the Brigade march past.

Behind the infantry came a most unusual and very spectacular body, camelry. There were in India a very limited number of irregular camel troops, used for carrying the tentage and stores of troops on the line of march; they carried all their kit and on completion disappeared whence they had come, the drivers, hubble bubble in hand, slowly trudging along holding a cord attached to their camels' noses, until they all passed out of sight and out of ken.

Here they were, huge unwashed villainous looking desperadoes from the Salt Range, some with beards dyed bright red with henna; I do not know if they took kindly to drill or to cleanliness; they had been enlisted together with their own personal camels on the more or less rough understanding that they would carry baggage when so required and while serving, refrain from murdering each other or anyone else; today they were sitting on their camels and dressed up like the cavalry with coloured turbans and scarlet sashes under their leather belts and on their faces expressions of lofty disdain, the exact counterpart of those on the faces of their camels.

During the cold weather in Lahore we were always visited by a number of people, some on missions, others quite unashamedly sight-seeing, for in the days before the Welfare State there did exist honest people with the time and money to wander about the world and enjoy themselves.

An entrée to one Government House usually meant a letter of introduction to the next and it was a pleasure to show interested people the way in which India was run.

The guests found themselves accompanying each other round India in batches, starting off with Government House, Bombay, where they would be taken round the sights, bathe in the Indian Ocean, and so on. They may have been rather startled by the Parsee Towers of Silence. Parsees dispose of their dead by laying them on the flat tops of these tall towers to be devoured by the birds of the air. Older residents of Bombay are apt without much encouragement to produce a revolting story about a tea party, held on their very own lawn, at which a vulture flying overhead absent-mindedly dropped a human toe into the milk jug.

Having stayed their allotted spell at Bombay, the guests went on to Viceroy's House, New Delhi, that vast creation of Lutyens.

The Delhi area is one in which one can go sightseeing for months on end but one of the least known spectacles was that provided by the well divers, a living relic of Mogul entertainment. This was a family who had for untold generations held the unusual Court post of producing a constant supply of men who were prepared to jump down a well at the behest of their masters.

This well among the ruins of the fifth Delhi, was constructed with a narrow staircase spiralling down between the earth and the brick lining of the well shaft, with here and there a window looking inwards, down as far as water level. For the modest sum of one rupee an old man would divest himself of all but his loin cloth, sit on the parapet muttering a rather theatrical prayer and then with a blood-curdling shriek leap in feet first to whiz down and hit the water with a most almighty splash, climbing the stairway again for a repeat performance.

Since the well was eighty feet deep, narrow at the bottom and only contained eight feet depth of water in summer, the performance was far too dangerous to be countenanced by a British Government; it was, however, recognised as being improper to deprive a family of their livelihood and, as a special dispensation, all the men then jumping were allowed to continue on the strict understanding that no more were trained. I can only observe that either these old boys had been born a hundred years ago or else that the law was being observed more in the spirit than in the letter.

Our potential guests, their minds already broadened by one or two things, now headed for their next port of call, Lahore. Behind them lay the real India with its small dark men and its coconut trees; ahead was the Punjab, now mostly in Pakistan, the land of the five rivers, populated by the descendants of all the warrior races who had in turn swept down in successive waves from the shores of the Mediterranean, the Caspian, Persia and Central Asia. From the window of the railway carriage things began to look quite different; in place of the endless barren vista of miles and miles of dusty thorn bush-studded country they began to see fields of wheat, of sugar cane and of cotton as far as the horizon on either side.

On the wayside platforms, too, were men of a totally different race shouting to each other in gutteral Punjabi; soon the train passed into the land of the Sikhs, those ferocious sons of battle, all the men wearing the insignia of their sect, the iron bangle, the long hair done up in a knot, the beard often tied in a net, all, too, carrying that most cherished emblem, a sword.

The Punjabi bull-frogs, too, were bigger and better, for their croaking could actually be heard above the roar of the train.

On arrival at Government House we had many things to show our guests according to their tastes. An early entertainment which could always be relied upon as a sure-fire winner was a trip round the teeming bazaars of the picturesque old city on the back of Primrose, the elephant; shopping from her was far more oriental and romantic than from a motor car, as any merchandise that a visitor wished to inspect could be gently wafted up out of a shop window, examined and carefully replaced with the minimum of effort to anybody and with great pleasure to Primrose, who loved showing off.

Another way of entertaining our guests was to take them off for the day to see the Golden temple of Amritsar. This temple, entirely covered in gold leaf, was reached by a causeway across an ornamental lake in the middle of Amritsar City and was the Holy of Holies of the Sikh faith. The city itself was insalubrious, streets being narrow, winding and dirty, and the inhabitants lacking in that friendliness which could always be counted upon elsewhere. It must not be forgotten that but for the British the Sikhs would still have been masters of the whole of the Punjab and they were resentful at our curtailment of their power. The city had a bad name for communal riots and general seditious tendencies.

The inside of the temple was small and in the centre sat an old white bearded priest reading aloud in a monotonous drone from the pages of the Granth Sahib, their Holy Book which was read aloud ceaselessly night and day by one of the priests.

On only one occasion did I see the temple treasure and that was when accompanying the then Viceroy, Lord Willingdon, for whom it was displayed. It could only be seen on very special occasions, as seven keys were required to unlock the treasury, each key being held by an important Sikh leader living in a different part of the Punjab.

It was not only we who entertained our guests, for it was very often they who made us smile. One of the very first during my tour of duty was Major Yeats-Brown, the author of 'Bengal Lancer.' Neither Pat, the other ADC, nor I knew more about mystics than one could write on the back of a stamp and were slightly alarmed by a hint from Viceroy's House that he was prone to going off into trances; he had, of course, written about studying yoga in Hindu temples and living in caves with the sort of people whom we would not expect to find on our calling list.

Luckily, we had staying in the house a very understanding fellow guest, Lady Beatrice Pole-Carew, who had come out on the boat with him, so to her we took our problem. We explained that we did not want him going off into a trance in the middle of some public ceremony and we did not know if it would be safe to stop him, in the same way as one is not supposed to waken a sleep-walker. She assured us that we could count on her, so, when an evening or two later we suddenly saw him looking rather intense and glassy-eyed, we quickly hurried him over to her.

Demanding the Indian Railway Guide, she thrust it into his unwilling hands.

'Oh dear Major Yeats-Brown you are so clever and know India so well. I feel I should go to Darjeeling and see the snows of Everest, so beautiful at sunset they say; can you look up the trains for me? I am such a dunce at Baedeker.'

Waiting until he had solved this extremely complicated

journey she lightly put her hand on his arm:-

'I did tell you that I would like to start from Secunderabad down in Central India didn't I? I have an old school friend down there whom I haven't seen for years who has asked me to stay and perhaps I might persuade her to come with me.'

Having got her to Secunderabad and then from Secunderabad to Darjeeling, all cross country changing here and there at stations with unpronounceable names, the gallant Major, now slightly sweating, waved the guide for one of us to remove but the lady gave a radiant smile.

'Oh Major Yeats-Brown, do you think I should see the jungle cities of Ceylon? From where would it be best to take a ship? I am sure you must have been there yourself.'

Yeats-Brown thumbed through the pages.

'Oh well, if it is so difficult I won't go there, lets start again, how does one reach those wonderful temples in Madras?'

By now he was quite convinced that she had no intention of going to any of those places; he had after all come out from home on the same P&O, and there had been no mention of it, but the therapy went on until she was perfectly satisfied that his astral body was firmly tethered for the night and knew what was in store for it should it feel restless during the next few days.

Another of our celebrated guests was General Evangeline Booth of the Salvation Army.

Her personality was terrific and her handling of the big monster meetings which she held quite masterly. I was sitting close behind her on the platform with, beside me, a very senior Salvation Army Officer, Commissioner Blower; at her every trenchant, ringing phrase which succeeded, as was calculated, to maintain the high pitch of religious fervour which quickly permeated the place, Commissioner Blower turned to me and said, 'God be praised,' which put me in a quandary as to whether to reply, 'Hear, hear!' or 'Hallelujah.'

One of our most colourful guests was Rosita Forbes, the traveller and novelist, whose visit came during the period of Court Mourning for King George V when we had to wear black ties in civilian clothes, black armbands in uniform and black waistcoats and ties with our evening Staff Coat Livery and were forbidden to attend any public festivities whatsoever, including for a short time even the cinema. She rather surprised us, for we did not then know her ways, by appearing at a small official dinner the first night clad in a bright scarlet dress when all the other women were in deepest black but put things right by explaining to the room at large that she 'did not know our social status, but that in London only the Court were in mourning.'

The Viscount and Viscountess Chetwynd struck an original note by arriving from Bombay by car. I went along to their suite their first morning to ask what they would like to do, where I was informed in rather shocked tones by the chuprassi that they already had gone out – they had not said where, but in very dirty clothes indeed. I was frankly puzzled; they had seemed such a normal pair; but all was explained when I ran them to earth in the garage; all I could see of her Ladyship was a pair of shapely ankles sticking out from below their car whence came the noise of hammering intermingled with profanity; my Lord, in dirty dungarees, oil on his face, was standing keeping at bay the entire garage staff who were all extremely and justifiably indignant at any guest insisting on or even touching his own car. It turned out that they were a pair of well-known racing drivers.

VII

The valley of the Gods

In April the plains get very hot. A dry searing wind starts blowing that soon shrivels up all green vegetation and the air loses its wonderful winter sparkle. It becomes fatiguing to take vigorous exercise at any time but in the mornings and evenings, and trying to write anywhere but directly under a fan is unpleasant, as sweat trickles down the arm and onto the paper. At night it becomes too hot to sleep until late and the heat wakes one up in the morning; flies appear in swarms from nowhere and the malaria-bearing mosquitoes start making their unwelcome appearance. The more intelligent birds migrate and with them migrates the Punjab Government to the cool of Simla.

It was, however, convenient for HE and Lady Emerson to have a short holiday between leaving Lahore and arriving at Simla (heaven knows they deserved it), and they chose a different place to go to each spring. My first spring it was decided to visit Kulu, a delightful valley famous for its scenery, away up in the mountains beyond the hill state of Mandi.

Moving from Government House was highly organized. At GH one walked out of the office leaving one's files spread about the desk and, on arrival, there they were neatly stacked on it. One walked out of one's bedroom to get into the car leaving one's clothes draped over the back of the chair, or more likely on the floor and, on arrival, there they all were hung up in the cupboard awaiting one. There were certain compensations in employing a whole army of servants.

The journey to Kulu entailed a train journey followed by two days by road. Special police arrangements had to be made and all executive civil authorities warned about HE's movements as it was their duty to meet him on the border of the area for which they were responsible and escort him through.

On the day of departure normal work went on until after dinner when, still in evening dress, we motored down to the ceremonial platform at the station where we were received by the Agent to the North Western Railway (The Managing Director), the Station Master, the Commissioner of Lahore, the Deputy Commissioner, the Deputy Inspector General of Railway Police and a host of lesser officials. Walking up the strip of red carpet from the platform entrance to the coach door, we entered first a brass railed observation platform and then a small drawing room where the more senior officials were entertained for a few minutes.

The two coaches used by the Governor had been specially built for the visit of the Prince of Wales in 1921; the one we had entered contained a drawing room furnished with cretonned armchairs and sofa, occasional tables and a writing desk; on a side table were the current papers and periodicals and a few new library books; in a little cabinet were an ice bucket, glasses and the necessary bottles. Leading out of this compartment was the dining room with a highly polished table and room to dine about eight people; further along were the kitchen and accommodation for a limited number of personal servants. Returning the way I came, I walked through the heavily ornamented observation platform into the other private coach; here was a row of bedrooms with proper beds, full length looking glasses, bathrooms etc. These two coaches spent most of the year garaged by the Railway, a goodish sum being handed over in garage fees. The remainder of the train was made up of normal passenger coaches for the accommodation of servants and police: at the end was a flat truck on which were P2 and the GH lorry.

The proper courtesies having been observed, our guests bade

us farewell, HE indicated that he was ready for the train to move, and off we steamed into the night.

I awoke next morning to find that we had already arrived at Pathankote from where we were due to continue the journey by car. The place for me had very mixed memories as it was railhead for our regimental depot at Bakloh and since from there this was three days' march, all of it downhill on a very hard road, we usually arrived with sore feet. Here outside the carriage window was the dusty area in which we sat on the ground on arrival, waiting for the slow swaying baggage camels with our possessions to catch up. Waiting for camel transport to arrive is unenjoyable; having marched for most of the day, one wishes to sit or lie but, there being nowhere but the hard ground on which to do it, there one sits or lies, no matter whether it be awash with rain, baking hot under the sun, covered with sharp stones or merely scattered with goat droppings. Just there was the area of sand and cinders upon which, rolled in our blankets, we used to try and sleep, eddies of dust stirring our hair while all around the village dogs bayed the moon, disturbed by the unexpected sounds and smells of camels and the tramp of sentries.

Just out of sight was the military siding. Visions rose before my eyes of the scenes attendant upon loading dozens of squealing, frightened, kicking mules and horses into open trucks, all under a blazing sun, after a sleepless night and with sore feet; of the Colonel when he learnt that I could not give him a compartment to himself.

The first day's drive up the Kangra valley was uneventful until the evening when we entered the State of Mandi, as guests of whose Ruler we were due to spend the first night; rounding a corner we nearly ran into half-a-dozen Lancers in full dress, lined across the road; as we slowed down they saluted and, turning their horses, galloped along the road in front of us ventre-à-terre; this was His Highness's Body Guard come to escort us.

His Highness had beautiful manners and great charm; his family had ruled Mandi for eight hundred years. While we dined in the Palace a string band played classical music and I noticed that they were nearly all Gurkhas, military pensioners, many having been trained by our pre-war German bandmaster.

Leaving Mandi state, we crossed the border into Kulu where we passed under a triumphal archway decorated with 'Welcome' spelt out in flowers, beyond which we saw school children lining the road, waving and cheering and in the distance a crowd of officials, garlands in their hands.

One day I went for a walk and found a camp of Gaddis, looking quite different both in features and in dress from the locals. They are nomadic shepherds spending their summers in the high hills from whence they bring vast herds of thousands of sheep and goats down to the foothills when forced to do so by the approach of winter with, on the high ground, its nine months of deep snow. They dress in grey felt-like tunic, rough trousers and puttees, but their distinguishing mark is a very long piece of brown rope woven from goats hair wound round their waists. With them they bring huge and extremely fierce hairy dogs to guard their flocks from the panthers which follow them about. The gaddis, a hardy lot, dispense with tents and sleep in the open beside their flocks, no matter what the weather may be.

There was a hand ful of British settlers scattered about Kulu typical of what one might expect in such a remote place, and some families have been there since shortly after 1846 when we took over Kulu from the Sikhs and appointed a British Commissioner. Since then officers came up to shoot and fish, keen to escape from the heat below. Finding the climate and scenery to their liking, (there were flowers everywhere in profusion, changing as the valley gained height, pale pink oleanders, feathery spiraea, dark red and pale pink and yellow potentilla in between great banks of rhododendrons), some decided to retire here and brought up their families from India.

In course of time some descendants married local hill girls, who could be very pretty, while other families intermarried with each other; this, however, did not prevent them from having constant vendettas with each other over the most trivial things.

There was one family which was unique and remained very much aloof from the others, for which reason they were under deep suspicion. Their name was Roerich, which is Russian, and they were highly talented, musical and well read. Their house was hung with paintings by the head of the family; they could discuss the intricacies and subtleties of such things as archaeology, ballet, folk-lore, theology and. theosophy. They had been up here for about eight years and both the locals and the Punjab Government could be pardoned for wondering exactly what they were doing.

Any Kipling enthusiast will know that throughout the nineteenth century and to a lesser degree after it Great Britain and Russia had been playing a hallowed game of espionage and counter espionage in Central Asia; more than one officer was murdered in these largely unknown wastes, while others simply disappeared complete with their escorts, drawn chiefly from the ranks of that famous regiment, Queen Victoria's Own Corps of Guides, who were raised for this role and recruited men from the Frontier, Afghanistan and Central Asia.

The Punjab Government's surprise was not excessive when it discovered that Roerich himself had been to Moscow and had wandered about all over Asia, always well supplied with money. There was, however, no crime in this and the picture became clearer when it transpired that he had visited Mongolia only a year before to investigate some types of grass which it was hoped would combat soil erosion in America, financed by the Americans.

I heard an extraordinary story much later from another source that the highly intelligent Mr. Roerich was the founder and High Priest of some kind of mystical cult of which Henry Wallace, the American Vice President was a disciple. It seems that Wallace was accustomed to write to Roerich in the most extraordinary theosophical jargon addressing him as 'guru' and alluding to 'meeting the seven stars under the sign of the three stars' etc.

Unfortunately, this correspondence got into the hands of the rival political party, the Republicans, who naturally made the most of it and that was the end of poor Mr. Wallace's aspirations to Presidency; one sincerely hopes in all charity that this was not the end of the Roerick's comfortable income from America.

While on this topic it might give food for thought that the gurus who practice in India among Indians are perfectly sincere men living simple lives. It is one of their tenets that whereas a man is entitled to charge for his services so that he may live, his remunerations must be sufficient only for his needs; should he give way to greed his mystic powers will be removed from him in the same way as they were bestowed.

After a few more days in this camp we moved higher up the valley to a spot called Minali where we happened to come in for an interesting annual festival in which the Gods are paraded in public for all to see, bedecked with flowers and borne on litters on men's shoulders. These little tinsel covered dolls between two and three feet high were treated with the utmost reverence and it was not politic to approach too close. Each was accompanied by his own mouthpiece, an otherwise ordinary person who went into a trance when his God wished to communicate with the mortal world.

Everyone was there, dressed in his or her best clothes, forming a series of little processions, each headed by their village or temple bands.

The instruments too seemed at first glance to be entirely indigenous, some drums gently thumped by the heel of the hand, others whacked with a curved stick, to the accompaniment of various reedy flutes and piccolo-like instruments. One's attention was, however, caught by what looked exactly like those long curved eighteenth century 'serpents' which one does not see outside military museums and which are said to be of Turkish origin, for Turkey brought the novelty of military bands to Europe, at least as far as Vienna, in her invasion. Had they come up into the hills as a result of the Turkoman invasion of Northern India, or down the other way through the high passes?

One's attention too was drawn to what looked like wooden Alpenhorns as used by Alpine shepherds but these were made of silver and immensely long, so long that they had to be supported on the shoulders of one man while another did the blowing.

They emitted a series of fog-horn like notes of deafening intensity at indeterminate intervals which in this setting seemed perfectly natural and even musical.

In the civilised world spiritualism is practised by a mere fraction of the population and suspected by the remainder as being odd, possibly slightly dangerous and, in any case, largely in the hands of charlatans.

In the more remote Himalayan valleys things are seen rather differently. There are Gods able to deal with every human contingency and occurrence. Their visible habitations are these dolls to serve as focal points for the attention of worshippers and for their prayers. They make no pretence of speaking: since, however, they must be able to communicate to perform their functions properly they select human mouthpieces.

Communication with a God is regarded as a perfectly normal matter of fact every day affair. Thus, for instance, if rain is badly wanted for the crops, the human mouthpiece of the Rain God is induced to go into a trance wherein he is questioned by the village elders as to how the God has been offended.

The God will in turn answer, reveal the cause of displeasure and if he can be appeased and things put right there will be rain.

All perfectly logical and straightforward.

There are too in the Himalayas stern practical reminders of where duty lies; the Gods must be placated by gifts, even heavy sacrifices, to produce freedom from floods and from plague, to give the sun and the rain: the dead must be compensated for past wrongs.

No money in the offertory box, no jam for tea.

In Sultanpur town, to dignify a small village by that name, there is an example of how one of these purely local Gods came to be defied.

Back in the mists of time a woman called Neoli Rani was

Queen of one of the Kings of Kulu. Since she could produce no children the King took a second wife to whom the rather upset Neoli Rani prophesied that her first two children, a girl and a boy, would die in infancy.

When this prophesy came true the second wife complained to the King that Neoli must be a witch, for which the penalty was death, so the King, not wanting blood on his own hands, was considerate enough to leave her to take her chances in a valley near Kulu where it was well known that a giant came down every night to eat people.

When the giant justified the story by appearing, the resourceful Neoli quickly cut her finger and smeared the blood on his wrist. At this the erudite and gentlemanly giant who knew his folk-lore and abided by the conventions said:-

'I cannot eat you now as we are blood brother and sister. Instead I will look after you in this dangerous place until the King comes along in the morning to see what has happened.'

The King, once his mind was made up, was not the man to change it easily, so he had Neoli buried alive but not before she had told him that if he dug her up in 12 years time she would still be living.

All then went quite well for several years until one day Jahanni Mahadev, at that time Senior God, for even Gods have their pecking order, appeared looking rather worried and said to the King:-

'If you dig up the old Queen after 12 years she will still be alive, as she said, and the people will rather naturally start worshipping her as a Goddess and forget all about me; if, however, you dig her up after 10 years have elapsed she will be dead which will suit us both much better.'

The King accordingly dug her up after the stipulated 10 years and finding her indeed dead started remembering her good qualities and was rather belatedly struck with remorse. Indeed when she appeared to him in a very vivid dream he asked her to let bygones be bygones and come back to him; the lady, however, only gave a rather enigmatic smile.

From breakfast the next day all food set before him was immediately covered with ants and the water in his soup turned to blood.

Having given the lesson time to sink in the late Queen appeared again before her Consort and declared her terms.

'You must build a temple in my honour, elevate me to the rank of Goddess and come to my temple every morning to drink holy water before you touch any other food, or else . . .'

The terrified King built her a temple, her image was placed in the sanctuary and ever since then she has come to the Rai of Rupi, his direct descendant, spoken through her mouthpiece and stated her wants or complaints.

Shortly before our visit she wished to visit the Rupi Palace so the image was brought on its palanquin and placed in the middle of the drawing-room floor where she stayed for six days, while the family brought her offerings of flowers and lit lamps round her and did all the honours.

Deoli had no interest in blood sacrifices in contrast with the demon Goddess Hidimha whose temple was a very sinister edifice above Minali.

The joke about the Verger asking the Vicar to pray for rain and being told 'Not when the wind is in the East, you fool!' would in this valley be regarded as blasphemy and whereas I doubt if the utterer would be murdered if a European, it is certain that in some strange way he would subsequently see no more game to shoot nor fish to catch.

A whole book could easily be written about the faith in these hills. Sir Herbert told us two stories of his own which illustrate its salient points.

When he first received his commission in the Indian Civil Service, he was, after an initial period, sent to a remote place with the charming name of Pooh, in Bashahr, up on the Tibetan border, where the only other European within many marches was a Moravian missionary. Being destined to rise to the top, he was not slow in picking up the local dialect, a sort of bastard Tibetan, and in gaining the confidence of the very conservative and quite unspoilt local inhabitants. The able-bodied male inhabitants of Pooh formed the habit, after gathering in the harvest, of trekking down to the Simla Hills every year to earn a little extra money by felling trees and taking on general forestry work; among these men was one called Gappu.

One year the old men of Pooh received a message from Gappu saying that he felt extremely embarrassed in having to tell them that he had been possessed by the spirit of an Indian Goddess and that he did not like to return home without their permission as she might not get on with the others. The village council quickly held a meeting at which they decided that it would be churlish to bar the lady, forwarded their official letter of approval and, on his arrival, sent down the village band to play her in with musical honours. A holiday was then held, a shrine built in her honour and on occasions Gappu would go into a trance, speaking, of course, in high flown and grammatical Hindee as befitted an Indian Goddess, Hindee being a language which neither he nor any other man in the village could speak and which they understood only imperfectly.

All went merrily as a wedding bell for a year or two, when suddenly, without any warning, another young man in the village went into a series of trances in which he spoke pure Hindee, demanding in the voice of the Goddess that her shrine should be swept out more frequently, the flowers were not fresh and other complaints of a like nature. Everyone in the village at once explained to Sir Herbert and the Moravian, who were quite mystified, that poor Gappu must be dead. So it turned out to be; a messenger arrived hot foot a few days later with the sad tidings that Gappu had been killed by a falling tree.

The second story also concerns the Bashahr district. A young married man was having an affair with another lady, much to the annoyance of his wife who eventually considerably embarrassed him by jumping into a well and drowning herself. A very few weeks later this unhappy man was smitten with a most undesirable combination of dysentery and boils which considerably sapped his vitality and manly strength; try as they might none of the local doctors could cure him, and it soon became reasonable to think that this could be no normal illness but the result of a spell cast upon him by some enemy. The village elders summoned a small boy and girl, both under eight years of age, and rather reluctantly held a seance. The little girl commenced trembling under the sheet in which they had covered her, thus demonstrating that they had to deal with a female spirit; the small boy was turned out and the seance began.

From under the sheet, and recognizable by all, came the voice of the late lamented wife upbraiding her husband for his infidelity and mental cruelty, his general insensitiveness, his lack of appreciation of her good cooking and many other virtues, his untidy habits, his lazy ways, his unpunctuality with the housekeeping money and all the usual rigmarole until the elders got bored and testily asked her what she wanted.

She wanted quite a lot; first and foremost, her husband must build her a shrine in the very centre of his best field, which he must then visit daily, bringing fresh flowers in summer and lighting candles in winter; there were a few other little things as well.

The day the shrine was completed and the first bunch of flowers produced, the man's dysentery and boils began to clear up and by the time Mr Emerson was due to leave, the man was completely cured; pure coincidence possibly.

Some thirty years later His Excellency Sir Herbert Emerson was pondering upon where to go for a few weeks for a short holiday as he had not been very well. Where better than Bashahr? He had never had a chance of seeing the place again.

It had hardly changed at all, he easily recognised several old grey beards as men he had known in the prime of life. But who was this skinny doddery old creature dressed in rags who kept on looking at him obviously hoping to be recognized and greeted? At length the figure spoke up:-

'Do you not recognize me? You knew me well; I am Rin-Tin-Ting whose case you very carefully investigated when my wife committed suicide and I was afterwards so ill.' Was this the gay and dapper young blade he had known? Why was he in rags? He used to be quite well off. 'I married again after my first wife died; my second was young and pretty and I was forced to go down to the Simla Hills every year and make extra money to keep her in new clothes. One year I was away when an Indian who said he was a magician arrived in Pooh and said he could turn silver into gold and five rupee notes into ten rupee notes; my pretty wife, anxious to seize this wonderful opportunity of helping me to become rich, dug up all my life savings from under the hearth and gave them to this man, who said he would take them away for a few days to where he could increase their value undisturbed. He never came back; but this was not the worst. I could no longer afford the candles or the time to pick flowers and I eventually had to sell my best field with the shrine to pay some debts which my wife had run up; ever since than I have kept on having attacks of dysentery and boils.'

Before we left I took the opportunity of going off to see the temple of the demon Goddess. One left the flower carpeted little valley with its tinkling little stream dashing over the bright pebbles to go up a narrow side valley and then climbed a little hill.

On the top was a circle of tall dark old cedars, shutting out the light from above with, between their trunks, huge boulders piled one on another. They fulfilled their obvious intention of cutting out light, sound and contact with the sunny free world outside.

I entered through a narrow gateway. There in the centre of the dim little open space stood the temple, a wooden pagoda-like structure about 80ft high.

The woodwork was heavily carved with the usual Hindu Gods and Goddesses, sprays of foliage, birds and animals, among which I was astounded to recognize interlaced scroll work of the exact pattern one sees cut on old stones in Ireland. There existed a tradition that Raja Bahadur Singh, who had the temple built, ordered the hands of the carver to be cut off so that he could never produce as beautiful work elsewhere.

There was no one in sight anywhere but I had the sense of being watched and not too kindly.

Peering in rather apprehensively I wondered whether it was really only animals that were sacrificed here.

As my eyes got more accustomed to the gloom I caught sight of a large flat stone above which was hanging a thick rope tied to a beam above. Whatever did go on there, it had all the hallmarks of being extremely sinister and nasty and this, indeed, was its reputation.

A mile or two away along our so called motor road the little track took off to the 13,000ft. Rohtang Pass, over which the long plodding lines of pack ponies and yak-cow crosses had for centuries been carrying their loads of grain and salt and firewood. Up zig-zagged the path, following the contours, up through the snows of the 16,000ft. ranges which I could see through the gaps in the trees, up to the wild windswept treeless unvegitated wastes of Spiti and Lahoul and finally to Tibet itself.

I had read somewhere that the early shepherd tribes of Tibet had solemnised two oaths to their Chiefs.

A yearly Little Oath when they sacrificed sheep and dogs, and every third year the Great Oath when they sacrificed oxen, horses – and men.

Contact with Tibet was close.

Our holiday in Kulu was over all too soon and the time came to leave the wonderful scenery and the fresh mountain air and motor slowly down the narrow bumpy road to Pathankot where our train would be waiting for us.

VIII

Heaven's outer portal, Simla

The petrol-driven rail motor buzzed and clattered up from Kalka on a line reminiscent of a scenic railway. Winding through the foothills, it clung to the edge of ravines, crossed viaducts shot through tunnels of which one lost count. There are said to be a hundred and seven.

For the 60 miles of its length it is in a continuous succession of reverse curves of 160 ft radius which no doubt gave a tremendous sensation of pride and joy to its designers but are less popular with the passengers; on some of the sharper corners one cannot see any ground below one and gets the impression of being launched into space.

This rail motor, like a motor coach on railway wheels, did one trip a day for the important. For the hoi polloi, there was a very slow train.

The scenery changed from the dusty open country round Kalka with its clumps of mango trees enclosed by cactus hedges, through variegated green scrub-covered foothills intersected by dried-up water-courses full of great boulders, up to the huge rounded pine-clad hills of Simla.

Simla, 'Heaven's outer portal, full of knights and angels' built on the very top of a ridge seven thousand feet high is a place to which the motor never seems to get any closer. Visible from far down the line, it gives promise to the train-sick that their troubles will soon be over, only to vanish as the jolting rail car lurches into a tunnel and emerges into some quite different valley facing the opposite direction; the air gets cool and then positively cold, windows are shut and passengers start donning the heavy overcoats they have not worn since winter.

Lahore which we had glided out of the previous night may for some reason not immediately apparent have been called 'the Paris of India' but what was I to expect of Simla? Knights? We had several in the Punjab Government whom we were bringing up to add to their numbers but I sincerely hoped that they were not the hallmark of the place. Angels? I do not remember Kipling mentioning them as being present in large quantities.

Simla had been the temporary residence of a colourful character in the person of a Mrs James who arrived with her military husband with whom she had recently eloped.

Unfortunately for the aforesaid military character she eloped again and next appeared in Bavaria bearing the name of Lola Montez. Here she captivated the King of Bavaria, and soon became the power behind the throne. She died in America.

On quite a different plane would be any throwbacks to those serious soldiers who had apparently first fallen upon their knees and then upon the natives.

From Simla railway station we drove at a snail's place along a road congested with pedestrians, people on horseback and dozens of rickshaws. Up here a car is something at which to turn and gape, since the gaze will be rewarded by the sight of either the Viceroy, the Governor of the Punjab, or the Commander-in-Chief, with their ADCs basking in the reflected glory beside them.

On the Mall which runs along the top of the ridge the scene was quite unique. At any time of day the entire road was thronged with a mass of well dressed Indians in the garb of every corner of the sub-continent. European women, parasol in hand, dressed up, as far as the male eye could judge, as if for Ascot, picked their way on high heels a few paces in front of a servant carrying a small parcel, and pretty good some of them looked too; a lounge-suited European passes us on a horse, he is probably going out to lunch.

As we pass Davico's restaurant a crowd of girls cease chattering over their coffee for a few seconds to glance down at us through the plate glass windows as we pass; since there were no regiments stationed in Simla, the only men under thirty were the ADCs and there were only eleven of us at that.

Once the crowded Mall has been safely negotiated we increase speed as we take the road for West Simla. Here all the windows have wire netting across them as a preventive against the swarms of monkeys which descend from the monkey temple on Jakko whose lower slopes we are now reaching.

The resident Priest of the temple was an old Belgian turned yogi who lives on the premises with the monkeys and it was firmly believed, at any rate by all the Simla servants, that suitable offering in hard cash would ensure any garden being left unmolested for the entire summer season. Of course, no European ever believed this kind of nonsense but it was a very singular thing that whereas certain gardens were constantly being ruined, other seemingly identical gardens next door to them were never once visited and seemingly protected by some strange invisible fence.

A short time before our arrival in Simla, Pat's tenure of office drew to a close and a new ADC had to be found to take his place. It has somehow always been my fate that when confronted by something new that needs experience, my guide philosopher and friend on whom I am expecting to rely is immediately removed out of my ken; this was turning out according to the usual pattern; in Simla everything was on a far vaster scale than in Lahore and I knew none of the Government of India Officials and only very few of the senior officers in Army Headquarters, moreover, as senior ADC I not only had to learn but teach someone else too.

To my great relief the newcomer was one Walter Skrine, a Gunner and the future idol of the British race course crowds. He became the amateur jockey who was so seriously wounded while a Major in the Commandos that one leg was 2½ ins shorter than the other and who later had the other leg shortened to match and thus went on to ride in the Grand National.

When he arrived I found myself handing over the wines, the catering, the cars, the clothing, the garden, all the jobs, in fact, which nearly ran themselves, and taking on Invitations myself.

Originally Simla was merely a group of charcoal burners' huts set in a dense jungle inhabited by wild animals and it was not until 1816 that a British Officer passing through with some Gurkha troops noticed how cool it was and what a nice place it would be in which to live. In a short space of time Captain Kennedy, the Political Officer, had built himself a spacious house at Simla, for Political Officers were chosen for their intelligence, and here he entertained his friends.

Monsieur Victor Jacquemont, a charming young adventurer, gives a delightful description of a visit to Captain Kennedy:

'He is a Captain . . . with a hundred thousand francs a year and commands a regiment of Highland Chasseurs (Gurkhas), the best corps in the army.'

Running invitations in Simla kept one quite busy. I would not care to say how many officers were employed in Army Headquarters; they used to emerge in the evening in their thousands like bees leaving a hive, while the various departments in the Government of India were legion, added to which there were the Embassies; also the Punjab Government that had come up with us.

Anyone resident in Simla for a few days whom it was desired to have in for a meal was at once contacted.

The names of the remaining callers were gone through with care and their precedence established. The most senior, to the number of about six hundred, were placed on the Dinner List; next came the slightly more junior who were placed on the Luncheon List; then came the younger who were put down for the Annual Ball. Finally came everyone else for whom there remained the Garden Party. There were also cross references against people's names who might prove to be tennis or bridge players, for we had formal bridge and tennis parties once a week.

Simla was a whirl of gaiety; almost every night someone or

other gave a cocktail party and there was a big dance at both Davico's Ballroom and the Cecil Hotel four nights a week, attended in force as a matter of course by all the youth and beauty in the place. The Simla Amateur Dramatic Club, whose off-shoot, the Green Room, was quite a social centre, had been started in 1838 and was a most flourishing concern.

The prettiest girls were always to be found acting in these plays and since the obvious way of seeing rather more of them was to act oneself, which I could not do, my only alternative was to take on the job of Assistant Stage Manager, which I did very badly. Horror of horrors, somebody fell sick and I had to double up as a French sailor in 'Tony Draws a Horse.' I only had to fire a pistol and say one word. I don't think it was 'merde' because I always forgot it, while the leading lady screamed. In the next act we both had to do this off stage for the benefit of the actors on stage and the only spot where we found that the noise was sufficiently muffled was in the tiny loo into which we had to cram and shut the door. Even then I had to take half the charge out of the cartridge and she had to scream into the loo pan. Thus one gets to know people.

Each unattached girl had, until a claim had been established, a dozen unattached men waiting to wine, dine and dance with her, eyeing each other jealously; no mother could have wished for better chaperons than these.

Once a claim had been established and the unlucky eleven shooed off, the ultimate deterrent was that 'the pill' had not been introduced.

Official entertainment up here was on a far vaster scale than down in Lahore. The Viceroy had six ADCs, while the Chief made do with three. There had in previous years been ADCs who had become important people later, Lord William Beresford, Sir Ian Hamilton, Lord Ronaldshay, Lord Birdwood and the Earl of Cromer, to name a few.

Apart from 'Invitations' our office work remained much the same. We used to get some extraordinary letters. Most went to the Home Secretary; those threatening HE's life and sometimes signed in the originator's blood went straight to the Police. Others should have been framed. The following gems, the one so typical of semi-educated simplicity, the other of frustrated fury, must, I feel, go on record . . .

Hoshiarpur

May it please His Excellency,

In a dream I came to know that I am attending your Excellencies leisure for a request. My request in the dream was that I should be made Deputy Commissioner of Hoshiarpur District. Your Excellency readily accepted my request in the dream and ordered me to submit an application for the job. Your Excellency said 'It shall be considered favourably and the order for the appointment shall be sent within a week'.

I don't know how far is the dream substantial and true.

As far as my qualifications I appeared in the B.A. Examination of the Punjab University but as ill luck would have it I got plucked. I have passed the examination in First Aid to the Injured. Moreover, I can play upon harmonium and sing very nicely.

Thanking your Excellency in anticipation and hoping to be obliged with a favourable reply.

I have the honour to be
Sir,
Your obedient servant,
Rattan Chandra Prashad.

To the Agent   Ernakulam
North Western Rly   17th June,
Lahore

Mr. Agent

About three weeks ago I had to stay in the retiring rooms above the Rly Station in Delhi. On my arrival there I was asked to pay Rs 3 for the first twelve hours and for the subsequent twelve hours I was made to pay further Rs 3 i.e. Rs 6 per day!!!

Mr.Agent, put your hand on your conscience and say for yourself if this is not robbery, it is bloody robbery because expecially in this season at Maiden's Hotel in Delhi one can get a fine suite of rooms, beautifully furnished, with hot and cold bath as much as one wishes, excellent meals, servants etc., and all this for Rs 9 per day and you extract from us Rs 8 for rotten rooms badly furnished and if we want to have a bit of hot water, for this we are made to pay an extra 4 annas per bucket.

Recently I was in Madras and in Trichinopoly where I occupied very fine rooms, much better furnished than those rotten rooms of yours, yet I was asked to pay only Rs 2 for a day of 24 hours. Now then compare this amount with the one your are robbing us and see if you should not be called a criminal cheater. Shame, bloodly shame and you should hand yourself before it is too late.

Copy to the Governor.   A TOURIST

Here at the Cecil Hotel Ballroom, I talked to and danced with my first Indian girl, the daughter of the famous Mr Jinnah, the architect of Pakistan, who had been educated at Roedean or some such establishment, and probably finished in Paris. She talked wistfully of all the London night spots.

It was while at Simla that we received, in the very early hours, the news of the terrible Quetta earthquake.

The first news was scanty and further detailed information difficult to obtain. It seemed that the bazaar portion of Quetta had been completely wiped out and all rail road and telegraphic communication cut. It soon became obvious that the resources of the Punjab would have to be mobilised and, within a matter of hours, arrangements were being made to organise hospital trains for the injured, medical supplies and food, relief workers and accommodation in all the big hospitals.

Of the first 15,000 bodies to be disinterred only 5,000 had not been killed instantaneously. There had been some amazing cases of survival among animals; the longest survival of a human being had been a woman who had been dug out alive and conscious after five days; but a living and healthy cow had been unburied after 27 days without food or water and a cat was rescued after twenty days in the same condition.

The rescue parties would have been happier had the earth contented itself with shivering and heaving, but huge fissures opened up at their very feet swallowing up men, animals and even motor cars and as suddenly closing up again. The surviving dogs too had formed into large packs and gone completely wild, becoming a source of danger at night. One of the leaders was a bull terrier bitch so cunning that she constantly outwitted every effort to capture or shoot her.

The Royal Air Force, who were making constant sorties to find out whether there had been damage elsewhere in Baluchistan, reported that even at ten thousand feet the stench was terrible as to be quite nauseating.

There were, of course, a few lighter incidents to relieve the monotony of horror. Some British troops, digging out the dead, were approached by an old Baluchi peasant woman who indicating a heavy iron chest of which one corner was visible through the rubble, made signs that she wished it opened for her. Always ready to oblige, the troops set to work with a crowbar and soon she was stuffing handfuls of gold ornaments, jewellery and bank notes into her voluminous clothes. Next day the troops still working in the same area were rewarded by the sight of a fat and prosperous looking Hindu Banniah in floods of tears at the sight of the empty chest that had contained a large portion of his savings.

The Governor, together with the Viceroy, later paid a visit to the injured evacuated to hospitals in the Punjab. We walked down through ward after ward of men with broken backs, men with legs suspended by pulleys to frameworks above them, internal injuries, shock cases, injured children who had lost all their relations. It was estimated that there were about twenty thousand killed; there may have been more.

One of our earlier Simla engagements was a mass Jamboree for all the local Wolf Cubs on the lawn at Barnes Court; by far the most unruly pack was that composed of the sons of British officials who, with an excess of initiative in their make-up, got up to every kind of mischief; if a small boy had to be shooed off a flower bed, be sure it was the son of someone very senior in the Government of India; if a child had to be rebuked for going round and kicking all the little Indians, be sure he was the pride and joy of some unfortunate Brigadier; Khidtmagars bearing trays of ice cream ran the risk of being torn limb from limb; my clothes were later found to have jammy finger marks from knee to chest.

We later held what must sound rather an unusual social activity: we gave a tea party at which none of our guests was either able or expected to take tea with their hosts: There were in the Simla Hills twenty-three little independent States, each with its own Ruler, which were for some reason looked after by the Punjab Government and not by the Political Department of the Government of India. These States range in size from Bashahr which covers three thousand square miles of high rough country broken up by precipitous ravines through which the mountain paths were scarcely negotiable even for pack mules, and the bulk of merchandise is carried on the backs of sheep and goats, down to little Bija, Rawai and Dadhi with areas of four, three and one square miles respectively. Their rulers looked rather a mixed bag when they arrived for tea; some were perfectly turned out in the conventional ceremonial dress of the upper class hill Rajput; others, not over-clean, wore loose, badly cut European clothes of undyed homespun, together with the rough unpolished heavy country shoes of the small farmer, which, indeed, many of them were despite their titles.

To comply with the very strict caste restrictions of these very orthodox Hindus, all kinds of unusual arrangements had to be made. Special Hindu cooks had to be engaged even to boil the tea, since all our own cooks were Mohammedans and, to make matters worse, no Mohammedan was allowed into the kitchen while the cakes and scones were being made. Hindu khidtmagars had to be engaged to serve, since all our khidtmagars were also Mohammedans and no Mohammedan or European was allowed either into the drawing room during tea or into the passage leading from the kitchen while the food was being brought through.

Most difficult of all, some of our guests were so holy as to be forbidden tea even in the presence of some of each other without breaking their caste and thereafter paying vast sums to their religious advisers for purification; there was, however, one loophole, to drink tea out of a silver tea cup provides an unfailing antidote against contamination by the presence of the lower orders; we, therefore, found ourselves trying to find someone who could lend us a set of sixty silver tea cups for the afternoon; we eventually found HH The Maharajah of Patiala; even so, we heard later, some of our guests only nibbled a few nuts and one or two ate and drank nothing.

An annual party with rather similar restrictions was the Purdah Party. The vast majority of Mohammedan leaders and officials kept their wives in Purdah but, as the latter were largely semi-educated and brought up to the system, they were perfectly happy about it. They could not, of course, come to any of the normal official entertainments, so a special party had to be held for them to which only women were invited.

Together with the actual Purdah ladies it was usual to ask a few Indian ladies not in Purdah and any British ones able to talk sufficient Urdu to be useful. A portion of the lawn having been entirely enclosed by canvas tent walls some eight feet high, everything for the tea party was left ready and all the men withdrew. Once inside the safety of tent walls, boorkahs were discarded, veils thrown back and, judging from the noise and laughter that we could hear from as far away as the house, the ladies seemed to have plenty to discuss, despite the fact that the majority of them lived their lives enshrouded in the folds of a garment like a tent.

There was a not unamusing incident in connection with one of these Purdah parties at Viceregal Lodge. An important telephone message arrived for Her Excellency Lady Willingdon in the middle of tea; she, of course, being busy among her guests inside the screened off arena on the lawn. It so happened that the ADC-in-Waiting was Reggie Freeman-Thomas from a British Light Infantry Regiment, very new to the job, very new to India and apparently knowing nothing about Purdah.

Reggie, confronted with this message and holding Lady Willingdon in considerable awe, as we all did, decided that his only safe course was to deliver it as soon as possible, despite her being involved in some sort of women's tea party or other. Entering the screened off area he looked round for a moment at the sea of upturned faces then, spotting Her Excellency, started to pick his way among the tables towards her. There was a moment or two of complete stillness, for he was a remarkably good looking youth, then suddenly all was confusion; faces were quickly hidden behind hands, there was a general dive for boorkahs and quite genuine shrieks rent the air bewailing the undoubted fact that their Purdah was now broken, their husbands could do nothing less than divorce those married, while the unmarried must now remain in that unhappy state for ever. Mercifully, one serene old Dowager, I think it was the Begum of Mamdot, kept her head; calling sharply for attention that she was well used to receiving, she first smiled sweetly at Reggie to whom she had already been introduced, for she herself was not in Purdah, and then announced in ringing tones, 'Ladies! please, my sisters! you must calm yourselves. You are in no way compromised! Your reputations remain unsullied! Fear not, for this is no one but her Excellency's new eunuch!!'

Walter and I were usually busy helping to organise something or other by day but the more monotonous parts of the work were being in Waiting in the evenings when nothing was happening.

His Excellency, the Governor of the Punjab goes to the Races in his camel carriage once a year.

We proclaimed King Edward VIII's accession although to be summarised

On some evenings the telephone never ceased and there might be members of conferences who had to be shown in and afterwards shown out; at other times nothing happened at all. There were, however, plenty of friends living not far away whom we used to 'phone up and ask in to have a drink and a chat.

One evening a young lady dropped in to swap gossip; she was one of our particular friends who had a standing invitation and knew that she would always find one or the other of us in; but on this occasion she struck the wrong night as Walter was out and some political crisis or other was brewing which caused the telephone to ring ceaselessly; apart from the telephone, there was a big committee meeting of some sort on at half past six and, what with one thing and another, I was rather too busy to give her that full attention, which, on account both of her personal beauty and her charm, she was undeniably due. Finding that I was listening to her with only half an ear, she began to get bored and rather noisy and, since I had my work to do, writing down important messages and the like, there was nothing for it but to deal with her firmly so, since she was becoming a nuisance, I with great reluctance locked her into the ADCs' lavatory which adjoined the office, intending to release her after she had promised to be quiet and good. Then the telephone rang and as I was finishing taking the message a chuprassi came in to say that HE wanted me; as I came back from HE's office a few minutes later I glanced through a passage window and saw a rickshaw arriving, which caused me to make for the front door by the shortest route to welcome the people attending the conference. Taking up my stand in the porch, I started receiving the earlier arrivals from among our own Ministers, some Government of India officials and a Judge or two.

Having seen a few out of their rickshaws and as far as the door of the conference chamber, I was waiting in the porch watching the next little batch drive up when I noticed them all gazing up at the front of the house. The facade, as far as I knew, was no different from usual, the wisteria was not in bloom, and when I noticed one or two quietly smiling I thought I had better take

89

the next opportunity of investigating. Showing that little lot in and quickly walking out, I was horrified to see young Joy, about whom I had completely forgotten, in the act of swarming down a drain pipe — she was, in fact, stuck about half way.

To pile the Pelion of embarrassment upon the Ossa of apprehension, the next arrival was the Premier himself, Sir Sikander Hayat Khan, who, highly diverted and perhaps with memories of his Cambridge days, suggested that it would be wiser were he to see himself in while I assisted the lady either to go up or to come down. This was not so easy but, eventually, having extracted her from a bed of carnations, the apple of Lady Emerson's eye, I hustled her in by the side door and fled back to my post; I knew that Sir Sikander and his Ministers were far too good sportsmen to give me away but they would no doubt chaff me unmercifully about it afterwards. Checking up with the chuprassi on the door that the full number of people had arrived, I went along to warn them that I was about to bring HE in, whom I then fetched and announced.

At dinner that night HE kept chuckling to himself in a way I did not altogether like, but started to lull my suspicions by saying that he had just made the biggest faux pas of his life: it seemed that the committee meeting had been going for a minute or two when the side door of the conference chamber very slowly opened and in sidled an apologetic looking little stranger who, twisting some papers in his hands, stood as if quite bewildered and at a loss as to what to do. HE, wishing to put him at his ease, said 'Please sit down over there, will you, with the other stenographers. It is not your fault for being late as I think we have started a little early.' The little Indian blushed, scuttled over to a chair and replied, 'Excuse me, I am the Chief Justice of Madras.' I laughed politely. What HE was never able to make out was how the poor little man had got past me at the door and had lost himself wandering about the house. I saw no good reason to enlighten him.

IX

The Tibet Road

Simla was a place from which it was nice to get away during the weekends. Ordinary people not being permitted cars owing to the narrowness and paucity of roads, and bicycles being out of the question even had they been allowed, the only methods of travel were by rickshaw, on horseback or by walking.

Sunday morning saw a vast number of European officers and officials, their wives, children and dogs setting out upon the Tibet road. The majority of people walked, three or four abreast across the narrow road, with behind them a coolie balancing on his head a picnic basket and all those parasols, rugs, cushions, magazines, hot water bottles and strange impediments that women seem to find essential for such a pioneering enterprise as a day in the country.

Those few who had horses in Simla could do the thing in style; they could reach Wild Flower Hall first and be sure of getting a table, this being a hotel which made a speciality of slap-up Sunday lunches. One had, of course, to keep two horses so as one could take along the girl friend, or better still three, so as a servant could ride behind and hold them all while one wandered off into the woods and admired the wonders of nature.

It may not of course have improved one's promotion prospects when one clattered past more senior officers puffing up the hills escorting less attractive women.

For horsemen who were possessors of anything but an armchair ride the journey held one rather major hazard. A couple of miles from West Simla, beyond the cemetery which Kipling mentions in such a macabre manner, is the dank dark and lengthy Sanjauli tunnel, a place where every simple coolie whistles and shouts his loudest to scare off the ghosts. It is nearly two hundred yards long, very dim inside, the walls are green and slimy, and drips of water of abnormal size and intense coldness plop without warning onto horse and rider; the floor, which is of tarmac, is wet and slippery.

Lord Kitchener fell and broke his leg when riding a horse through that tunnel and lay there for quite a time as no coolie would come to his assistance because they thought that his shouts for help were the cries of some evil spirit.

Once beyond the tunnel the scenery became more and more lovely; the road wound through fragrant sighing woods of deodar to emerge among sunlit strips of flower-covered pasture; steep ravines plunged to valleys so far below that there was hardly a murmur from the rushing torrent precipitating itself from rock to rock in its headlong course to the plains; on the slopes opposite tiny green fields were terraced one above the other and tucked into any space big enough for a tennis court, for flat ground there was none.

Over the nearby hills, range after range carried the gaze up to the distant skyline where on a clear day could be seen the jagged peaks of the roof of the world clothed in their perpetual covering of snow.

On any day of the week there was a constant stream of traffic on the road. Small wiry peasantry whose seemingly frail legs had already carried them miles along narrow winding mountain paths from some little slate-roofed village perched up on a far hillside; heavily built skull-capped Kashmiri coolies, stick in hand, carrying across their shoulders planks so long that, until they turned sideways, no one could pass; charcoal burners, both men and women black from head to foot carrying on their backs conical baskets of charcoal for the braziers of the bazaar, walking in single file singing as they came; an occasional more prosperous farmer ambling along on a tubby little hill pony, sure footed as a goat and with a strange preference for trotting on the very edge of the road nearest the precipice. Further up the road lay the rough track down to Sipi in the territory of the Rana of Koti where a big annual fair was held, an outing attended by all the hill folk and by a few interested Europeans from Simla. In a small cup-shaped valley encircled by deodar and spruce everyone collected from miles around and as little parties of villagers approached they could hear the beating of drums, the whiz and crackle of fireworks and the choruses of dancers as yet hidden by the trees as the path wound its way down. Rounding the last corner there came into view a milling throng of people, dressed up in their brightest and best, seething about among the stalls and booths, being cajoled to buy glass beads and necklaces, bright clothes of every description and sweets of every degree of stickiness. This was the real holiday atmosphere; jhimpanis who every day, rain or sun, had been pulling rickshaws about Simla from dawn till dusk had now cast dull care aside and were dancing, shouting, leaping, laughing as if they had not a worry in the world; bazaar-made rockets spluttered and crackled as, with a train of sparks and blue smoke, they ricocheted among the tree tops, marriage bombs exploded with a deafening bang that reverberated round from all the little side valleys, brassy wails and the thud-thudding of tomtoms rose from small bands of musicians dotted about among the crowd.

Threading one's way through the booths and being greeted on all sides by the Simla coolies and rickshaw wallahs all of whom knew one as well as they knew each other (for had they not observed one's daily and nocturnal goings and comings throughout the season?) one came to the opposite side of the arena where, sitting on natural terraces on the hillside, were rows and rows of hill girls of marriageable age, decked out in all their finery, hung with turquoise necklaces and gold or silver ornaments, chattering and making eyes at the young bachelors who self consciously circled round them. This is the big marriage market where the young people meet and decide whether they like one another's looks, while their parents talk of dowries and settlements.

Besides this, which is the main business of the day, there are side shows such as archery in which the target, oddly enough, is a man, possibly a rather sinister survival of the times when targets were human prisoners. The 'target' places one hand on top of a stout stake driven into the ground, round which he may cavort, duck and caper as much as he likes provided he does not remove his hand; the archer from a distance of about fifty yards shoots with a barbless arrow padded with cloth, amid barracking from his friends and a flow of wit and repartee from the target.

At Mashobra, further up the road and some six miles from Simla, the Viceroy had a weekend 'cottage' called the 'Retreat'. It was not quite the conventional idea of a cottage, as it had a dozen or more rooms, including a billiard room with a full-sized table, and also a large conservatory. I once spent a very unhappy afternoon there. There was only one path to this house, which was on a spur surrounded by very steep slopes and precipices down to the foot of the valley far below, and when Lady Willingdon announced that she wished to go out for a ride and that I would escort her, I naturally assumed that it was this one path that we should take. Two fat tubby hill ponies were produced and I was horrified to find that she proposed riding down a hitherto unsuspected little path fit only for a hillman or a mountain goat; no one had ever yet argued with Lady Willingdon, and I could only suppose that, having become bored with taking the stuffing out of her own ADCs she wished to test out the Punjab variety; this was obviously one of those occasions on which it would be better to die than to betray emotion and I prayed that she would leave her pony's head alone and let it jump down from rock to rock, for it was, after all, Himalayan born and bred; this, however, was not to be; catching it an imperial clout with her stick, Her Excellency urged it into a canter and disappeared over the edge amid showers of stones and small boulders which threatened to start an avalanche; some fifteen minutes later, with chalk white face and palsied hands, I reached the Tibet Road close on her heels and ceased rehearsing apologies to the Viceroy for having permitted his wife to break her neck while in my charge.

The Governor himself had a permanent summer camp at Naldera four miles further along the road and to this we would come to spend Saturday night under canvas and he would entertain his old friends informally. At this height brown oaks grew beside ordinary English yew trees and great clumps of rhododendrons, both scarlet and the ordinary ponticum, made one feel at home.

The portion of the road nearer to Simla was the favourite walk of the thousands of Indian clerks and their families; here, the day's work done and the typewriters back in their cases, the ink scrubbed off their fingers and wearing their best clothes, they would come in family parties of twenty and thirty, the men walking hand in hand in front, a swarm of mothers, sisters, aunts, cousins and their innumerable children behind. Indian babus are amusing in small quantities; they talk an extraordinary patois of their own composed of equal portions of Urdu and English officialese, all mixed up, and are very polite in an old fashioned stilted courtly way.

The children were to be pitied, especially the better class small boys who, dressed up to the nines in Little Lord Fauntleroyish velvet suits and gold embroidered caps, were cuffed and scolded by at least a dozen female relatives every time they went near a puddle; they must have hated the whole thing.

Even though the small boys got little amusement out of these constitutionals and their fat women folk, too ponderous to be comfortable at any pace faster than a waddle, must have felt exhausted after the first few hundred yards; there was one individual, a senior British official of the Punjab Government, who made the most of them.

Tom Bollinger, Esq, CSI, CIE, ICS, was the possessor of that most-to-be-envied but rather dangerous of gifts, a talent for mimicry which, added to a keen but sometimes warped sense of humour, made him very popular with all but his victims. He too after tea would sometimes take a stroll along the Tibet Road to admire the view, returning just as the shades of night were falling, after drinking in the beauty of the far snow, stained pink by the setting sun.

Choosing a time when he found himself well away from the crowd and some distance behind one of these large family parties, he would entertain himself by imitating the peculiar harsh sawing cry of a hunting panther. Panthers were common in these hills; they were constantly taking goats and pi-dogs from the villages; every babu knew by repute exactly what noise they made and how ferocious they could be when accompanied by small cubs or when unable to kill their legitimate prey because of an injury.

On hearing this awe inspiring noise the family in front would spin round to see in which direction danger lay, and noticing our friend looking apprehensively over his shoulder at the road behind him would quicken their pace. Letting the party in front walk on a little further, he would let out another roar and start running towards them. Fear being infectious, they would break into a brisk trot with the younger and more athletic taking the lead and the ladies losing ground some way behind, bumping into the next family party in front to whom they would transmit their alarm; in course of time half the Indian population of Simla was pounding along the road heading for home, any slackening in pace being immediately counteracted by more panther noises.

Eventually, Mr Bollinger, feeling sufficiently exercised and entertained and knowing that nothing could now stop the headlong rush, would pause to massage his sorely abused larynx and continue his stroll in peace.

X

A monsoon tour

Directly the rainy season started in July and the plains got slightly cooler it was usual for HE, a great believer in seeing things for himself, to go on a short tour.

By far the most interesting tour on which I accompanied him was to the Eastern part of the province which was quite unlike the rest and infrequently visited by Europeans, as there were no military stations in the area, no towns of any size and nothing to attract tourists. This was the country of the Rajputs who claimed themselves a royal race, and also of the less aristocratic but more hardworking Jats; sturdy cultivators all, of the type that makes soldiers, they were heavily recruited in cavalry and infantry.

Hindu and Mussulman were very tolerant of one another, often sharing the same villages, and there was no Purdah except among the upper middle class.

In the country round Delhi which we first visited, the bigger landowners were of Afghan or Persian origin, being the descendants of the leaders in the various invasions that had swept down from the North West; the direct descendant of the last King of Delhi still lived here in poverty and obscurity.

One of the pet projects of the Punjab Government was 'Rural Reconstruction' and for this mammoth task a special Commissioner had been appointed who now joined us for the tour.

Broadly speaking, the Punjab agricultural methods were back

in the stone age. They still ploughed with wooden ploughs, pulled along by a camel or a couple of oxen. Iron ploughs were obviously far more expensive although one would have supposed far better. 'Not at all' argued the peasantry, 'we and our fathers before us have always used wooden ones, they plough to exactly the right depth, they are light, they are cheap, they are easily repaired, they are this and they are that.' Counter arguments had to be produced showing iron ploughs produced better crops, and the Government subsidised ploughs which were then produced in bulk; but even then I doubt whether these ultra conservative farmers ever took to them.

Normally when on tour we would move on every two or three days, leaving early in the morning, inspecting something on the way and timing ourselves to arrive in good time for lunch at one of the Government bungalows dotted about the country for the use of touring officials, forestry officers, canal engineers, circuit judges and the like; there our servants would greet us and re-dress us in freshly ironed suits, we would be handed the morning's post, and I would find the drinks ready and the table laid out for a lunch party we would be just about to give. It was a matter of a moment to make a quick mental table plan and put the name cards in the right places and our guests would start arriving.

Typical of a normal day's work when on tour was our visit to Gurgaon where we went on arrival to look round a hospital, followed by a lunch party; after lunch a cattle show, a tea party, a meeting of a branch of the Indian Soldiers' Board and a dinner party followed by a firework display. The cattle show was attended by the thousands of small farmers from the area, all keen cattle breeders anxious to scoop the quite valuable cups and prizes offered by the Punjab Government. HE, who loved talking to the peasantry, gave us a worrying afternoon by insisting on disappearing into the very centre of all the thickest crowds which immediately closed round to crack jokes with him, the various uniformed police, the plain clothes gunmen and myself weaving about in a series of vain pursuits. No sooner had we taken up strategic positions where we could watch and protect than he would be swept off in the midst of a crowd of enthusiastic laughing Punjabis to see someone's wonder heifer or the progeny of some champion bull; the danger was, of course, infinitesimal, but we were always faced with the possibility of the presence of some unbalanced person with a grievance and a knife.

We encamped for a couple of days at Hissar where there was a big Government cattle farm run by rather a genius called Larry Smith, an ex-Cavalry Officer. The trouble with Indian agriculture has always been the conservatism of the peasants, with neither the money nor the initiative to buy the newest and best seed, nor the inclination to bother to use the services of the best available bulls. This latter was a serious matter in an area like this where cattle were the mainstay of the population; the cows provided milk, the bullocks ploughed and dragged carts and their dung, when dried in the sun, provided fuel for cooking and an ingredient of the mixture they used for plastering their walls.

The Punjab Government had a scheme whereby bulls of the native Indian breed were scientifically bred here from carefully selected stock and then sent round to all the villages where their services were given free; at the same time every effort was made to track down and destroy all the 'scrub' bulls of unknown ancestry and no virtue, and which did so much harm to the breed.

Larry had vast paddocks full of bulls of varying sizes and ages, all carefully tagged and documented, among which he would wander with nothing more lethal than a walking stick; he had the commonsense theory that any animal kept chained up in a dark byre for much of its life becomes vicious and dangerous chiefly through boredom and sex frustration; here his bulls had thousands of acres in which to wander at liberty, with plenty of congenial companions and he never had trouble with any of them.

Larry's house was built among the ruins of a picturesque old Moghul fort of vast size and had a rather gruesome incident in its history. At the outbreak of the Bengal sepoy mutiny of 1857 Hissar had many more Europeans than now, there being a magistrate, a police officer, two military officers and the farm manager, all with their families.

The bazaar, as is always the way, heard the news first, and this having been transmitted to the Europeans by their servants, it was thought a wise precaution to gather the familes together in the largest house, that of the farm manager. Since bazaar rumours have always been a byword for inaccuracy, no one was unduly apprehensive; no officer could believe that his own troops would be anything but loyal. A few days went by without any untoward occurrence except the arrival, unknown to the Europeans, of some mutineers and agitators from Delhi; then hell was let loose, the officers were shot down by their troops on the parade ground, the magistrate was murdered sitting in his court and the police officer killed on the way to the bazaar; only the manager got warning and, dashing back to his house, gathered together the women and children and bolted and barred the doors.

Soon the angry roar was heard of the approaching mob, the scum of the bazaar led on by the armed and fanatical mutineers; the front door could not survive the battering for long and soon the murderers poured in, the women and children fleeing shrieking from room to room before them; the manager himself jumped out of a back window into the branches of a tree whence he escaped into the scrubby thorn jungle which extended for miles in all directions; the women and children, finding every other avenue of escape blocked, sought sanctuary in a small bathroom at the end of the large rambling house, but this gave refuge only for a few moments, the door was battered down and every single person hacked to pieces, irrespective of age.

Larry cheerfully showed us the original bathroom door, slashed with bayonets and sabres and finally broken down, apparently by an axe; leading us to the dining room, he pointed out the haunted mantelpiece upon which the mutineers had placed the severed heads of the victims.

Wherever we went one of the main festivities was a garden party in honour of HE and we had seven in a fortnight, all taking exactly the same pattern. The Deputy Commissioner who had met us at his boundary and who might have been showing us round for the last two days, would introduce us to the local Superintendent of Police, the Medical Officer of Health, the Veterinary Officer, a few Magistrates and one or two other worthies, and we would then be conducted to a table under a big tent roof with open sides, where we would be plied with plates of sticky coloured cakes, friut, nuts and Indian sweetmeats. If given an opportunity, I would then quietly disappear and look round for the tables at which sat the old pensioned Indian Officers, for they were always to be found together, irrespective of race or religion, and kept aloof from civilians. The old soldiers were a fine looking lot, some with medals of very long forgotten campaigns.

I knew exactly what was coming; leaning forward with finger on lip, one of these old men would say 'Captain Sahib, you are in a position to help us; all is not well here; we have an Indian Deputy Commissioner and an Indian Superintendent of Police; replace these two by Europeans and send the former off elsewhere and we shall have no complaints; it is a very small thing to ask of you, but it will mean a lot to us.'

'But Captain Sahib' these old warriors would say, 'it seems to be the accepted thing that India will get self-government one day, but what will people think of it when they get it? Will things be the same? Here we are, drawing government pensions, but in the old days before you British conquered the country no Indian ruler ever gave a pension to common soldiers; Hindu now sits with Mohammedan – did that happen before? We can go back to our homes safe in the assurance that they have not been looted and burnt in our absence; our grandfathers could never do that: even twenty years ago this land was desert: now look at the crops, all the result of these canals, your doctors have stamped out plague: could our hakims ever do that?'

'Listen, Sahib' an old Jemadar would whisper, 'what good do you think that fat Hindu Deputy Commissioner from Delhi who favours his own relations is? This is a bad place to live, Sahib.'

Visiting the villages was always the same: they had changed little in the last thousand years: since, however, there were no longer plagues, pestilences and civil wars to keep numbers in check, they were now far bigger than of old: masses of small mud huts, ill lit, ill ventilated, between them filthy little narrow unpaved streets onto which were thrown all the slops and refuse straight out of the doors. The Government had devoted much time and money to pouring out propaganda extolling the virtue of sanitation and cleanliness of which we now saw the effect. In the villages which we were officially scheduled to visit miracles had been performed; we walked or drove up a street so spotless that it had obviously been closed to all traffic for several days; we were shown into a house which had obviously been rebuilt, and introduced to villagers all of whom had carefully been primed as to what they should say, and do.

It was amusing watching HE taking every opportunity to go down the street which he was not meant to go down, to see the real prosperity or otherwise of the village, and talking to worthy citizens who were not supposed to be on view and would, therefore, blurt out what they thought.

Leaving this area, we continued our tour across the Nili Bar or Blue Desert lying to the West. Here all was sand with occasional woods of stunted camel thorn, and the climate got hotter and hotter; we could not travel in shirts and shorts: convention demanded our appearance in tropical lounge suits, collars and ties, for the oriental is a great critic of dress and would be very shocked were we to be informal on an occasion such as this.

Spending a few nights on the way in little known places such as Fazieka and Pakpattan, visiting canal systems, schools and hospitals and attending garden parties, all in the shimmering heat, we finished up at Ferozepore, a hot little military station on the edge of civilisation and occupied by a whole brigade of troops and an Indian Cavalry Regiment.

We had barely sat down to a little dinner party our first night in Ferozepore when Scott, the local Superintendent of Police, who was one of our guests, was suddenly called away to go and hunt decoits, an informer having most inopportunely come in to report that a gang which had been eluding him for months was spending the night in a village only twenty miles away, the track being passable only for camels. While hurriedly finishing the meat course, for he did not propose fighting on an empty stomach, Scott told us that this particular gang was led not by some renegade soldier but by, of all men, a village sweeper, of the lowest caste of all; he pointed out that sweepers, being the people who got all the kicks, were provided by divine providence with the quickest brains, and when they turned dacoit speedily rose to the top of their profession.

These gangs of dacoits or bandits still existed in outlying places on the fringe of the desert, their trade being highway robbery and armed burglary, and presented a problem until they were rounded up which in the end was inevitable. Composed of a dozen or so of desperate ruffians armed to the teeth with rifles, guns and pistols, they would lie in wait for rich men known to be travelling home at night, or raid villages, descending on the bunniah's shop and torturing and bunniah until he disclosed where he had hidden his wealth. By daylight they would have departed with the booty and perhaps a bunniah or two to hold to ransom and disappeared into the desert no one knew where.

Away went Scott, with his force of camel police, and after a very stiff fight, for men with a score of murders for which to account do not give themselves up lightly, he settled the score; the sweeper and his two lieutenants cheated the gallows, but as Scott had promised, before he rode off, he would get them dead or alive and he fancied it would not be alive.

One winter HE was bidden down to New Delhi to discuss affairs with the Viceroy, taking myself with him. Alighting from our special train on a cold January morning we glided past the Mogul City, the Red Fort and the Jama Musjid, all founded by Shah Jehan in 1638, then on to our own Lutyens' New Delhi, where every roundabout gave us new vistas to right and left of the magnificent residences designed by him for the rich and the mighty, made ready for occupation by 1929.

Eulogies have been written about Viceroy's House, the masterpiece of Edwin Lutyens, one of the three leading British architects of his day. It may, therefore, be tactless to suggest that while his houses are incontroversially superb as coups d'oeil, they are nightmares to live in.

The ADC in Waiting conducted us to one of the State Suites of which there were several, skirting on the way about five of the twelve inner courtyards each with its own particular little whirlwind; while negotiating a series of passages and corridors down which the draught seemed to blow from all directions, he told us that the front of the house was two hundred yards long and that the actual building covered four and a half acres which we could well believe.

A recollection of the late Sir Charles Duke can best illustrate the hazards of the place which lay waiting to entrap the uninitiated.

Arriving to take up his appointment as Assistant Private Secretary he was shown his quarters in some far corner of this maze and told he would not be required to put in an appearance until dinner, when he was to be present in number three State Drawing Room before 7.45, preparatory to the entrance of Their Excellencies at 7.55. The time came to seek out the particular drawing room which was his rendezvous.

All went well along the first few passages and round a corner or two until he found himself walking round three sides of a courtyard which he could have sworn he had only just left. He quickened his pace until glancing out of a window and seeing the Evening Star he realised he must be walking North when he thought he should be walking South. He broke into a brisk trot his coats tails flying and was practically galloping when he discerned in the far distance the giant figures of the Bodyguard, standing at attention lance in hand. Then came the welcome sound of distant chamber music.

He had arrived at a landing below which, at the foot of a flight of marble steps, were his fellow diners sipping sherry. At the top, however, were arranged the Viceroy's Band, some 40 retired British military bandsmen, sitting shoulder to shoulder, sawing away at their instruments, their music stands touching. How he got down he never knew, but he did by 7.54.

I felt I could not follow this procedure with my own 'His Excellency'.

The routine of the place was very like our own but all was on a far bigger scale; they certainly needed their six ADCs. They observed one barbarous custom which we did not: formal afternoon tea for everyone over which Lady Willingdon presided in her inimitable fashion, making it impossible for anyone to relax.

One must give the lady her dues. There was no one better at raising funds for her particular charities, be they the RSPCA, the Simla rickshaw coolies, or whatever. She was quite unscrupulous in the way she bullied the rich, the Maharajahs and the like. As they wrote out huge cheques with assumed smiles on their faces they realised, as did all other men with whom she came in contact, that to oppose her was a pure waste of time.

This brings us to the rather revealing story of the swimming bath. A swimming bath was the one amenity Lutyens had not thought of providing. Perhaps they were not fashionable in his day, although we had a beauty at Lahore. Unfortunately Lady Willingdon saw one somewhere and decided she must have one like it but, of course, bigger and better.

She accordingly dictated her wishes to the Comptroller of the Household who must at the time I think have been Major Britten Jones of the Black Watch, the only man known to be able to handle her, and then not always. The latter unhappily pointed out that there had been all that redecoration earlier in the year, the Building Fund was badly in debit and that, in modern parlance, there was no more money in the kitty.

Up to Simla went the Viceregal Court in the spring to escape the heat and he thought that the whole thing was forgotten. He may have had other things on his mind, the ex-King of Greece had recently been to stay and become a fervent admirer of his very lovely wife.

Back in Delhi once more in the autumn not even a day had elapsed when Her Excellency swept into the room and said:- 'BJ come round the garden with me and we'll see how these new flower beds are going to do this season.'

Steering him round a corner behind some tall shrubs she said 'Look! Isn't that lovely.'

There in front of him stretched the cool blue water of an enormous and well appointed swimming pool that had certainly not been there before. Dabbing at his forehead with his handkerchief he blindly tottered back to the sanctuary of his office and summoned his Public Works Superintendent for an explanation.

'What is the meaning of this? Who permitted you to build that pool? I gave no order for one!'

'The Lady Sahib told me to,' whispered the unhappy man through ashen lips.

'Well then, why did you not immediately report the matter to me?'

'The Lady Sahib threatened me with instant dismissal if I did.'

XI

Long johns on the Highland chief

One winter in Lahore the army were asked to lay on a big Tattoo at the Fort. Tattoos do no differ very greatly, and here we were to see the normal displays.

For the final night, however, it had been arranged that HE and Lady Emerson should drive down to the old fort and watch the show, so in accordance with our usual practice, Mr Rowson and I motored down the day before, stop watch in hand, timing ourselves over the three or four miles so as to ensure arriving at the actual minute that we were required. It had been planned for the car to be driven into the arena and then make a three-quarter circuit lit up by coloured searchlights until it reached the little gateway in front of our box, where we would alight. Then the searchlights would be switched off and the empty car would be driven away.

Next night we drove through the main gate of the fort exactly as the clock struck and entering the arena, full of confidence, were immediately blinded by the coloured searchlights one of which seemed to be directed straight into our faces. By picking out the white posts on my side as they came, we wove a slightly drunken course along the front of the old palace buildings and negotiated the two right angled turns at the end of the ground.

As we entered the final straight somewhere in the centre of which should lie the little gate leading to our box, I could see nothing but shafts of light which served only to intensify the surrounding darkness in which could be heard the cheering multitudes close alongside; after what seemed to be endless driving I began to feel that we must have come too far and got into a frenzy of irresolution wondering whether to tell Rowson to drive all round once more and try again or to stop and await rescue and guidance. At last to my relief, I saw a little knot of policemen standing by a white post which must presumably be the gate, so I told Rowson to halt and stepped out in as dignified a manner as possible to open the rear door; out on my feet among the searchlights and with my hand on the door handle, I suddenly got the feeling that this was not the gate at all, my horrid suspicion being confirmed by one of the police.

There seemed nothing for it but to get in again but Rowson, straining his eyes forward to pick out the real gate, did not realise that I was not in my seat and moved the car forward. My shiny sword hanging on its gold slings, my tight overall trousers and straight-jacket blue frock coat, my long box spurs and my loops of aiguillette were no doubt designed to strike fear into the hearts of the foe, but never to jump quickly into cars, and I was left running alongside holding onto the handle, picked out by the searchlights.

The next occasion when I took part in a public ceremony at the old Fort was at a Durbar held by the Viceroy, Lord Linlithgow. His whole visit lasted a week and was a busy time for us as, for a start, there were thirty-eight extra guests staying. There was, as well, the Bodyguard to be accommodated, a spectacular squadron of Punjabi-Mussulmen and Sikhs with a height limit of six foot two inches, mounted on black horses.

Police arrangements for guarding the Viceroy were infinitely greater than those for the Governor. Posted all round the wall encircling the grounds was an outer cordon of constables, their business being to see that no one scaled the wall. Inside, unobtrusively posted behind the trees and bushes, was an inner cordon, again all within sight of one another, and within hail of the outer cordon. Finally, round his own suite was the 'isolation cordon' inside which no one could penetrate with the exception of his own staff and personal servants. A further innovation was the introduction of police gunmen inside the house, dressed up in our khidtmagars' red livery, but looking nothing like khidtmagars. If the house was not now proof against assassins, then it never would be.

The Viceroy was received on the Ceremonial Platform with all the honours, including a Royal Salute of thirty-one guns, everyone carefully counting the reports in case the battery inadvertently let off thirty or thirty-two. There was quite a crowd on the platform, about fifty people in all, everyone in Levee or Full dress, including the Premier and his Ministers, the Chief Justice and full Bench of the High Court, the Bishop and an Archdeacon or two, military officers of the rank of Colonel and above, Secretaries, Heads of Departments and many more besides.

We all, of course, arrived early, and it was in front of all this assembled throng that one of the Commissioners, a rank junior only to that of Governor was, to every one's unbounded delight, whisked off by his wife to the waiting room temporarily to divest himself of his splendour and exchange his warm winter woollies for some lighter texture, the morning having been frosty while the day promised to be warm; on retirement he so manipulated things as to become the Macnab of Macnab and from then on never wore trousers at all, let alone long woolly pants, which goes to show to what lengths pride of race will suddenly take people.

Hardly had Their Excellencies reached Government House, having carried out a State Drive than hard work began. The Viceroy himself started granting interviews while Lady Linlithgow was taken off to visit first the Mayo hospital and then the Aitchison hospital. After lunch we set off to see our Boy Scouts at Kot Lakpat, where, preceded by their Pipe Bands, three thousand scouts marched onto the field to give a physical training demonstration followed by rhythmic exercises, in which ideas they were several years ahead of the army.

The first night of the visit we started off with a dinner party for seventy-five people; we were, however, spared the normal after dinner talks and went straight out on the lawn where we were holding a reception for a few hundred others, the latter being temporarily held in play by our three Indian Honorary ADCs who travelled from their homes for big occasions such as these. These other guests having being presented, and I felt as if I should be presenting people in my sleep for nights, we watched a display of Khattak dancing by Pathan troops.

Khattak dancing is a spectacle which, if once seen, is never forgotten; oil was poured onto a huge fire of logs and round it whirled and spun about thirty Khattaks, recruited from the Frontier; tall, lithe, fair men, some with classical Greek features, their oiled and combed bobbed hair hanging to just below the ear, they are said by some to be descended from the garrisons of Greek soldiers which Alexander the Great left behind him to await the return which never took place. All the time their orchestra of drums and serenais, the wild harsh pipes of the Frontier, throbbed and screamed in increasing tempo.

On the second day of the visit took place the real pièce de resistance, the Durbar which was the occasion for all the nobility, the landed gentry and the leading men of the Province to pay homage to the King in the person of the Viceroy.

Their Excellencies drove off from Government House to the Old Fort in a carriage drawn by six white horses, escorted by a considerable cavalcade of both the Governor-General's Body-guard and a Field Officer's escort of the 6th Duke of Connaught's Own Lancers; on arrival they were greeted by a Royal Salute from a Guard of Honour of the Dogra Regiment while the 5th Field Battery crashed out a further thirty-one gun salute.

Next we formed up for a procession, Walter and I in front, two Viceregal ADCs next, two Private Secretaries, the Governor, the Viceroy and finally the two Military Secretaries behind; one does not need to have taken part in a procession to guess how hard it is to keep step up a flight of stairs.

Now began the real ordeal; we ADCs had to stand up on the dais round the Viceroy for a period scheduled to be just over an hour; behind us were two mace bearers and four chobdars or bearers of yaks' tails which are the symbol of Sovereignty in India. One by one the hereditary Durbaris mounted the steps and, on their names being announced, held out a gold coin on a white handkerchief for the Viceroy to touch with his finger-tips, this being their 'Nazar' or symbolic tribute.

Here were all the elite, the Maliks and the Khans, the proud hawk-beaked border Barons from Mianwali and Shahpur, the ringletted Baluchi tamindars from Dera Ghazi Khan, the Chieftains of the near Pathan tribes in that portion of the Punjab across the Indus, the Sikh Sirdars from the Doab, the Rajahs from the Sikh States, the Jats from Hariana, the Rajput nobles, the Nawabs and the Rai-Bahadurs. These were the backbone of the country, these the men who had risen in arms and led their tribes to our assistance at the very perilous time of the Mutiny, here were the men who had mustered their kith and kin and themselves fought for us in the Kaiser's War, and were to do the same in Hitler's. Were we to surrender them into the hands of the shrill mouthed politicians in Delhi? These loyalists? These men some of whom had travelled hundreds of miles from their estates for the honour of paying homage? We could not guess it then, but this was exactly what we were to do.

As, however, I was standing near the front edge of the dais watching the Durbaris ascending the steps one behind the other, jewels flashing in their turbans, jewels scintillating from the hilts and scabbards of their curved swords, my attention was caught by something else shining on the red carpet below; it looked like a spur, it was, in fact, a spur, a straight necked box spur with a spike for sticking into the heel of a boot, but who else wore straight necked spurs? It is not easy when standing strictly at attention to investigate the decoration on one's own heels, nor was I much happier after proving beyond doubt that the object now shining in the sun like a heliograph did indeed belong to me!

When the last of the Durbaris had presented his 'Nazar' the Viceroy rose to deliver an address which was replied to in Urdu by the Chief of the mighty Tiwana Clan, the blue blooded Honorary Major General Nawab Malik Sir Umar Hayat Khan Tiwana, GCSI, KCIE, MVO. Then amid more fanfares of trumpets, more Royal Salutes from the Guard of Honour and a further salute of thirty-one guns from the 5th Field Battery, we drove back in our carriages surrounded by the Cavalry escort.

I discovered years later that the Viceregal party had been treated to a good laugh. We on the dais had been instructed to stand at attention for as long as we could and then to stand at ease. I was right out in front where I could be seen by everyone and decided to try and stand at attention for the whole period, because it looked better. The ceremony lasted an hour and a half by which time I reckoned I had just had about enough; what I had not realised was that Willy Goschen, a Viceregal Grenadier Guards ADC, who was parallel with me out in the opposite corner, had decided that anything I could do he would do also, for the honour of the Guards, and that it had very nearly killed him.

The remaining days of the visit were devoted to a variety of things, most of which were interesting but few restful. The day after the Durbar, being a Sunday, was comparatively slack and the Viceroy contented himself by being taken round to see a typical Punjabi-Mussulman village, a ploughing match, some selected bulls, a District Board Middle School, a review of military pensioners, a co-operative credit society and, finally, Evensong at the Cathedral. Monday was almost a day of rest too, as after a morning spent in interviews and followed by a big lunch party, we all went off to watch the sports of the Aitchison College, a British staffed establishment on public school lines. Here were two items not generally found on the programmes of schools sports, show jumping and tent pegging with the lance, for horsemanship was considered an essential part of the education of a young Indian gentleman.

On the Tuesday, the final full day of the visit, we really earned our pay. Starting off with the Veterinary College, we saw among other animals more bulls; indeed, Walter and I had specially mugged up all sorts of cattle breeding jargon, such as 'she goes well to the bucket,' determined not to be caught unprepared.

Leaving the bulls behind, we drove off to the Irrigation Research Institute, where we learnt of the measurement of silt properties, of uplift pressures of water table slopes and the mechanical properties of soil and, finally, with our heads buzzing with words like 'cusec', were driven away to the University Chemical Laboratories.

Here we started off all right, for Dr Bhatnagar, the brilliant Indian Director, commenced by explaining his experiments in connection with the addition of the juice of some common hill shrub to paraffin oil to increase its luminosity; we were soon, however, to get into deeper water, as he started explaining the use of those well-known waste products Calotropis and Mombax for improvement of gloss and his method of obtaining fibre from Agave; I soon gave up.

After lunch we called in on the King Edward Medical College; the day was then rounded off by the Viceroy laying the foundation stone of the Memorial Library at Government College.

A light touch was provided that evening by one of our chuprassis; we had three of these orderlies for the ADCs office, a Dogra, a Punjabi-Mussulman and a Sikh, all much bemedalled army pensioners. It so happened that Kishen Singh, the Sikh who had been away on sick leave after an operation for appendicitis, re-appeared on duty and reported at a time when Willy Goschen happened to be having a drink with us in our office before dinner. We were glad to see Kishen Singh back and asked him how he was feeling. 'Feeling? Why, simply fine! Just watch me!' Whereat he kicked up his legs and started walking, long scarlet coat, medals and all, round the office on his hands! Walter and I were rather tickled and congratulated him on his recovery, but Willy, poor Willy, the refreshing simplicity of the Indian soldiery was quite novel to him; brought up on the traditions of the Grenadiers, he speechlessly dabbed his lips with his handkerchief, eventually recovering only sufficiently to murmur, 'Remarkable, most remarkable.'

The final event on the Viceroy's programme was the presentation of new colours to the 2nd Bn The Dogra Regiment, and to the big brigade parade ground we motored with him; it was one of those hot autumn days with little eddies of dust rising up and settling again, usually a warning of something bad to come in the way of weather. Beside the parade ground the Dogras had pitched a huge shamiana, a vast square tent without sides, under which as we arrived were seated all the society, civil and military, British and Indian, of Lahore. In the centre was a small dais raised about three feet off the ground for the Viceroy and a few others.

As the parade commenced the wind began to get up, and the battalion marching past the saluting base raised a dust cloud so thick that figures were barely distinguishable; the shamiana too started flapping so violently that a squad of recruits who had been brought as spectators were speedily mobilised and employed two to a pole in trying to stop the whole contraption from taking off and sailing away. It seemed as if we were in for a real dust storm, for these things appear as a cloud on the far horizon and are on to one in a matter of minutes; soon the sky grew dark, a mighty rushing roaring sound was heard and with a tremendous heave the shamiana pulled out its remaining tent pegs, rose a few feet in the air and then collapsed on to all our heads.

Crawling about among the chairs, which were all that saved us from being flattened and striving to disengage the spike of my helmet from the canvas, I heard the muffled voice of Colonel Hugh Stable, the Military Secretary to the Viceroy, saying rather anxiously, 'Are you all right Sir?' and the Viceroy's reply, 'Never felt better in my life; how are you, my boy?'

As we stood a minute or two later sorting ourselves out and consoling our hosts, our attention was caught by the antics of the tall flagstaff which stood beside the saluting base; it was whipping backwards and forwards like a fishing rod while the big Union Jack on the top was making a series of cracking noises as loud as pistol shots; there could be little risk of the staff falling down: it was embedded in a square concrete base with four wire stays attached to a ring about a third of its height, but if the storm got worse something was bound to give; the dust was now so thick that we could only see the Union Jack at intervals through our watering eyes as it plunged about as if on the mast of a small ship during a storm; the sky was quite black and visibility was reduced to a few yards. Then came a final, vicious, stinging, dirty yellow blast of dust and with a resounding crack the top half of the mast broke away, whirled off and then crashed down on to the ground where within a few seconds, a little drift of sand and dust started piling up and promising to bury it, flag and all.

India is a land where much weight is given to omens and I doubt if the significance of what we saw was lost on anyone present.

XII

How to take a bribe safely

HE owned a gun but had worked so hard all his life, as did all Indian Civil Servants, that he had hardly ever fired it. What is more there had never been anyone in his immediate circle to show him how interesting shooting could be.

In Britain tired business men requiring to relieve tensions are said to find the antidote in viewing strip shows. In India we went off shooting with a similar result, added to a sense of achievement presumed lacking from the former activity.

Hill shooting round Simla had very grave drawbacks for my purpose, the main one being the 'size' of the country; vast mountain ranges interesected by valleys a thousand or more feet deep, sheer and covered with dense jungle which as one got higher gave way to deodar forests and eventually the bare hills and snow. The main quarry was varieties of magnificent pheasant, tragopan, the monal and the kalij, together with the jungle fowl not unlike our game bantams and finally that crafty bird the peacock which can fly like the wind through the thickest jungle.

All these birds were highly intelligent, far too intelligent and up to every trick. Since it was unsafe to use a dog because to a panther a dog is a delicacy they would sit tight and let one pass them unnoticed. If, panting and puffing up the slope one did get a shot, the remainder would whiz off like rockets over the valley onto a parallel ridge, never to be seen again.

Tremendous fun for a young officer needing fresh air and

exercise but out of the question for a middle aged Governor and his friends.

Of big game to be shot with a rifle there was virtually nil, although I had been fortunate enough to bag a tiger on our Eastern border. It was probably an unlikely visitor from the United Provinces jungles.

In those days not even the most hysterical anti-blood sport enthusiast could object to tiger and panther shooting. Goats were major items in peasant economy. With a panther about, one would be killed almost every day; the village firearms were limited usually to that of the headman who would be the proud possessor of some lethal old muzzle loader infinitely more dangerous to the sportsman than the quarry and really kept for prestige purposes. Thus when the villagers came in to report the presence of a panther it was really up to someone to take action, so off would go some enthusiastic young officer ready to do battle. Panthers were very cunning and he usually came back empty handed.

One season in Simla the Sub-Inspector of our police guard told us that a panther had formed the habit of walking across one end of the garden at night, presumably on his way to some favourite hunting ground, probably the abode of the half tame mouth- watering scabrous Jakko monkeys round Sanjauli bazaar.

Walter was keen to sit up for it, not so myself; one could find panther anywhere but not girls, not up to the very high standard of the Simla ones, and especially mine, who was by far the prettiest in the place. She had taken me a great deal of time and trouble to appropriate and with so many single men about, any neglect and I should lose her. My spare time was not my own.

Walter did not really appreciate the potentials of girls, he preferred horses and since I know nothing very amusing that one can do with a horse at night, he was unopposed. Walter got the enthusiastic staff to hoist a native string bed up into the fork of a tree overlooking the route the panther was seen to take, then, lashing a long electric torch to the barrel of his rifle, shinned up the tree at dusk.

There were several considerations to give him food for reflection. Many houses and paths lay within range of his heavy rifle and it would never do to pick off a Member of the Viceroy's Council on his way out to dinner in his rickshaw.

A greater tragedy could have occurred had he wounded that panther, as it would have sought refuge in some thick cover and woe betide any woman or child unlucky enough to disturb it while gathering sticks. Had its injuries prevented it from seeking its natural prey and faced with starvation it would turn its attention to easier quarry and become ultra-cunning like all man eaters.

Above all he must not wake up Lady Emerson after she had got to sleep.

Sitting up in a tree for a panther is never very comfortable. The method most likely to bring success is to watch over the odiferous corpse of a donkey, goat or what have you, sometimes even a human one, that the panther has killed and made a meal of a night or two before: then you can hear him when he gets down to his second helping.

One cannot move a muscle, one gets attacked by every kind of noctural stinging, biting or merely crawling insect without being able to counter-attack, one cannot apply anti-mosquito cream because of its smell, and while on the subject of smell one must sit down-wind of the carcase which may have been out in the sun for several days; one cannot smoke and one cannot show a light; to crown it all if in tiger country it is not safe to come down until dawn.

We spent several evenings half expecting to hear a rifle shot and preparing to congratulate a triumphant Walter but the panther never materialised; it had obviously heard or scented him, and he got tired of waiting for it. It was of little importance to him; his interest was race riding; that summer he could think of little else but the steeplechaser he was importing from the Wexford bogs which would provide him with fame and fortune on the Indian racecourse. I am glad to say that eventually in moderation it did.

I have little doubt that as he sat up in the tree amid the sighing and soughing deodars, the light night breeze bringing the heavy scent of all the nocturnal flowering shrubs on all sides, the bobbing fairy lights of far distant rickshaws twinkling back at the cold stars, he was happily pre-occupied with his dream of race horses, their idiosyncracies and their ailments.

Down in Lahore shooting prospects were far more promising but here again there were snags.

In British India where one could wander anywhere in search of game, the quality of one's shooting depended largely upon one's enthusiasm in finding it and, of course, the time at one's disposal.

I had now to find a place where the shooting was really good enough to take the Governor and his friends. There was no question of laying on something similar to the skilled slaughter on a really good pheasant shoot or grouse moor at home; we required somewhere not too far away where they would see and shoot enough game to keep them amused and interested. Recourse to the GH Game Books was not fruitful. There had been little shooting in past years.

My next act, therefore, was to ring up all the Deputy Commissioners, Superintendents of Police and the like within an hour or two by car to see what sport was to be had in their particular areas. Unfortunately they too, like HE in Lahore, were very busy men who never got a chance to shoot and could only refer me to their subordinates.

These minor officials did not themselves shoot either, if one discounts blowing the occasional duck on the village pond to pieces with a blunderbus, but wily men, they did have an eye on the main chance. They invariably sent in reports that their own particular area was alive with birds but it nearly always transpired that their object was to get themselves noticed by higher authority, so instead of getting down to shooting we would have a tea party.

We did, however, much later encounter one huge fat Sub-Inspector of Police with far more savoirfaire and also imagination than his fellows. He was known by all and sundry as 'Tarzan,' the latter series of films currently appearing in the vernacular cinemas with Urdu captions and very popular too.

'Tarzan' had mixed enough with Europeans, as most minor officials had not, to realise that when they said that they wanted to come and shoot that was exactly what they wanted to do, and nothing else. Furthermore, it was immediately obvious to him that the fewer local dignitaries there were that got to hear about it and insisted on appearing, the more individual attention would be focussed upon himself.

He laid on a most excellent partridge shoot all day with flighting duck to follow, engaging the expert services of a well-known burglar to accompany us. This latter, a quiet unobtrusive little man, was not too wrapped up in his work to have a hobby and on his appearances from jail, to which he paid regular visits, spent his leisure in snaring game. Tarzan did not seem to think it the least incongruous to produce this sportsman to accompany His Excellency and a Government House party. The little man certainly knew his stuff and must also have been rather witty for directly he discovered that HE spoke fluent Punjabi as well as Urdu he attached himself to him and kept him in fits of laughter all day.

Tarzan was a very colourful character. A story was told of him, vouchsafed as being true by all the senior Police Officers, of his method of dealing with bribery, a charge levelled too often against the Punjab Police.

It seemed that a go-between provided with a considerable sum of money had been instructed to ask him to so interfere with the course of justice as to withdraw a case involving a certain murderer against whom the evidence was so overwhelming as to make a verdict of 'not guilty' quite impossible. Tarzan unhesitatingly agreed to accept the bribe but on one condition; it was to be handed over in used notes at mid-day on the flat roof of the Police Station where he was accustomed to take his siesta,

Mahsuds with a Government go-between.

A Waziristan Village —
all were fortified.

Mahsuds — descendants of the Lost
Tribes of Israel, so some said.

nor would he budge from this extraordinary proposal.

The money, a few thousand rupees, was brought and handed over as desired, no receipt, of course, being asked or given, and the go-between went away to tell the jubilant relations. In due course, however, the sessions were held, the man convicted and hanged for a most brutal murder and the public agreed that justice had been done; not so the friends and relatives of the late lamented who had put up the money.

'But the behaviour of that Sub-Inspector is quite scandalous! Has he no sense of honour? Or of justice? This is intolerable. We had better go as a deputation to the Deputy Commissioner.'

The DC was prepared to receive them; only recently the Chief Justice had been making severe complaints about the sudden acquisition of wealth by various subordinate policemen. He must investigate.

'Where did your man hand him over the money? What? On the flat roof of the Police Station? At mid-day? And with some of you together with a lot of other people watching from the courtyard? An insult to the intelligence! Chuprassi! Show them out! Next case!'

Tarzan need never have worried about catching the eye of the high and mighty. Nobody could ever have kept him down.

Soon I was given carte blanche on my free days to take out a GH car and chauffeur and a friend or two just to explore the country and find new places for all of us to shoot every Sunday. Thus of a Sunday morning when we were not required to go to church we would set out in P3, usually driven by Ganpat who always liked to be in on everything.

This suited everyone. The Secretariat approved because HE had been in the habit of working on Sundays and presented them with baskets full of files early on Monday morning; Walter could work his race horses from dawn till dusk and Lady Emerson had a whole day's peace without either husband or ADCs.

The only discordant voice was that of my girl friend. Shooting and dancing do not go together. If one goes out before dawn and shoots all day one falls asleep very early in the evening.

Out of deference to members of the Lord's Day Observance Society it must be pointed out that firstly this was not a Protestant country and secondly it was the only free day that HE ever had, or for that matter that many others had either, for in India there were no leisured Europeans.

P3 was a big car, they were all huge, designed to transport six in perfect comfort, so off we went just after sunrise muffled up in thick coats as in those days cars lacked heaters and there could easily be a hard frost.

First we sailed smoothly and silently down the Mall, passing the occasional equestrian getting his exercise along the tan. Then passing through one bazaar or another with its horrible early morning smells we came to the main road. After a few miles we dismissed the police motor cyclist pilot and the escort car; there was now no danger since we were quite unexpected, and sped along the tarmac until the time came to turn off onto the rough unmetalled village roads, no more than cart tracks.

The sky was fleckless blue, the sun's rays fell upon fields, green with the winter crops, sky-larks sang in mid-air. Near the villages vultures and kites wheeled and whistled overhead. Cheeky little grey striped Indian squirrels, known rather unkindly as tree rats, dashed across the road. King crows, the 'subaltern's pheasant,' resplendent in their black and chestnut livery, hopped about from twig to twig on the trees lining the road. Brightly feathered little bee eaters sat in couples on the telegraph wires.

Reaching the selected spot, with not a soul in sight to have disturbed the game, there was no problem in finding people to carry our cartridges. It took about two minutes flat for small boys to appear out of thin air. They turned out to be a far better bet than most of their elders, who had to work too hard to be interested in what went on in a swamp and were apt to say anything that they thought would please us. Not so the small boys; being principally engaged in the not very exciting task of herding goats until they were old enough to work, they knew every inch of the surrounding area and the habits of its denizens and were only too delighted to have something new to entertain them; furthermore, they were far quicker at interpreting my mixture of Urdu and halting Punjabi.

While we unpacked our guns, the urchins would be sent off to produce all their little friends and soon we were plunging knee deep into the bright green mossy warm swamp, each closely followed by his posse laden down with game carriers and spare cartridges of which one could easily shoot off a hundred each in the day.

Vivid blue and bright scarlet dragon flies go up with a whiz from the edge of slimy pools and kingfishers resenting our intrusion darted off further into the reeds. Magnificent ring-tailed fish eagles, sitting on the branches of dead trees, would greet us with raucous screams like an unoiled cart wheel; they alone would find our shooting to their advantage.

With a whirr of wings a snipe suddenly rises from a tuft of grass and as one fires one hears a scuffle from behind as one's own small boys assert their rights to the ownership of the empty cartridge cases. Fighting had to be sternly suppressed as they had to be taught to act as retrievers and watch where the birds fell. Once trained they hardly ever lost any dead or wounded game.

Wading on a little further, the moss sinking at every step and great evil smelling bubbles rising and bursting round one, another snipe would rise out of range and zig-zag away, a little dot in the sky, carefully watched as he would be making for some other swamp which we must find later.

Now a heron, getting himself airborne with a few awkward bounces, flies off with a long slow wing beat uttering his harsh cry of protest. We soon find ourselves firing rights and lefts as the snipe get up in clouds, so that there are often nine or ten birds in front of us awaiting collection. As the sun rises in the sky our guns get unpleasantly hot to hold, but who cares for such small inconveniences on a day like this?

By mid-day the last of the snipe had written off this particular group of bogs as being a noisy and dangerous feeding ground and departed elsewhere, so there was nothing for it but to splash our way back to the car. Here we would consume not the packet of soggy sandwiches one would have were one alone, but a real lunch spread out on a snowy tablecloth under a shady tree by Ganpat.

The afternoon was usually devoted to looking for partridge, of which there were two varieties, the grey, *Francolinus Interpositus* and the black, *Francolinus Francolinus*, each with different habits. Here again it was necessary to have done one's homework and one's reconnaissance, because the grey preferred dry, thorny, scrub country with cultivation nearby whereas the black liked grass six or eight foot high with plenty of water.

The crops yielded a few quail and we usually brought back one or two, but they gave us easy shots flying quite straight for short distances so we spared them. They are excellent eating, being served for breakfast.

When shooting near the foot hills we would find peacock very worthy game when in their correct habitat, dense scrub and deciduous jungle. They are possessed of phenominally keen sight and hearing and they too prefer when disturbed to slink away unseen rather than fly. When, however, they do fly, and they take care to get airborne well out of sight, they accelerate to a terrific speed, giving one a tantalising half second flash of bright colour through a gap in the foliage.

Pea-fowl have to be shot with some circumspection as near villages they can be semi-domesticated. If the village should be a Hindu one they may be protected by religion or sentiment; or on the contrary the local small farmers might come and implore one to shoot them on account of the damage which they do to the crops.

I once had quite a lot of trouble talking myself out of an embarrassing position after shooting a couple of large peacock in answer to an appeal from a group of villagers. They knew full well, which I did not, that the Brahmin in charge of the local temple would be absolutely furious. They had also calculated that by the time he had heard the bangs and rushed out with his avenging acolytes, the foul deed would have been done, they would have been rid of these particular pests and would be the picture of wide eyed innocence. It was more than lucky that this happened before I was connected with Government House as otherwise it would have been reported by some ill-wisher and made headlines in the vernacular press.

Having disposed of the partridge it was time to move on to what could be the best and most exciting shoot of the day, flighting duck. With duck as the quarry the search for a good spot was infinitely more difficult.

The only obvious haunts of duck to be found on the maps of this part of the Punjab were the chain of marshes and small lakes formed by the ever changing course of the mighty River Ravi. Everyone, of course, knew about them and on arrival at any of them one could count on finding parties of disconsolate sportsmen walking about with nothing to shoot at.

I eventually got advice from an engineer in the Canal Department, who was himself too busy to shoot, to investigate the possibilities of the canal system. These canals, of which there was a vast network, supplied irrigation water to nearly every corner of the province. Taking off from the headworks near the Himalayan foothills where the five large rivers of the province debouch onto the plains, these massive canals lead towards the deserts in the South, with every few miles a branch to the left or right carrying water to the area on either side. They were, of course, all linked up so that if some vagary of the melting snow on some high mountain range caused one river or another to fall low and fail to supply its necessary quota of water, requirements could be met by diverting from the next; that terrible disaster, drought, thus vanished.

They had one very great advantage. Being closed to the public the heavy iron gates giving access to them were always locked and in many cases also guarded by a watchman dozing in his little hut. Government House took care to have a master key.

The majority of the canals were lined with stone but not all and here and there at intervals of perhaps thirty miles were places where the water had seeped through the bank to make pools and marshes a few hundred yards broad and a mile or two long. A major headache for the engineers but an ideal place for duck to feed undisturbed both by day and night. Here too were the acres and acres of mossy swamp land so beloved by the snipe but not for the solitude because one of the best little snipe shoots I knew lay in a bog a few yards from the Grand Truck Road with lorries hurtling past every few minutes. Further away from the canal as far as the eye could see would stretch an unbroken line of crops, for not a square yard of irrigated ground could be wasted.

Accordingly before the shadows lengthened we would take up our positions concealed by high grass on the edge of our pools and await what fortune might bring.

Fortune might bring a variety of duck, all migratory, spending the winters with us and flying back over the Himalayas to their breeding grounds in spring.

The most common to fall to our guns were the Mallard or Wild Duck with their glossy green heads and chestnut breasts, exactly the same birds as one sees on so many stretches of water in Britain. Next came the Pochard, both the spectacular Red Crested and the ordinary: tubby little diving ducks which secure most of their food from deep water. They usually keep to large sheets of open water, and for some reason often swim along side by side in lines fifty or more yards long; it seems possible that since they feed on weed and the various grubs clinging to it, they are, in fact, practising strip grazing.

With the Pochard are the other diving ducks, the Golden Eye, also purpose-constructed with their legs set further back on their bodies which makes them very ungainly on land.

To add variety we had Gadwell, very fast on the wing and giving good sporting shots, Common and Gargany Teal and very occasionally the, to us, rare Scaup and Pink Headed Duck. Sheldrake and Ruddy Sheldrake or Brahminy were not fit for the table and did not give sporting shots so we left them alone.

As the sun was setting we would see a dozen or so Mallard describing an arc across the sky, circling round us in a wide sweep to get into position to land into the wind. Crouching down until we are nearly sitting in the water we peer out under the brims of our hats, exposing as little as possible of our faces, until they are within range when we straighten up and fire. The dead birds fall like plummets into the water raising a huge splash, the signal for some of the boys to launch themselves like torpedoes across the swamp, running lightly over the surface where a grown man would sink to the knee at every step.

As it gets darker more and more birds come in, unseen until they momentarily appear as dark shadows above, barely allowing time for a quick swing and an instantaneous pull of the trigger before they disappear into the gloom. By now the positions of the other guns are disclosed only by vivid crimson flashes as they fire and all too soon we can see nothing and stand listening to splashes on all sides as yet more and more duck pitch in beside us and start feeding and quacking quite unconcerned by our presence.

Out come our electric torches and the search only stops when we have accounted for the last of the duck which we know to have been hit. Now for the first time we begin to notice that we are very cold and very wet and slowly flounder back to the car.

Sitting on the bank of the canal and paddling our feet in the water we peel off out filthy stockings and shorts and scrape off as much of the black glutinous mud that can be dislodged from our bodies before putting on something warm and dry.

Dispensing eight annas each to the small boys, far too much but in keeping with our exalted position, we promise that we will come again and waving until we are out of sight sink back into the luxurious comfort of the car.

Being driven home in the dark beside the canal we eventually emerge through the iron gates onto a public road where speed has to be further reduced in deference to the bullock cart traffic. Creaking along on their huge wooden wheels in convoys of about half a dozen, each with its driver muffled up in a blanket asleep somewhere on the top of the load, these carts would travel all night with their bullocks or buffaloes patiently following the cart in front unless they took it into their heads to walk with two carts abreast which was all that the width of the road would allow.

There was little danger if one allowed for the fact that as often as not they carried no lights. If the road was blocked one stopped the car and the bullocks stopped and the driver momentarily woke up sufficiently to howl some endearment to his beasts who automatically pulled into the left, and the traffic eventually continued on its way.

On occasions such as these, provided it was sufficiently dark and HE was not in the car, I would put on my most homely Punjabi accent and enquire tenderly:-

'Does the road then belong to your mother?'

This seemingly simple enquiry, taught me by Akhtar, was fraught with hidden depths of such shocking innuendo that it never failed to bring a smile to the face of any of the drivers or orderlies with whom I might be, while the effect on the sleeping bullock drivers and even the bullocks was electrical.

Bazaar lorries were a far greater menace then bullock carts, especially at night. Our roads were the best in India, tarred but only single tracked, leaving a drop of about two inches either side into thick powdery dust, down into which one was forced to put one's nearside wheels when passing. Were there no wind, or were the wind from the left, one was inconvenienced, but were it to be from the right and the approaching vehicle to leave the tarred surface too soon, one immediately became enveloped in a huge dust cloud which rendered even one's own bonnet invisible and made one stamp on the brakes and remain stationary until it had been blown away.

As we approached Lahore we would see the slender spires of the tombs at Shadra standing out white in the moonlight and soon would come broad streets flanked by pavements behind which were two irregular rows of tiny dilapidated open fronted shops dimly illuminated by single electric light bulbs.

Brief glances were given of the vendors sitting cross legged among their wares dispensing tired looking fruit, fly blown sticky sweets, rolls of bright cloth, heavy shoes with long curled up toes, biris with all but a written guarantee to give lung cancer; betel nut wrapped in green leaves which imparts that fetching reddish yellow stain to the teeth, bottles of coloured patent medicines chiefly aphrodisiacal, as if they needed it.

The best shoot in which I took part was not, however, in the Punjab, but as a guest of His Highness the Nawab of Bahawalpur with whom we stayed for a couple of days in his shooting lodge beside a vast lake called Bhugger, situated in the desert country which forms part of his territory.

Soon after arrival I was handed two books of tickets and, on glancing at them, found tear-off tickets clearly marked with the numbers of our state cars, our boats, our hides, our loaders, our spare pair of guns (the ones I was offered were by Purdey,) our boxes of a thousand spare cartridges, our basket with 'elevenses' (mine contained, among other delicacies, chicken sandwiches and a bottle of Champagne) and our human retrievers who would swim about among the clumps of tall reeds near our butts and fetch in dead and wounded birds.

On the morning of the shoot we were motored across country to points on the lake opposite out respective butts, there taking to the boats, which threaded their way for several hundred yards through channels among eight or ten foot high reeds and deposited us on our very carefully camouflaged platforms of logs. On the first shot having been fired by HH at the appointed time, the sky became black with different varieties of migratory duck which whizzed over and past me at full speed at every height and from every angle for about three hours, by which time both my guns were too hot to hold, my right shoulder and upper arm were black and blue and I was very deaf from concussion. On the morning's bag being counted, the eight guns had between us shot nine hundred and forty-two ducks.

In the evening some of the keener shots went out after partridge, bagging ninety-three partridge, twenty-six quail, two hare and Sir Bernard Darly KCSI, CIE, who fell to the gun of a young British Political Officer and whom I listed in the GH game book under the heading 'various'.

Another memorable shoot was on the occasion of a visit by Lord and Lady Baden-Powell. The Baden-Powells had brought with them as Secretaries their daughter Heather, and her friend, Rosemary de Renzy-Martin. In the evenings, the day's work done and our seniors safely in bed, I would collect a fourth, as Walter hated night life, and these two young ladies would honour us with their company at whatever hotel was holding a dance. One night we went on to the one and only night-club, no less amusing for not being by any means respectable; it made the headlines a year or two later when a serious young amateur pilot, jilted by one of the cabaret, tried to fly in at her dressing room window, after which what remained of the place was closed down by the police.

The night club was great fun and when we looked at our watches to discover it was half past five we were still as fresh as daisies, fresh enough to go back and change into old clothes, climb into my own old but swift car and drive back to the nearest duck jheel. The sun rose in all its glory; covering the swamp with wide bars of red and gold; the duck came over in their dozens; we shot a sufficient number not to be laughed at by the girls and we got back in time to appear at breakfast clean and properly dressed.

Having taken good care that we had a perfectly blank day which could be devoted to dozing, we were not particularly surprised when Rosemary and Heather failed to appear in our office for some beer at half past twelve as arranged, assuming that they were fast asleep.

When, however, we all met publicly at lunch they both looked pale and strangely worried; it seemed that they had some information to impart and that it was not wholly good. It transpired that Heather's . . . father (and she used an unfilial and unladylike adjective) had grabbed her directly after breakfast and dictated a very long speech which he was due to give on the morrow and which had to be typed out this very day for the press; things might have been better, she wailed, had there not been great gaps where she had fallen asleep and where she was not able to read her own shorthand.

After lunch we got down to work; there were sentences without beginnings and sentences without ends, there were strings of words that could not be made into sentences at all, and the only intelligent course seemed to be to scrap the whole thing and start again. The girls knew all about policy and anecdotes of scouting in other parts of the world; I for my part was conversant with the history of the movement in the province, local doings and the names of those who required thanks and recognition of their work.

Between us we produced a really wonderful speech, full of ringing phrases interlarded with topical allusions and little jokes; messages for the future followed on references to the past, no one's services were overlooked, no prize winning troop went uncongratulated. There remained, however, the acid test. As he got to his feet next day I do no know which member of the quartet felt the most apprehensive, but once started he went on without a flaw, although I did notice a rather puzzled expression at times, especially when he found himself making jokes that he had never heard before. The applause was colossal, no suspicion ever fell on any of us and all the leading Indian newspapers printed the speech in toto. What more could be desired?

XIII

Not pussy, but the hounds are down a well

In India horses, their equipment and upkeep were all so ridiculously cheap that anyone could ride who had the inclination. In the Indian Army all officers were mounted; they had to produce their own chargers after which the government paid all expenses.

At the top end of the equestrian scale were the Cavalry Regiments. Some of their officers hinted darkly that they made more on the race course than they were paid by His Majesty, others that they made a handsome living making championship class polo ponies out of young remounts, and then selling them to Indian Princes.

I could never thus understand why so many were heavily in debt all their service.

There was indeed one famous and gallant Brigadier, an international polo player, who was so much in debt on account of horses that he could not leave India, his creditors waving bills and forming a solid wall between him and the gangway every time he tried to get on a ship. He had to retire in Kashmir.

I bought a horse from the Executors of a Political Officer who had committed suicide, not, one was told, on account of any disillusionment with the horse, although one could easily have understood and condoned his action if it had been. With it, however, came a slit eyed red cheeked Turkoman groom, an obsolute treasure who stayed with me until I left India. He had fled to escape massacre when the Russians invaded his country.

Finding myself not entirely suited, mount-wise, I started looking about for another, and early on in my first season in Simla noticed rather a showy liver chestnut mare which was being hired out to all and sundry by a dealer in the bazaar.

One evening I met it and another horse coming towards me, each ridden by a slim young Anglo-Indian girl; probably typists and from their air of anxiety not exactly born horsewomen.

Just as they got abreast of me the liver chestnut gave a slight start, probably at the look in the eye of the beast I was riding, and deposited its rider, a remarkably pretty girl, gently onto the road where she lay with closed eyes moaning softly and with graceful gestures indicating her hip.

With perfectly pure intentions, thinking I should find out if she had broken anything before organising her removal to hospital, I started unzipping her jodpurs.

Never have I seen a girl recover quicker. I had no opportunity of making any further progress with the lady, but I did shortly afterwards buy the mare and started hunting her directly we got down to Lahore.

It was a nice change to have a mount that did not spend its time reaching out with bared teeth with the intention of seeking whom it might devour. We had a pack of foxhounds out at Mian Mir, the cantonments of Lahore, run and maintained by the garrison and with a Lady Master, the wife of the Home Secretary. Some of the hounds were generously presented by packs at home, others bred in kennels. One cannot pretend it was up to the standard of the Shires in the palmy days, but at least we had no wire and it was very exhilarating. It provided sport for a good cross section of the European community but not the Indians who somehow did not take to it.

Hunting was enjoyed for a bare three hours, twice a week, on Thursdays and Sundays, starting at dawn, as the ground would carry the scent of a jackal only in the early morning before the sun had risen properly and drawn up every drop of moisture left by the night air.

This suited everyone as on Thursdays people had to be back at work after breakfast and on Sundays there were family claims, church and shooting. Sending out our horses at sometime during the very early hours, we would be wakened with a cup of tea at about 5.30am and then struggle into our hunting kit and wrap ourselves in sheepskin coats before sleepily getting into cars.

Climbing aboard one's mount, which had every excuse for a cold back and the consequent display of buck jumping, one moved off behind hounds in the half-light towards the first covert.

We were rather dressy, permanent hunt members generally in pink or sometimes rat catcher and everyone else in tweed coats and field or polo boots. I myself was quite smart, if viewed from a distance, as I had fallen off in a field which must have been dressed by some kind of fertilizer, with my horse on top of me, ensuring that I was pressed well in. The result was that by the next meet my beautiful red coat, an heirloom, had developed great crimson patches like a herald's tabard, which even the laboratories of Lahore University could not remove. My top hat, like my coat, was of equally antique cut; I had found it in a box in the attic along with my grandfather's last coachman's livery — a very good line shoot — I was delighted when people asked me where on earth I had got it from.

The little grey Indian fox leaves no scent, but jackal, which was what we hunted, were plentiful and had the advantage over the British fox in not living in earths and seldom going to ground. It was thus a matter of laying hounds onto a patch of sugar cane and it would not be long before a hound spoke and we would all be galloping hell for leather over the light sandy plough and as often as not straight into the rising sun; here, it was essential to get out either in front or well to a flank as the leading horses kicked up such a dust as to make it unpleasant and dangerous for those behind.

Obstacles there were in plenty, ranging from wide and deep irrigation ditches which were jumped with the heart in the mouth, to canals which could sometimes be forded; here and there was a thick hedge of prickly pear or a sunbaked mud wall or a tricky narrow lane with high mud walls on either side.

As the morning wore on and the sun rose higher scent worsened until it became non-existent; it was then time to find water for the hounds before taking them back to their lorry standing at the meet.

After the horses had cooled down we would usually stop and water them at an irrigation well. These were up to ten or twelve foot in diameter at the mouth, and thirty or forty foot deep.

When these wells fell into disuse and the parapets crumbled away, they became a menace to strangers at night or when riding a horse fast across country.

There was another type of well, not dug for irrigation, which was very infrequently encountered and had been constructed for the enjoyment of rich families, where they might sit throughout the hot summer's day some thirty feet underground in a little chamber just above water level; one wonders if the children were continually falling in.

It was due to a well of this latter type that a sad incident befell the Lahore Hunt which must be unique in hunting history. We were having a bye-day in one of the few places where we could meet when the crops were getting high, a vast tangle of scrubby trees and thorn bushes where hunting was usually confined to trotting about the little winding paths and continually flattening oneself on one's horse's back to avoid being swept off. This wilderness was inhabited by a profusion of jack far too intelligent to ever consider leaving it, who would cross each other's lines with such rapidity that sooner or later each hound was hunting a jack of his own.

This particular morning it never ceased raining cats and dogs as it had done throughout the night, and a bare half dozen enthusiasts were out. After the usual procedure of finding myself along with the jack and a couple of hounds, then meeting the Master without the pack, followed by encountering half the pack without the Master, then meeting stray horsemen who were lost and looking for everyone else, I decided that the chances of a proper hunt were negligible, so slowly started making my way in the rough direction of where we had left the cars.

Having gone a couple of miles, I heard the thudding of hooves and the swish and tear of small branches as one of the whips appeared across our bows, shouting something unintelligible and pointing his crop in the direction whence he had come, before crashing on through the undergrowth.

Someone must have had an accident, so trotting back along the hoof marks of the whip, I was not surprised after about a mile to see a riderless horse grazing beside a bush. Leaving the horse I recognized as belonging to Jack Morton, a Police Officer, I started to look for him and, skirting a clump of bushes, suddenly saw a whimpering hound puppy, one of the new entry, standing up on its hind legs and peering over the rim of a very old and disused looking well.

Poor old Jack, he had been a nice fellow; I hoped he had bashed in his head and died instantaneously and not drowned slowly in, of all gruesome places, a well.

Peering in apprehensively I saw far below me, swimming round and round very slowly and obviously in the last stages of exhaustion about a dozen hounds; more surprisingly still, from an archway the floor of which was a couple of feet above water level, protruded the head and shoulders of Jack, on his stomach on the floor, one hand dangling into the water.

It was only too obvious that something needed doing urgently, and the corpse, screwing round its neck, supplied the answer. 'There is a passage entrance about twenty yards away in the bushes; come down and lend me a hand, as I can't pull any more of these . . . out.'

I had thrown off my heavy red coat and was about to divest myself of my top boots, in case I should find myself swimming, when I remembered that a tunnel of this nature was almost bound to be simply wriggling with snakes. A narrow little passage, rough and slippery, led down very steeply into darkness in which there was water; turning the corner at the bottom of the steps and finding the latter no more than ankle deep, I splashed along quite happily, for I could see Jack silhouetted in the archway in front of me, and had just answered what I took for a shout of welcome when I fell into a waist deep pool of stinking slimy green water where the floor had apparently caved in; Jack, however, really had nothing at which to laugh, for he too was soaked to the skin and on him now stood a couple of hounds anxious to keep their feet dry.

I do not know the weight of a good solid English foxhound, but I do not need to consult a reference book to know that they are heavy, especially when one is lying flat on one's stomach over the lip of a well and pulling them up out of water a good two feet below; to make matters worse, the rescued refused to assay the passage to the world above without us and were soon occupying every inch of space, and even standing on us. The final count showed two and half couple drowned, and we estimated that the pack must have been swimming in the well for an hour and a half.

At the end of the season when hunting was over because of the height of the crops, the hunt held its point-to-point, a big social occasion and one to which people brought their horses from all over the Province.

All the jumps were reasonable, mostly irrigation ditches of various widths with and without water, together with baked mud walls. There was, however, one wide and deep irrigation channel which always looked unjumpable and never failed to scare me. The real bugbear, however, was the awful dust which made it imperative to get in front immediately to avoid being blinded.

On the last occasion that I rode there, as a regimental officer once more, the lead was almost immediately taken by an officer of another regiment whom we loathed. Eventually he seemed to have disappeared so far into the distance that I could not spot him at all, but I had forgotten about my old friend the terrifying irrigation channel; as I cleared it I looked down on him struggling in the murky depths below, his horse on top of him, wedged up by the sloping sides.

I rode on my way rejoicing.

Since I lived cheek by jowl with Walter and our desks were only a few feet apart; and since we had many of the same friends, Frank Cundle, then a young officer but later the well-known trainer, and Geoffrey Frith, the Races Secretary, a live wire sent up by The Royal Calcutta Turf Club, to name two, it was inevitable that I should start race riding, at the very lowest level, of course.

I should already have known much more about it than I did owing to two colourful family skeletons in the cupboard. As I have already said my grandfathers were not honest infantrymen like my father and myself but in the British Cavalry and thought and talked of little else but steeplechasing. One had actually won the Grand Military Steeplechase of 1864 with his left arm strapped to his side because of a fall two days earlier.

The 18th Hussar was, making the necessary allowances, quite a keen soldier, the 12th Lancer less so, but neither would have appreciated the dictum of the great Duke of Wellington in one of his more jaundiced moods: 'British Cavalry is no good except for galloping.' It gave me great pleasure to be reminded of the reminiscences of the 12th Lancer's ancient batman who maintained that his officer could never master the words of command and that the only order he was ever known to utter was: 'Follow the tail of my horse' which had to serve all purposes.

After seven years, however, this feat of memory proved too exhausting and he transferred to the Territorial Army commanding the 9th Lanarkshire Rifle Volunteers for twenty-one years in accordance with the extraordinary usage of the day. God help them.

My second winter in Lahore I invested in a far better class of hunter than I had ever owned in my life. He was from Australia and had but one eye but could see well enough out of the other and could jump excellently. I was soon to discover that he pulled like a train but in the Plains of the Punjab there is plenty of turning space. If in danger of over running hounds when they were heading North, all one had to do was to point the horse East or West.

There were a series of open meetings, known as the Northern Circuit: Meerut in the beginning of November, the Army Cup and the Grand Military Steeplechase at Lucknow at the end of November, followed by our big Four-day Lahore Christmas meeting with the Indian Grand National, the Stewards' Cup, the Governor's Cup and the Gold Cup; after Christmas came three more meetings.

Since Walter used to ride for various owners at all these places I used to find myself very busy as I was permanently In Waiting night and day. He, however, did a lot for me at all the other times of the year.

The accompaniments of racing here were luxury itself. During open meetings a military band would play on the lawn of the members enclosure, the flower beds were a blaze of colour and between them were dotted little tables each under its garden parasol to which smartly dressed and above all attentive khidtmagars would bring trays of tea or drinks.

The highlight of the racing season was the Indian Grand National on Governor's Cup Day, as for this meeting horses were brought from all over Northern India and people congregated for the big social event. Government House too had a part to play, and what a part!

We were the proud possessors of a camel carriage, a singular vehicle the existence of which I had never before suspected, nor do I suppose that nine people out of ten have either. It was in the form of an open landau towed along at a fast trot by six postillioned dromedaries, and was used once a year on this occasion only. Its history was that in the good old days before the province was blessed with roads and railways it or its predecessor was used to carry the Governor on tour through the sandier portions of his domain denied to horse-drawn vehicles, he and his staff actually abandoning the carriage and mounting the camels in districts where the going was really bad.

On Governor's Cup Day the black landau was polished until

it shone like a mirror, the camels were draped in gold saddle-cloths and flaunted crimson muzzles, the six postillions were dressed in scarlet and blue and gold, two scarlet and gold dressed chobdars stood on a little platform over the rear springs waving yaks' tails and inside was His Excellency the Governor, his Consort and an ADC.

Preceded by a drummer, mounted on an especially big camel with, slung on either side of the saddle, a pair of bass and tenor silver kettle-drums on which he played a continuous tum-tum tom-tom tum-tum tom-tom, we would appear between the first and second races through a gate opposite the five furlong mark and proceed, lurching and swaying, surrounded by a whole squadron of Lancers, at a brisk trot up the course.

Our arrival would be twice heralded by fanfares from trumpeters posted on the roof of the grandstand, after which we would sweep up and the camels be pulled back onto their haunches opposite the wicket gate leading from the course into the Members' enclosure. Then, covered with a thick layer of grey dust and flecks of foam from the Cavalry Escort, pea green from the horrid swaying motion of the vehicle and feeling ourselves smelling strongly of camel, we had to climb down a contraption like a very springy hen ladder in front of the assembled multitudes.

Lady Emerson did what she could with her frock, H.E. desperately clutched his grey topper, stick and gloves, and the unfortunate ADC took what steps he could to prevent his sword from getting between his legs, his long spurs from sticking between the rungs of the ladder and his various golden cords from lassooing the door handle and suddenly suspending him in mid-air. Our safe arrival on terra firma was the signal for the band to strike up 'God save the King.'

On arrival in Simla I hacked Skate about the roads and although he pulled off some most alarming shies and spectacular buck jumps we never quite went over a cliff. We had never considered racing him at Annandale; the course was only about four furlongs round and required a handy horse with a quick turn of speed. Walter thought that the course was only safe for polo ponies as at one end to the left of the stands only a low stone wall separated it from a precipice; it was at any rate quite unsuitable for Skate, who with his long ungainly stride was probably faster than some other horses there, but who was a 'one pacer' and at the mercy of any small animal who could get inside him at the bends.

I had been down to several meetings as a pure spectator and Walter had had a few rides on other people's horses when we were prevailed upon by a cheerful Gunner Colonel, who ran Annandale races during the summer months, to make up runners in a distance handicap. Walter could never refuse a suggestion like this so enter we did, although I was on the point of entering hospital for an operation. Obviously, Skate could have no chance over such a distance but Walter took the precaution of giving him one or two short half speed gallops round the course early before breakfast, so that he would recognise his way round and not disappear into space over the wall.

We entered the horse at 10 stone 7lbs which just suited Walter nicely. The great day came and the whole population of Simla, European and Indian alike, headed by the Viceroy and the Commander-in-Chief, thronged down to attend and have a flutter. The runners were from all parts of Northern India, some ridden by professional Indian jockeys, some by Eurasians and some by jockeys of indeterminate nationality. Huge crowds milled round the tote and the bookies, for the Indian dearly loves a gamble of any kind. Skate was by no means composed and although Fateh Khan, my groom, who was an ex-rough rider in Hodson's Horse IA had brought him down as late as possible and tucked him away in a far corner, he knew exactly what was taking place and was in a white lather of excitement.

Eventually it came to our race and after a slight display of temperament in the paddock, Walter got on board and down they all trotted to their various posts.

They all careered past the stand sending up showers of loose clods and there was a wild rush to hug the rails at the next bend, the 'precipice' turn. I could see him disappear into the scrum at this point but then a horse ridden by a little Australian jockey that had been hugging the rails, swung out at the bend and cannoned into him sending him flying over to the left but fortunately not over the wall. By the time they were heading up the final straight Skate had lost many lengths and there was no hope of catching the leaders. The obvious solution was to enter him for his next race with a further two stone to carry, which we knew in a short scurry like this was unlikely to slow him up. We also knew that the Annandale handicapper was not in the same class as our friend Peter Brooke in Lahore and was unlikely to realize that Skate was a weight carrier and a one pacer.

There was a fortnight to go before his next race and in this time Walter practised short darts round the turns of the Annandale course before breakfast, deciding not to gallop him except for one morning three days before the race, as early as possible before anyone else should be about.

With the arrival of the race card we saw that we had secured a handicap of plus forty-five yards in a field of eleven horses. The two horses of which we were most apprehensive were an entry by the Rana Sahib of Dhami and a horse called Peanut entered by HH The Rajah of Faridkot, both carrying light weights but starting well behind us.

The same evening HE The Governor took a party to the theatre and since both Walter and I wanted to see the show we both decided to be In Waiting. There we met some of the Viceroy's Personal Staff who declared that they thought that we had a very good chance of winning on handicap. In vain we replied that the race was too short for the horse; in vain we pointed out that there were two or three horses which although they were starting behind us were a great deal faster; in vain we told them not to back us, or if they did, not to risk more than a few rupees. They seemed quite convinced that we had a dark horse and were going to bring off a major coup and openly told us that not only would they be backing us but that the Viceroy and Lady Linlithgow would be having some money on us as well. Furthermore they divulged that they had been in touch with the Commander-in-Chief's ADCs and both he and they proposed backing us. This was by no means what we wanted but there seemed nothing that we could do about it. Even more fervent supporters were all the servants at Barnes Court and despite our warnings, for we were even more loth that they should lose their money than that all the other ADCs should lose theirs, we could not shake them in their conviction that we should pull it off.

On the day of the race when I entered the ring, I found the odds standing at only four to one whereas I had expected them to be at least fifteen to one. Hanging about to see it they would lengthen before the 'off' I was horrified to see them shorten down to two to one at which I had to lodge my modest wager.

Skate stood like a rock at the starting post and soon got into his stride when the flag had fallen. There was no bumping match at 'Precipice Bend' for by that time he was out in front though hotly pursued. They gained on him all the way up the straight but failed to head him off at the final bend and from this point gave up pursuing him seriously.

Walter hastily glancing over his shoulder and seeing no one behind decided that he could ease Skate up a bit; but the old horse, however, was enjoying himself far too much to pay any attention to Walter. The sun was shining, the birds were singing, the going was good, the crowd were roaring, he was full of expensive oats and he liked being in front of all the other horses. He went it anything a little faster, flashing past the post with no other horse anywhere near him.

We were astonished and delighted; the old nag had beaten all comers; he had shown his heels to these various combinations of expensive horses and professional jockeys; he had won on his merits; Walter's intelligent idea of carrying extra lead to gain distance had paid off its dividend: if only I had staked a month's pay on him; my friends congratulated me; those of our servants who were off duty were all grinning from ear to ear in the background; they had as I suspected staked far more than they could afford; all was right with the world.

We soon, however, discovered that the Stewards held a very different view. While Walter was unsaddling and before he had even weighed in, he was warned by the Secretary that the Stewards wished to see us both in their room in a few minutes. We were staggered. We had moreover little time to think up what to say.

On entering the Stewards' room we were confronted by quite an imposing bunch of senior officers and officials; among those present were a couple of Cavalry Brigadiers from GHQ, our Inspector General of Police who always owned a string of good race horses himself, and four other senior officials who were big time race horse owners. They all looked grim and many looked rather embarrassed, for either one or other of us was known to most of them personally. In the centre sat the acting Chief Steward, a Brigadier whom neither of us knew: he betrayed no signs of embarrassment and his tone was menacing, an accuser as well as a judge.

His initial remarks were addressed to Walter.

'I understand that you rode this horse in both these races?'

'Yes, Sir.'

'You won to-day with a lot in hand and it appears to us that the improvement in his form is about two stone, how do you account for that?'

'The horse was quite unaccustomed to these sharp bends on the first occasion nor had he ever run in a sprint race before. He is a long striding horse and we had been running him under entirely different conditions at Lahore over hurdles in a race of 1½ miles.'

'Oh! So you ran him at Lahore did you?' (In a tone of surprise) 'Where did he finish?'

Walter told him. The Chief Inquisitor glanced at his brother stewards with a look as if to imply that we had accused ourselves out of our own mouths. Walter went on to explain, with mounting heat, how the horse had received a bad bump in the first race etc, etc. The evidence for the defence thus concluded we were shown out of the room while the stewards considered their verdict.

On being re-admitted we were treated to a tiger-like glare from the acting Chief Steward and told that they were not prepared to accept our explanation, to which Walter replied that before accusing us they should at least have heard the story of the jockey who bumped us. This, however, he was not prepared to hear, on the grounds that the next race was already late. This made us both lose our tempers, and Walter is an Irishman; he, throwing discretion to the winds, suggested that half the stewards present were ignorant and that in any case he was prepared to bet that most of them were on our side. Wasting no time he started walking round the room jabbing his finger into their faces one after the other saying 'How about you now? Do you honestly believe that I pulled the horse in the first race?' The big-wigs of Simla were not used to this treatment.

The Secretary went out and returned with a tiny weather beaten wisp of a man looking rather like a startled shrimp, his little bow legs like matches in their racing boots. He had suddenly been pulled out of the jockeys' changing room, we had been given no chance to brief him about our troubles, and the luckless man, twisting his jockeys cap in his muscular little hands, obviously did not know for what past indiscretion he was now being hauled up; he was all of a shake and his past misdeeds were obviously coming before his eyes one after another; he stood, moistening his lips with his tongue, surveying the awe inspiring half circle in front of him until asked about any particular incident in connection with his race in the last meeting.

'Oh yes, Sir' he piped up in broad Australian, for he was a temporary migrant who had just finished a season's racing in Calcutta. 'At the first bend there was a bit of a mix up, Sir, all I remember is that there was a bigger horse outside me and he gave me a bump that all but put me over the rails, Sir, fair knocked the stuffing out of me, Sir, very dangerous riding, Sir, I could never get going after that!'

Had we had any sympathisers before this little speech we certainly had none now. The Brigadier, assuming the manner of a judge pronouncing sentence of death, said that they were not satisfied with our explanation, that they did not, however, propose to take the race away from us but that we must both watch out in future. With that we were ushered out, confirmed black sheep.

We were rather mystified until Walter, schooling a polo pony down at Annandale a few days later, ran into his friend the Secretary who said that he was sorry we had been in trouble, adding with a twinkle in his eye that he understood that we had made a pile out of the bookies! On Walter giving him the facts he said that the Chief Steward had been told by one of the bookies that he alone had taken a bet of the equivalent of £120 at fours and had had to pay out £480, that the other bookies had all been in much the same boat, and that the whole lot were whooping for our blood. This was the story and the Brigadier putting two and two together had made five or six out of it.

We immediately got our spies to work. We were on good terms with all the race course riff-raff, the tipsters, the stable boys, the superannuated Indian jockeys and the rest so that it was not long before we got the answer. It seemed that a professional backer from Calcutta used to spend his time sitting high up in the woods overlooking Annandale, stopwatch in hand and powerful glasses trained on the course, timing all the horses as they did their early morning gallops. He had been up in good time on the morning of Skate's final gallop and it was then merely a question of sending his agents into the ring to place his big bets for him. One lives and one learns.

More was to follow; the less reputable Indian papers, always anxious to embarrass the Government, came out with headlines about 'Government House ADC carries out his nefarious work under the very shadow of the Union Jack.'

I gave up racing for a while.

XIV

Indian history can hardly be philosophy from examples

We are indebted to the great Henry Ford for the dictum that 'History is Bunk'. Some may agree, others have reservations.

Having said that, perhaps a little potted 'History without Tears' might give us some clues as to why firstly anyone who has fought with or against them, considers the Northern Indians to be the best natural soldiers in the world, why 2,000 British administrators backed up by a seemingly inadequate army could have ruled such a large continent and kept its teeming 400 millions happy and contented for so long, and why Hindus and Mussulmen are busily continuing to fight each other again now we have gone.

In 327 BC we really do get some detailed history of the province for this was the year of the invasion by Alexander the Great.

Mounted on his charger, Bucephalus, he crossed the Indus and found the country divided into petty kingdoms, happily engaged in fighting one another. Their kings, well used to weighing the odds, and having had a good look at Alexander's forces, decided to be friendly. All except one.

King Porus, who had a very large army indeed and the River Indus between him and Alexander, decided to defend himself.

As the Macedonians tried to cross, Porus put in an attack with his 300 chariots which proved abortive. The reason was obvious and he should have known better. About two thousand years later I thought I could take a car near the river while looking for duck; the sand gave place to mud and extraction proved a lengthy and blasphemous business.

He then sent in his secret weapon, his 200 war elephants, creatures which must have been unknown and terrifying to the opposition. I have never been chased by a wild elephant but I know someone who has and he said that was once too many. But here again something went wrong; elephants are very nervous animals, hating loud noises, and for this reason have to be sent into battle drugged. Was the timing wrong? Were they given too much? Did they sober up too soon and have hang-overs? Was it the mud again? We shall never know. Whatever the cause was they took fright and with Porus on top of the leader made an exit over the infantry whom they trampled under foot as they went.

Alexander stopping only long enough to build a couple of cities marched on through Lahore and Amritsar, slaying and burning as he went until his troops sat down and refused to go any further. One can sympathise with them. The heat of a Punjab summer is simply awful both by day and by night.

It is inadvisable to march by day as the temperature, 119° or more in the shade, invites deaths from heat exhaustion whereas he who marches by night and rests by day gets no undisturbed sleep because of the flies. The flower of the fighting men had probably been killed and the remainder no doubt reckoned they had done their bit by Alexander; there was no place like home.

Seleukos his successor did, however, return to find that all the people of importance had murdered one another, including our old friend Porus, and that the place was in such a state of insurrection as to be ungovernable, so he too returned home. The Greeks or Macedonians, call them what you will, left, if little else, more than a drop of Greek blood which can be seen in the faces of the soldiers recruited from those areas.

Buddha was born in India in about 662 B.C. and is the St Josaphat of the Christian Church with a place assigned to him in the Roman calender. The religious confederacy representing the old coalition of the Vedic faith of the Brahmins with the rude rites, and some were pretty rude, of the pre-Aryan races.

On the rise of the militant faith of Mohammed there followed a series of eruptions through the North West passages to add to the fighting blood of the Punjabis, already not lacking in good red corpuscles.

Afghan, Turcoman and Tartar disciples of the prophet descended to form dynasties depending upon the power of the sword, unstable in their nature and liable to be overthrown by fresh invaders, by the war-like Hindu tribes or by military intrigues and palace revolutions.

It would be tedious to descend into any detail but the first, a Turki from Ghazni, invaded India seventeen times and earned for himself the title of 'The Idol Smasher'. During his twenty-five years of fighting he must have been responsible for the deaths of quite a number of people, 5,000 on one occasion.

Rather strangely, stories were told of his piety.

The next conquerors to arrive were the Afghan Ghors who did not have the reputation of handling enemies with kid gloves. To emphasize this point they captured the city of Ghazni, took the chief inhabitants back to Ghor, cut their throats and used their blood for making mortar for their new foundations.

There was one marked difference between the two. The Ghaznis were addicted to massacre and the looting of Hindu temples; the latter preferred massacre and the acquisition of territory.

Now came the slave dynasty distinctive even if for nothing else for producing the only female to occupy the throne in Delhi. She was, however, indiscreet enough to have an affair with her Master of Horse, an Abyssinian ex-slave, which so shocked her conservative and straight-laced generals that they deposed and executed her.

The last but one of these Slave Kings found himself in the awkwardly embarrassing position of having to liquidate no less than forty of his most intimate Generals, Viceroys and friends, with whom years before he had made a solemn compact when they were all slaves together. They now formed too powerful a confederacy and he could take no chances.

The next dynasty was that of the Khiljis who came to power in 1290 and whose second ruler also appears to have had a violent streak. Murdering the first ruler, his uncle, while shaking him by the hand, he defeated four Mogul invasions in succession, in each case taking the leaders to Delhi where he had them trampled to death by elephants. Still he was not allowed to rule in peace as it is understood that he had to blind and later execute several insurgent nephews who had in turn led various rebellions. Even then he was faced with more trouble, having to massacre 15,000 Mohammedan settlers whom he suspected of plotting. It can be appreciated that he must have made enemies here and there and the last we hear of him is when he was helped to his grave by poison administered by his favourite General.

The Tughlaks were in their turn ousted by Timur, or Tamerlane, who swept down through the Afghan passes at the head of the combined hordes of Tartary. Defeating the Tughlaks outside the walls of Delhi he entered and authorised a five day massacre during which some streets were rendered impassable owing to the heaps of dead. A religious man, he then gave a 'sincere and humble tribute of grateful praise' in the marble mosque and marched on to have another great massacre at Meerut.

Next came Humayun, best known by the British for his tomb, a favourite spot for moonlight picnics.

Humayun's son was Akbar the Great, the real founder of the Mogul Empire whose reign lasted fifty years and was exactly contemporary with that of Queen Elizabeth of England.

Akbar is remembered not only by sportsmen but by every educated Northern Indian as the monarch who speared and killed a tiger single handed.

Akbar while respecting Hindu laws put some of their inhuman rites down, such as trial by ordeal, child marriage and widow burning on the funeral pyre of the husband unless the latter was undertaken voluntarily, which strange to relate it usually was. He also legalised the remarriage of Hindu widows.

His son Jehangir added nothing to the Mogul Empire.

Marrying Nur Jehan 'The light of the World', a beautiful Persian from a noble family, he took to drink. One must not be cynical.

Jehangir's son Shah Jehan built the Taj Mahal. Described as blameless in his private habits, he murdered his brother with all the members of the house of Akbar who might prove rivals to the throne.

Shah Jehan in his turn had son trouble. His eldest boy Aurangzeeb kept him in prison till he died. Apart from this he first put to death his own elder brother, following that by driving out his next brother who was murdered and then had his last brother executed in prison.

After his death the Mogul Empire broke up, and Sikhs and the Rajputs renouncing allegiance as did various rulers to the East. The Mahrattas, a large and loose confederacy of Hindu chiefs swept North, gathering up Rajput and Jat forces as they came, and gained control.

In 1738 there was a return to the old style of living when Nadir Shah the Persian descended through the Frontier passes, sacked Delhi, massacred the inhabitants and after staying fifty-eight days left with booty worth nine million pounds.

Nor should one forget Ahmed Shah Duranni, the Afghan, who staged no less than six excursions after plunder, sacking Delhi and massacring its inhabitants twice. They seemed to have been a very resilient lot.

In 1761 with his mixed force of Afghans, Persians and Pathans he came down again and defeated the Mahratta army on the former battlefield of Panipat, killing thousands in the battle and then murdering his 40,000 prisoners.

During the anarchy that followed the British patiently built up a new power out of the wreck of the Mogul Empire.

Plain for all to see, the recipe for successful rule in India had been first to smash all opposition and then adopt a policy of religious toleration and political conciliation.

To those able to stomach more potted history, that of the Sikhs has a bearing on the racial antipathies present in North India.

They are a religious body, not a race, notable for their bravery, their cleverness, their martial spirit and their relish for intrigue.

In 1762 they were subjected to a great disaster when Ahmed Shah Duranni, the Afghan returning from destroying the forces of the Mahrattas at Panipat, routed their forces completely, destroyed Amritsar, blew up the Golden Temple, filled the sacred lake with mud, defiled the holy places by the slaughter of cows and continued on his way.

It was our policy to have a strong and friendly state on our frontier, as it was of Ranjit Singh to have us on his side, so we left him free to seize Multan from the Afghans after a siege of four months. He then invaded Kashmir in 1819 defeating the Afghan troops and annexing the country to the Lahore Kingdom.

One of the secrets of Ranjit Singh's success was his employment of European adventurers of every race, many of them veterans of the Napoleonic wars: English, Scots, Irish, Italian, American, Spaniards, French, Dutch, Swiss, Armenians and Eurasians.

One weakness of all the armies in India was the handling of their artillery. There were a number of excellent cannon foundries making cannon of all calibres but the actual gun drill was lamentable.

The European mercenaries sped up the gun drill to three and four times its previous rate, the crews achieving a shot every 20 seconds.

The Sikh hand was heavy upon conquered races. The Sikhs attacked and looted Peshawar, then an Afghan city after which Ranjit Singh put in his own Governor, an Italian named Avitabile so renowned for his cruelty that travellers mentioned it in their records and even the locals were impressed.

I myself had an insight into Sikh methods. We were out on column and had met quite stiff opposition in precipitous country quite close to Bannu. We entered a village which the enemy had evacuated with the exception of an old, old man lying out on his string bed in the sun. We told him we would look after

A typical camp in Waziristan.

Camels — the only form of local transport in Waziristan.

him until the village was re-occupied but he could not make out who we were and obviously did not think much of us: 'You say you are the British do you? The last army who came here were the Sikhs. When they arrived they asked for twelve of our best looking and strongest young men; they then hanged them; they really were a proper army!'

Ranjit Singh had bullied the deposed Shah Suja when he came to him for assistance and got the famous Koh-I-Noor diamond off him. Shah Suja was spared from worrying about his loss for very long as he was murdered soon afterwards.

The Koh-I-Noor, the famous Mountain of Light, had been seized from the Moguls by Ahmed Shah Duranni, along with the Peacock Throne. It weighed about 800 carats but was so damaged by cutting that it has now been reduced to 102 carats. The largest known diamond at the time was the Russian one of only 193 carats which became part of the Czar's sceptre. I wonder where it is now? More of the Koh-I-Noor anon.

On the death of Ranjit Singh his army, highly trained by his mercenaries became a conglomeration of mutually suspicious forces each with their own nominee for the throne, intriguing with and against each other and with the British.

The Queen Mother, or more correctly the Rani, a strong shrewd character, herself not unskilled in intrigue, decided that the only way of saving the throne for her young son was to have the army fight the British and with a bit of luck get defeated.

If the army were shattered she would be rid of her masters, if it won the Court would get the credit. Admittedly an appealing plan but just a bit dangerous.

In due course the Sikh army did fight the British. They had 50,000 excellently trained troops and on top of that double that number of ill-disciplined semi-trained fighting men. The whole lot were fantastically brave, a characteristic of their race. Besides this they had 200 guns with properly trained crews.

Against them we had 22,000 fighting men and 30 guns.

Nevertheless, we somehow defeated them after four pitched battles, after the last of which Sir Henry Hardinge, the Governor

General, who had himself been an officer under Wellington in the Napoleonic Wars and presumably knew what he was talking about, said:- 'Another such victory and we are undone!' This was the first war in which the British had to acknowledge that Asiatic troops could be every bit as good as our own. Indeed it was only because of the quarrels between the leaders of the various Sikh contingents which reached such a pitch, that not only would they refuse to support one another but actually passed on to us vital information about each others plans, that we won. It also seemed that some of the Sikh leaders did not mind who won the battle provided that their rivals did not.

Another portion of the indemnity was the Koh-I-Noor diamond. It was apparently handed over by its Sikh custodian to John Lawrence, one of Sir Henry's two younger brothers whom he had sent out to adminster the country.

John put it in his waistcoat pocket and promptly forgot all about it. When Queen Victoria ordered that it be sent to her it was rather fortunate that it was found, in a small box in one of his trunks. His Punjabi Mussulman servant having wondered why he had picked up a piece of glass put it away just in case he might want it!

XV

Communal Trouble

While HE and I and the Punjab Government were enjoying the cool breezes of Simla, communal trouble broke out in Lahore. Inter-communal strife was always only just around the corner in all the large cities of the Punjab. The three big communities: the Mussulmen, the Sikhs and the Hindus, had little in common except language, and there had been endless bloody war between them before the British came and conquered all opposition.

They were now living together side by side in the towns and the country, serving together in the army and police and with proportional representation and equal opportunities in all government departments.

The mosque at Shahidganj was ancient and dilapidated; it had been built centuries ago, no one knew why or when, and was too small to have been of any importance. In the time of the Sikh Empire, however, the Sikhs, no respecters of ecclesiastical property or freedom of worship, had built a large gurdwara or Sikh temple close by this very spot, so close that the outer wall of the temple also enclosed the mosque which was used by them as a coal hole, store and depository for unwanted lumber. With the Sikhs as the very heavy handed rulers of the province it would, of course, have been impossible to continue worshipping in the mosque had, indeed, any of the original congregation survived the sword, so, in course of time, hidden behind the high walls of the gurdwara, the mosque's very existence became forgotten.

155

There is, however, the Mohammedan law of Waqf, which lays down unequivocally that no religious building can ever be deconsecrated. It was, therefore, most unfortunate that the presence inside the temple walls of this long disused mosque came to the ears of a most unprincipled scoundrel, a Mussulman owner of a gutter newspaper whose sales were falling off; he at once made the most of it; his paper began to sell and he gained much personal popularity.

The Mohammedan community, as was only natural, demanded back the mosque, to which the Sikhs pointed out that it was inside the precincts of their own gurdwara and that they had now possessed the land for years without complaint.

Wiser counsels suggested that the matter be referred to the Courts; there were in the High Court British, Sikh, Hindu and Mohammedan judges and there would be no question of their judgment being anything but impartial; their ruling, however, proving unfavourable to the Muslim mob, the latter threatened to capture the mosque by force and, if necessary, burn the Sikh temple and its guardians in the process.

The threat was too much for the proud imperious Sikhs whose retort was they would raze the walls of the mosque to the ground at the first sign of violence and who started fortifying and garrisoning the temple for a seige as a sign that they were in earnest.

Tempers now rose on both sides; the stifling heat of June, up to 120 degrees in the shade at mid-day and at its worst in the airless city, did nothing to soothe the nerves.

HE realising the danger of full scale civil war took the unusual step of coming down to Lahore to be near the scene of action. On our arrival there was little for the Personal Staff to do but usher in conferences which, since all the carpets were up and the curtains down, were nothing if not informal. Whereas it would have been most incorrect for HE to show himself in the city, there seemed nothing to stop me from going down to have a look, which at the first opportunity I did.

The roads leading from the Civil Lines down to the Indian

City were strangely hushed; they had been cleared and barricaded by the Police and a curfew was in force. The Police Station, a very large courtyard surrounded by offices, barracks and other buildings, the whole encircled by a fortified wall, was full to capacity with resting police other ranks and a horde of Police Officers and Magistrates, both British and Indian, drafted in from all over the province.

At the end of a broad street a hundred yards beyond the Police Station a line of police standing shoulder to shoulder, their six foot brass shod staves in their hands, faced a murmuring growling mob of Mohammedans stretching back as far as one could see. Strolling off down a side street towards Shahidganj I turned a corner and was suddenly confronted by the high wall of the temple the top of which was manned by a whole row of Sikhs; they were chiefly the blue clothed and blue turbanned Nahangs or hereditary temple guardians, but among them fierce bearded faces under black turbans proclaimed the presence of Akalis, the most fanatical sect of them all; all were waving drawn swords and seemed spoiling for a fight and, on catching sight of me, flourished their weapons and raised a huge cheer.

The Police Station was full of old friends who were now complaining bitterly that, since they had been whisked away from their homes at a moment's notice several days ago, they were without European food, whisky, cigarettes or literature and were getting heartily sick of the Indian Police rations, furthermore, they were on duty continuously and could not go off and make proper arrangements.

I went back and arranged for the GH lorry to collect meals for 40 from Falettis Hotel, an arrangement which popularized me with all.

The position was at the moment static. The mouths of the streets leading towards the temple and the Police Station from the Mohammedan quarter were jammed tight with thousands and thousands of Mohammedans, densely packed together being addressed by their leaders and every few minutes roaring out some slogan.

The mob leaders were all the time playing upon the religious fervour of their followers who at intervals in response to some signal inexplicably transmitted throughout the vast crowd which would suddenly become silent, turn towards Mecca and prostrate themselves upon the ground motionless in prayer; the sight of these thousands of men squatting immobile with their foreheads on the ground gave more of an insight into their dangerous sincerity than did all their leapings and howlings. In front the lines of police stood leaning on their cudgels, forming up with them held horizontally and holding back the Faithful by sheer strength when they tried to advance. In the back streets leading to the Civil Lines the troops were held ready. In the fields and roads outside the city, Indian Cavalry and British armoured cars were patrolling to stop either side when, tired of its purely communal concepts, from moving in on the European Civil Lines, bent on loot and murder, as was often a later trend.

Watching the police was interesting. When any line of police-men looked like giving way under the sustained pressure of the mob against them a Police Officer would wake up his local reserve of thirty or forty constables and forming them up some distance away would charge the crowd, who would first start fighting, then waver, break and run for their lives with the police at their heels. The Officer's object obtained he and his men would run back dragging with them their struggling arrests and their injured comrades, hotly pursued by the bolder spirits among the crowd hurling stones and bottles at their retreating foes.

It seemed a pity to let slip a golden opportunity of securing some unique photographs.

A period when the crowd was comparatively passive gave me some nice steady stills of the packed mass of unintelligent, hot, sweaty, unshaven faces frowning over the fence of crossed cudgels; countless lean brown upraised arms fanned their owners with portions of newspaper or swatted at the myriads of dusty looking flies which crawled over them and the constables and myself, too lazy to fly more than a few feet. In among the

158

crowd the vendors of soda water, melons, palm leaf fans, elbowed their way about, fruit being passed one way over the heads of the crowd, money the other. 'Soda-pani, Soda-pani, ek paisa, soda-pani.' One hoped that they were sufficiently acute business men to retrieve their empties before the crowd again became violent.

There was not long to wait for action pictures.

The tremendous relentless weight of a crowd pushing forward inch by inch cannot be stopped by a line of men shoulder to shoulder. Many pairs of hands forced up the lathis and the dam was breached; as the crowd started to pour through with that never-to-be-forgotten roar far more menacing than any pack of wild animals the police closed back into little knots, striking out around them, safe-guarding themselves as best they might from being knocked down, trampled under foot, and in the case of the Sikh constables probably literally torn limb from limb as is the pleasant habit of Asiatic crowds when their victims are out-numbered.

Camera in hand I proceeded down the street at a decorous trot in the wake of a troupe of cheering yelling constables waving their great brass-bound lathis charging at the mass who were now halted and packed solid from wall to wall across the street and busy hurling bottles and bricks as fast as they could be supplied by those behind.

With the police only a few yards away there was a rippling and swirling among the crowd as the front elements dived back under the arms of their less quick-witted comrades; then all was flurry and confusion; some of the more stout hearted grappled with the police, seizing them and their weapons, holding them immobile through sheer numbers and the weight of their comrades behind; others panicked, surged back, stumbled, fell, admitting wedges of constables who forced their way forward in tight bunches of half a dozen, striking, parrying, lunging, warding off knife thrusts and blows from what I now saw to be a most effective close quarter weapon, the solid heavily nailed Punjabi country shoe.

It hardly made for concentration while peering into the view finder of a camera to feel that at any moment some muscular Punjabi might crash a club on to the back of one's head, or hit one in the face with a heavy nailed shoe or tickle up one's kidney with a dagger.

It was after pausing to insert a new spool that I realized myself to be violating what turned out to be a basic rule of police riot action; the crowd had broken up and were streaming away with their pursuers hot on their heels and here I was stationary and alone among a bunch of left-overs from the opposition, simply inviting a quick thrust between the ribs.

Just beside me a hulking Mussulman policeman knelt on all fours, his khaki turban on the ground beside him, blood pouring out from among his long bobbed and oiled black hair and forming a pool just in front of his eyes; an unshaven youth in dirty white clothes lay motionless on his back in the gutter a few yards away; propped up on one elbow another youth sat quite still staring vacantly; all over the ground were slippers, pieces of clothing, scraps of food, melon rinds and here and there a patch of blood; a small group of Sikh and Mohammedan constables were frog marching back a couple of arrests; there was, however, little time to reflect or stare about, as with a crash of nailed boots the police came running back, their khaki drill shirts black with sweat, amid a hail of road metal and earthenware; there was a potter's shop further up the street and the unfortunate man's entire stock was now being hurled down from the rooftops; flower pots bursting like bombs on the road around us; the wounded constable and two bazaaris were grabbed hold of and we retreated out of missile range as fast as we could.

In another quarter of the city where there was a large dusty park the mounted Police did a most spectacular charge; this mixture of Mohammedans, Sikhs and Hindus, all from stout peasant stock who had nothing but contempt for the degenerate city dwellers, made the hundreds of stone and bottle throwers flee before them like rats to the cover of the houses. I saw two mounted constables do what they must have been rehearsing as a turn for some tattoo; cantering up on each side of a fleeing rioter, they lifted him clear up in the air, then wheeled round and carried him back between them, struggling and shouting for help, without his feet ever once touching the ground.

As I looked through the view finder a shower of stones directed at myself made me look up and I saw a small bunch of rioters running towards me with the presumable intention of tearing me to pieces. It seemed best to remove myself.

Next day a fierce and most spectacular charge against a very dangerous looking mob was carried out by a squad from the Police School; these keen young NCOs, Hindus, Sikhs and Muslims, vied with each other in catching the eye of their superiors and paving the way to promotion. Charges like this, however, could not go on for ever; the temper of the crowd was getting worse, charges became more frequent and the police more tired; it was time that the military took over.

A day or two after the army had assumed responsibility, the unfortunate B Squadron of the 6th Lancers IA, under a Major Poole, was ordered to charge the mob using the flat of the sword, the venue being a narrow slippery tarred road. They themselves must have known what would happen, and it did; the leading horses slipped and came down, the rifles of the troopers were seized and borne off in triumph by the crowd and all was chaos.

Next I was approached by the Brigadier, B T Wilson, a tremendously tall Viking-like figure with long moustache and steely blue eyes, whom I constantly met in the hunting field. He instantly grabbed me. 'I say, I wonder if you would be a good fellow, one of the British Regiment platoons seems to be commanded by an absolute youngster just out from home, could you go and hold his hand until I can make some other arrangement? After all, you can understand both Urdu and Scotch and there may be nothing to do anyway!'

Off I went to a road junction a couple of hundred yards from the Yakki Gate, a tall pointed Mogul archway piercing the wall of the old city backed by its maze of narrow dark winding alleys.

The Jocks were sitting on the bare dusty pavement; they were in ill humour as they had spent a week living in a dirty smelly spit-stained street being tormented by flies; even while sitting still in whatever shade that was available they were drenched with sweat and their desire was to be allowed to go back to their barracks, their beds, their football and their beer.

Down in front of the gate a couple of Indian magistrates and some very tired police were confronting the mob. In the very front with their backs to me were three obvious leaders, each rousing the section behind him with inflammatory speeches. If these were the men who could rouse the crowd, it was they, if anyone, who could pacify them, and so it must be to them that I must address my remarks if I wished to interfere.

These three leaders were interesting contrasts; the first, a lean wild-eyed fanatic, hoarse from shouting, was quite lost to any form of reason, the second, with the professional patter of the confident public speaker was presumably in private life some kind of a huckster: I should like to forget the third; a tall striking looking man in his early thirties who, in a spotless white robe reaching from his neck down to his sandals, and hair combed down over his shoulders, looked startlingly Biblical; his eyes were steady and his voice was low and calm as he started to put forward the Mohammedan case and it was obvious that he was a man of importance who might save this particular situation if only he could be made to see reason. It looked, however, as if he considered it his duty to lead his followers to death or glory and one could only hope that he would not do it now.

I took the obvious line of telling each in turn that since the Courts had decided against the Mohammedans they were doing their cause a great disservice by rousing their co-religionists like this etc, etc. Having said my little piece there seemed nothing for it but to stroll back as nonchalantly as possible hoping that the crowd would stop any fanatic from rushing out and knifing me.

Giving them a few minutes' grace I returned to renew my arguments; I had a bright idea, and a piece of chalk was produced from somewhere with which I started to draw a line from wall to wall while I gave my personal assurance to all and sundry that provided that no one stepped over it there would be no shooting.

This arrangement seemed to meet with almost universal approval and I was about to turn and perform another nonchalent stroll back when suddenly a tremor ran through the crowd who, suddenly hushed, were glaring menacingly at some point behind me. Spinning round I saw a couple of soldiers levelling their rifles in our direction.

This must be stopped at once. My flow of persuasive Urdu changed in mid-sentence to yells of profanity in basic Scotch, and the speed with which they lowered their weapons made it absolutely clear that they now understood that I too was from North of the border. The damage seemed, however, to have been done. Confidence was lost.

As we stood and watched them the crowd gave a sign of being very seriously angry indeed, i.e. they produced and waved their private parts at us, the greatest insult they can give. Too late to help any more now; what must be must be. The subaltern ordered the platoon into the aim and the crowd checked; then out of the crowd appeared a little girl aged about five who in her birthday suit, thumb in mouth, started walking down the very centre of the road to get a closer look at us. This was awful; one could not let her be shot or trampled to death, so I as the only Urdu speaker had to go into the open, grab her by the hand and lead her back to the arms of the crowd. The crowd, however, had tired of my charms and my novelty had worn off; they passed back the girl but made no attempt to listen to me.

As the crack of the three bullets reverberated from the high mud walls, they echoed down the street like a whole volley. Those in front stopped but were thrust forward by the relentless weight of the thousands behind; bunches of people were momentarily bending over bodies where two of the leaders had been but on the left the man in white was apparently untouched and was cheering on his supporters into what would be the final rush on to the bayonets. They could hardly miss him again at that range; he staggered and spun round, the rest turned and fled, the whole mass trampling on one another as they went.

In a minute not a soul was to be seen in front of the big arch; an awful silence descended in which one could for the first time hear the distant roaring and chanting of religious slogans by the other crowds held back by troops and police in the streets to left and right.

Some days later we got a rather sad piece of information. It seemed that the saintly old caretaker of a mosque in some back street well away from the trouble had been warned by the police that there was likely to be danger and that he must at all costs stay indoors. He had obeyed their instructions, until he heard the screams of a wounded man on the steps outside; opening his door, he was immediately killed by a stray bullet; some soldier had been disobeying orders and firing over the heads of the crowd instead of directly at them.

XVI

Back to earth

All good things must come to an end and eventually it was time for me to go back and think about serious soldiering once more. My three years at Government House had been among the happiest in my life and the most interesting, but the scent of war was already in the air.

My opportunity seemed to have come when volunteers were asked for one of the two first ever parachute brigades, one to be raised near Manchester and the other in Delhi.

It was obviously a good arm of the service in which to get in quickly on the ground floor: we should get into action soon for certainty, the thing was bound to expand and for the eventual survivors there would, one hoped, be promotion, honour and glory. In the event this was exactly what happened although two of our three battalions were almost completely wiped out, officers and men.

We were to have a British, a Gurkha and Indian battalion and having studied the form of other possible contestants I thought that having all the necessary qualifications myself which included being a bachelor and under 35 on my last birthday, I might with luck get command of the Gurkha one. On arrival to my annoyance I found that I was to be second in command, the CO being Freddy Loftus-Tottenham of the 2nd Gurkhas who was both well over 35 and married: it so happened that there was a very senior and influential 2nd Gurkha General in GHQ in Delhi at the time.

Our Brigadier was Bill Gough, a nice chap too and obviously selected for his gallantry: he was, however, well over 35 and married.

He was certainly brave; when instructing in grenade throwing one of his Gurkha class had dropped the primed grenade on his own toe whereupon Bill had thrown himself onto it, saving the lives of the others at the expense of losing an eye, and a bit of his arm.

I had known him on the Fontier in the old days when his glass eye had not been a very good fit as when he leant forward over the bar it would fall out, bounce on the counter and roll off onto the floor. Having been retrieved by his friends from among the legs of the bar stools he would calmly wash it in his whisky and soda and carry on as if nothing had happened.

When I went to be interviewed by him as my new Brigadier he had just broken his leg parachuting and there he was sitting with his naked toes under his desk showing below his plaster. As we talked I noticed his gaze straying away over my shoulder and saw my one-eyed bull terrier, who was meant to be waiting outside, now limping in holding one paw stiffly out in front of him; as having recently been involved in another of his numerous fights one of his forelegs was swathed in bandages.

Extricating myself and my dog I went to meet Hutchinson, the Brigade Major, in the next room, to find him seated stiffly at his desk with the top half of his body swathed in plaster-of-paris. The pair of them hardly seemed a good advertisement for parachuting.

The work was new and fascinating but we had many troubles, not the least the absence of equipment. The aircraft from which we first jumped were ancient first war Vickers Victorias each with a huge hole cut in the floor from which to make our exit. While in the initial stages of parachute training they flew off to evacuate personnel from Singapore which was just about to be captured by the Japanese, leaving us with no planes.

There was no specialised equipment or clothing at all, unless one counts our so called helmets which were woollen machine-knitted balaclavas with rubber pads sewn into the back. One of our consignments of parachutes was loaded into a ship which was diverted to Singapore and unloaded presumably by the grateful Japanese; exact copies made in India hardly filled us with enthusiasm as when tested with dummy bodies they burst in the air.

We also had to restrain ourselves when dealing with certain of the more unimaginative senior officers who openly referred to us as exhibitionists performing a circus act.

Not only was the Delhi ground first rained upon and then baked by the Indian sun to the consistency of concrete, not exactly the softest of surface to land on, but an alarming number of casualties were caused. A parachute which failed to open and killed someone one day, would be re-packed and behave perfectly with a dummy the next and go indefinitely without giving any trouble in the future. Everyone had their theory, bad packing, high air temperature, etc., etc.

The fault was finally discovered to be "tired silk" but not till after I myself had made an indifferent landing and broken my back in a couple of places.

I was, however, alive, if not exactly kicking.

While we were training our troops and ourselves momentous things were happening in India on the political side.

There were two main political parties, the Congress Party which was Hindu and led by Gandhi and Nehru and the Muslim League led by Jinnah.

Everyone knew that India would have to be given independence some day, but when one looked round it was obvious that the time had not yet come: none of the Indian leaders had the slightest administrative experience at all of how a country was run and thought that all questions could be answered by a party vote. There were large numbers of perfectly competent doctors, vets, soldiers, civil servants, etc., but nothing like enough although we were training them as fast as we could. These things all take time. This, however, was not the view of the British Parliament, in particular the Labour Party which was much influenced by its own left wing to whom autocracy was a dirty word. Gandhi's aim for the last forty years had been to throw out the British and replace them by a Hindu government; the Muslims, however, who had no illusions about these sanctimonious Hindu politicians would never under any circumstances submit to Hindu domination. To expect these two sides to sink their differences rather savoured of wishful thinking.

Early in the war the United States of America, whose support was necessary at any cost, had possibly accelerated matters by voicing the opinion that all British colonies, however immature and irresponsible, should be considered for self-government, an opinion which the cynics declared to be not completely altruistic, adding that the United States might not be averse to taking over a large slice of our overseas trade.

Bowing to Parliament, Churchill sent out Sir Stafford Cripps in March 1942 with an offer to India of Independence. Since I was in Delhi I was, of course, in close touch with several of my old ICS friends, from whom I was thrilled to receive all the inside information. They told me that the offer would be for both the parties to come together to form a government but that any province, with the Punjab chiefly in mind, could opt out and govern itself if it wanted to. They also told me that Sir Stafford was wasting his time, the leaders would turn down his offer before he even saw them; Congress would turn it down flat because they wanted to dominate everything, while Jinnah would not have it because the demand for Pakistan was not to be conceded. Poor Cripps went home having achieved precisely nothing.

The Muslim League were co-operating fully with the British in winning the war which was much appreciated with the Japanese at the very gates, but not so Congress.

In August 1942 Congress launched their "Quit India" campaign which seriously disrupted plans for the defence of India against imminent Japanese attack. Their non-violent campaign included sabotage of railway bridges, tearing up railway lines, murders of British Officers, (two RAF Officers were I remember pulled out of their carriages and murdered by a mob on the platform of some wayside station) murder of Indian policemen, (some were burnt to death in their own police stations) and, of course, very violent picketing.

Part of this picketing included stopping food supplies including Indian civilian vegetable lorries from entering Delhi City. Since this obviously could not be tolerated, my brigade were ordered to place an armed paratrooper in the front seat of each lorry to ensure delivery and protect the driver from the murderous Congress-inspired mob and ensure safe arrival of the food.

Unfortunately for the murderous mob the parachute brigade had only just been issued with Tommy Guns, a novelty associated with Chicago gangsters and unknown to the rest of the army. Paratrooper Angel, I think that was his name, thus found himself sitting in a vegetable lorry with his new toy across his knees simply longing for the chance to fire it. His prayer was answered, a threatening mob advanced upon him which gave him the golden opportunity of giving them two whole drums to themselves, killing several and wounding many more. Food, however, started to flow into Delhi again without molestation.

Almost exactly eight months after my parachute accident I got back to active service and in due course went to Burma and then Italy. No more jumping out of aeroplanes for me; it still hurt even to jump out of bed.

To return to more politics, in June 1943, Field Marshal later Lord Wavell was nominated Viceroy by Churchill, probably with the intention that nothing much should be done about Independence until after the war when the whole thing could be gone into again.

In July 1945, however, there was a General Election at home resulting in a Labour majority of 200 or so, among whom Wavell thought there would be a lot of foolish, inexperienced and rather wild legislators in place of many stupid and tiresome Tories.

It soon became only too obvious that this Labour

Government seemed to be thinking more of placating public opinion in their own party and in the USA than of the good of India. They sent out Cripps, Pethick-Lawrence, the new Secretary of State, and Alexander, the First Lord of the Admiralty, to try again. It seemed that the new Cabinet were prepared to enforce the old Cripps offer because of the blow to Cripps' personal prestige, a highly dangerous proceeding.

Wavell flew home only to discover that the Cabinet were bent on handing over India to Congress as soon as possible.

In September 1945 it seemed that Congress were intending to launch another "Quit India" rebellion. In November, Wavell warned the Home Government that Congress might make a serious attempt to subvert by force the present administration of India. He also envisaged a possible mutiny of the Indian Army and feared for the lives of various European DCs and Police Officers dotted about the country in isolated spots.

Since he felt that he could not depend upon Indian troops to rescue these European civilians he was forced to use either British or Gurkhas and the obvious battalion to employ was my own which now the war was over happened to be the Demonstration Battalion and thus not earmarked for anything else.

I, therefore, found myself leaving it to carry on demonstrations under my second in command and taking half a dozen Jeep loads of Gurkhas on a motoring tour of the enormous area where trouble might start. It seemed that the main problem would be crossing numbers of rivers in the face of a hostile and presumably armed population who had taken the precaution of blowing up the bridges, and our getting to people quickly before they were murdered.

I soon discovered that the population was by no means friendly. This was the area from which the old Bengal Army had been recruited which spearheaded the Indian Mutiny of 1857 and where recruiting had since been discontinued in favour of the races from further North: the Sikhs, the Punjabi Mussulmen, the Dogras and the Khattack Pathans with, of course, the Gurkhas. They were thus the people to whom Congress' anti-British propaganda had been mainly directed and which they were not slow to absorb. It was an interesting trip, we motored about all day going through quite a number of towns of which I had never previously heard and whose citizens were obviously unused to seeing a white face. It was possible that hardly a white man and no troops had been there during this generation. The nights we spent camped beside some well out in the country.

I made tentative plans for rescuing several people whom, of course, I had to meet to sound out about the presumed location of ferries and motorability of unmetalled side roads and cart tracks during the monsoon.

I should not have liked to have been in their shoes: a few were a mite apprehensive. A rather farcical aspect was that my mission was so secret that I was not supposed to disclose it to anyone, although my cover story would hardly have deceived an intelligent child, and they were officials themselves.

By a twist of fate I found myself calling on and planning the rescue of someone whom I had never expected to meet again. I went to see the Deputy Commissioner of Lucknow and by whom should I be received in his bungalow but the girl friend, now his wife, with whom I had spent my eight months British furlough some twelve years before but who had jilted me shortly after I had arrived in the Malakand. Women are entitled to change their minds; who after all can stop them, but one could sometimes wish that they could time things better.

On my way back I took a couple of hours off to visit the Taj Mahal at Agra which I had never had a chance of doing before. Those who say that one must view it by moonlight are absolutely right, it is magnificent. They, however, refrain from mentioning that one should on no account actually enter the place, especially during the hot weather, as the accumulated smell of generations of sweaty bodies passing through those little airless rooms and up and down the corkscrew stairs is utterly repulsive.

I then went off my route to Delhi to spend a night with my old

171

friend Bill Robinson, the extremely tough Deputy Inspector General of Delhi Police, to find out exactly what Indians of all classes were thinking. The Army has such a mania about secrecy that officers are never told important things which they certainly should know and which are openly discussed by every educated person in the country, official or unofficial, British or Indian.

Bill said that Indians, both Mohammedan and Hindu were convinced that there was bound to be bloodshed amounting to civil war in Delhi and the Punjab, and that the feeling among ordinary people was that the only solution would be to split the country in two, Pakistan for the Mohammedans and Hindustan for the Hindus.

For himself he was quite prepared to stay on when the British had left, he loved the country and a bit more pension would always be useful, but he would never take on under the Indians. He had been responsible for putting a large number of people behind bars for every conceivable crime during his long service; whereas the Mohammedans would appreciate that he had only been doing his duty; this would not be the case with some of the quite unscrupulous Hindus. He foresaw that ill disposed persons of the latter religion would have no second thoughts about foisting some serious crime upon him, bribing all necessary witnesses and then the judge so that he would find himself in some prison where he might spend the rest of his life. Pakistan for him.

We talked far into the night. It seems that Cripps, Pethick-Lawrence and Alexander had had no clue as to how to handle Gandhi, who absolutely refused to be pinned down, which was his favourite trick. Cripps with his usual sloppy benevolence actually expressed penitence for Britain's misdeeds in the past; expressing penitence to this sanctimonious, tough old politician was simply asking to be brushed aside.

The next major event was the abrupt and very discourteous removal of Wavell as Viceroy by the Labour Government who in March 1947 replaced him by Lord Mountbatten; this appointment did not meet with universal acclaim as Lord Mountbatten was thought to be slightly pink politically; furthermore he brought a publicity agent with him on his Personal Staff which raised a few old fashioned eyebrows; the eulogies that this man wrote about him later made one absolutely sick.

On a less personal level it was obvious that he had been sent to do the bidding of the Labour Government which Lord Wavell was not prepared to do. Everyone agreed that he was a very gallant sailor but we knew nothing of him as a politician and even though he might be a most excellent and well meaning officer, Gandhi and Nehru would undoubtedly pull wool over his eyes at the expense of the Mohammedans, who had after all been on our side, not against us, in the war against the Japanese. It really did seem that the Congress Party under Pandit Jawarhilal Nehru advised by Mahatma Gandhi at the height of the war quite seriously regarded the Japanese as saviours who must be assisted in delivering India from us. In 1942 one such had said, 'We would rather be ruled by dacoits (bandits) than the British.'

XVII
The rot starts

To return to a less exalted level, it was 1947 and the Battalion with myself in command was in a horrible little outpost in North Waziristan, performing our post-war role of keeping the Frontier secure.

We were living below ground level in holes to give us cover from sniper fire from the hills all round.

We pitched tents over the top to keep out the elements so they were not uncomfortable. We were full of self-confidence, the ranks were dotted with Burma veterans and many men who had seen Frontier service before that; lots of us, including myself, had lived for over a year in identical little holes only a couple of miles away, so knew the country intimately.

All my officers were emergency commissioned but really much better for that as they were young and keen.

We were ready for a fight but whereas the Wazirs were quite happy to shoot at us from a distance no one would come and attack us.

Without fighting one cannot earn decorations so we trailed our coats by creeping about the neighbouring hills after dark, an activity which the Wazirs consider to be entirely their own prerogative and which they were by no means anxious for two to play.

On 17 July 1947 to our great surprise a signal came ordering us on permanent transfer to Wana in South Waziristan, a four days' journey by lorry and soon we were to be relieved and on our way.

174

Bannu, the first halt, was swirling with perpetual dust eddies and shimmering with blinding glare; no one could sleep and when dawn came I found that I had sweated through the canvas of my camp bed.

The next day took us to Dera Ismail Khan where we found that the Mahsuds had descended from the mountains in one of their sudden raids and looted and burnt down the city, whose stark ruins we could see from the camp. This was really the most dreadful cheek and I had never heard of it happening in recent years. There had been constant cases of them abducting Hindu merchants for ransom, driving off cattle and taking a girl or two back with them, but nothing like this. Jimmy Fell, commanding Skinner's Horse IA, had eventually pushed them out with a hastily raised force of his own armoured car regiment and two infantry battalions, but a few days fierce house to house fighting had not improved the looks of the place.

A very odd thing now happened. Jimmy's force was thought to be getting too big for a Lieutenant Colonel to handle and his final repulse of the Mahsuds coincided with the arrival of an Indian Major General to take over. Since there was now nothing for the latter to do he spent his time conspiring with the Deputy Commissioner and with the leading merchant to try and get Jimmy into trouble for allegedly mishandling the affair. The Deputy Commissioner had been the first in that appointment to wear a Gandhi cap, a political emblem, on official duty, and I had heard bad reports of that General before. All three were Hindus and it seemed as if this was their method of currying favour with the Congress party at the the expense of Jimmy in particular and British officers in general. We took note.

At Tank, our next halt, the Mahsuds had besieged the force of a hundred or so armed Constabulary inside their own mud fort and also the complete Wing of South Waziristan Scouts who had been rushed down from Jandola to relieve them. All was now quiet, but it seemed to have been rather a touch and go affair.

The latter, all Pathans (mostly Bhittanis, Khattacks,

Yusufzais and a small element of South Waziristan Wazirs with, of course, Pushtu-speaking British Officers), were absolutely furious at the indignity as they were the ones who always did the besieging and bringing in of hostile gangs from places where non-Pathans, such as regular troops, could not penetrate without raising the hornet's nest of the the whole country against them.

It had been a great surprise to everyone when in February 1947 in the House of Commons, Mr Atlee had made his statement that power would be transferred to Indian hands not later than June 1948.

Our last stopping place before reaching our destination was Manzai, with its well earned reputation of being the hottest and worst station on the whole of the Frontier. A cluster of mud huts and barracks, surrounded by the inevitable breast-high wall of boulders and a belt or two of barbed wire, and set in a desert devoid of even thorn bushes, it did not look exactly welcoming. Furthermore, it seemed that HQ Wana had not been expecting us for we stayed here not twenty-four hours but three weeks. One night, sitting out in front of the Mess after dinner, we had a sweepstake on the temperature which we found very hot, the official thermometer at the hospital read 110.5 at 8.20 pm in the dark.

There was now a rough single track lorry road the whole way from Manzai to Jandola, where there was a large Scout Post. For the next 45 miles from Jandola to Wana the ground was wicked, the worst section of the lot being the Shahur Tangi, far more unpleasant than the Khyber Pass where I had commenced my military career. If, however, there were no problems of military interest in Wana, political matters were coming to a head down in India. Mr Atlee's statement in February gave rise to much conjecture; once power was in Indian hands, what would be the fate of the Gurkha Regiments?

Would the War Office require us? We were cheaper to feed and to pay than British troops; we could fight at high altitudes and in jungles where European troops were completely out of their element; there were still thirty battalions of us and the British Government might see fit to employ us in our remaining colonies.

Since Wana was quite peaceful I accepted an invitation to a Commanding Officers' Conference at our depot in Bakloh, a three days' journey by road and rail and road again. Our depot had been in Bakloh for nearly ninety years and there was a vast accumulation there of regimental private property, such as the large and up-to-date Mess library, the silver, the furniture and the Mess funds. If we were to be disbanded, what would we do about our battalion and regimental funds for we were a rich regiment and to whom would we sell our expensive brass band instruments, our pipes and drums? It was with suggestions for matters like these that I arrived to find, and God is only one of my witnesses, that the Conference had been called principally to decide on which foot to give the 'about turn', to be in accordance with two new and conflicting manuals.

On 3 June, Lord Mountbatten, the new Viceroy, broadcast that the transfer of power would be made within the current year and that 15 August was the date; the public was also told that India was to be split into two unequal parties, the portion with the Hindu majority being called India and not Hindustan, which would have made things easier, while the predominately Mohammedan portion was to be called Pakistan. The poor unfortunate Punjab was thus to be cut in two with the border very near Lahore, the capital, which would be in Pakistan, while all the country to the South West of it would be the new India.

The politicians of the North West Frontier Province, however, were torn by dissension as to whether to join the Congress party and become part of the new India, or whether to unite with Pakistan: so in July a referendum was held under the auspices not of the Civil Government but of the Army.

Inside the booths on Polling Day were two boxes, one painted red and the other green, towards which a wild looking collection of cheerful illiterate Pathans, none of whom obviously had the slightest idea of what it was all about, were being directed. It seemed later that the pro-Pakistan party had told them that, if they were to be true believers, they must vote green and if infidels, they must vote red; since NWFP was fanatically Mussulman it was not surprising that 289,244 persons voted for Pakistan and 2,074 for India.

Tremendous problems had now been forced upon the Army: where all men of a regiment were of the same religion, such as the Sikh regiment, it was merely a question of moving it to its own side of the new border; where regiments had two companies or squadrons of Hindus and two of Mohammedans, as was the case with all the Frontier Force and Punjabi Regiments, then trouble arose; regiments were losing not only complete companies but a proportion of their specialists such as clerks, signallers, mortar men, armourers and, of course, officers; replacements were slow in coming.

One complete Mohammedan company of the Battalion of Rajputana Rifles here in Wana found itself uprooted and sent to join a regiment of which it had never heard and with it went the complete pipe and drum band to this new regiment which did not use the bagpipes but fifes. I saw the old Bugle Major driving away in a lorry his face streaming with tears, torn away at the very end of his service from the regiment in which he had lived all his life and which he loved.

Finding myself commanding Wana Brigade in the absence of the Brigadier, I discovered that the entire staff, less the Brigade Major, were Pakistani, and that they were imbued with altogether more of the national spirit than was wholesome in a Brigade which still had a very large Hindu element. I disliked the possible military implications. We still did not know the future of my own regiment. Then the awful blow fell, we had been sold down the river.

Recovering from the blow and finding that all we British Officers were due to be replaced by Indians before 15 August after which day we would not be required to serve on, I immediately pointed out to higher authorities that the North West Frontier was the last place for a replacement of this kind and extracted a promise that the first troop train available at rail head would transport us down to the peace and quiet of Bangalore. I had other reasons for wishing to get my Battalion back into India, for I had kept in touch with many useful civilian contacts, both British and Indian, from my ADC days and all were convinced that the country was on the verge of civil war; I also heard from one of them that Lord Wavell had privately and gloomily forecast the quite considerable probability of a general massacre of Europeans and a rearguard action to the sea, were the present policy to be brought into effect.

Current with this wholesale military reorganisation and disorganisation was a somewhat natural background of unrest. There had been a series of 'unfortunate incidents' which were known through every Northern bazaar and which had put the ever watchful tribes on the qui-vive, the really maddening aspect being that every soldier back from leave had a shrewd idea of what was happening. The Army, with its mania for secrecy, had thought it better to keep its Officers, including Colonels commanding regiments, in the dark; and there were terrible threats against anyone who discussed or even listened to rumours.

As far back as April anyone passing through Rawal Pindi district by train could see villages blazing at all parts of the compass and Henry Burrows rejoined the Battalion from a course with the information that he had been the only European on the train when it drew into Daud Khel and had been forced to watch a Sikh civilian being pulled out on to the platform and murdered with axes, his body being thrown under the wheels. What could he do against a mob of hundreds of wild fanatics, armed only with his pistol and a few rounds?

A few weeks later we were shocked to hear the news of the murder of the very charming Sikh Commandant of the transit camp at Bannu, who had been killed on the platform a few stations down the line; he had known his danger but he stuck to his duty. Almost on top of this came the news of the attack on a party of two Sikhs and twenty-eight Madrassi Christians belonging to the Indian Air Force; travelling by train near Kohat, they had been attacked by Adam Khel Afridis and while the two Sikhs escaped and hid in the high crops, eighteen of the Madrassis were killed and the remainder wounded.

In September an incident occurred which made us mourn for the glory that had departed, for an era in which the rank of Officer held a responsibility and had a meaning, when the fighting races of India were made to live peacefully side by side and the honour of wearing a military uniform forged links far stronger than those of race or creed. A fully armed Mohammedan company complete with Mohammedan King's Commissioned Officers, together with three Sikh private soldiers bound for another unit, were all travelling down together; at a small station not far from Bannu the three Sikhs were pulled out by a large crowd of Mohammedan riff-raff on the platform and murdered before the eyes of their Mohammedan comrades, who seemed to have been content to sit in the train and watch! It seemed that there had been serious trouble in Peshawar with the deterioration of civil control.

A very serious situation was said to have occurred when a Sikh section was apparently manning a post which was being approached by a large body of Pathan tribesmen bent on loot, when, as luck would have it, round the corner appeared a fighting patrol from some Mohammedan company. Waiting until the patrol were close enough to join in, the Sikh sentry opened fire expecting it to advance to his assistance. Unfortunately, the Mussulmen may have thought that he had opened fire on them and their immediate reaction was to attack and wipe out the entire Sikh section with the exception of one man who escaped wounded back to his own lines and told his comrades, who immediately assumed that the overwhelmingly Mussulman portion of the Peshawar garrison had joined in with the tribes against the Sikhs. All troops were immediately confined to barracks which left the city riff-raff free to sack the bazaar, including the quarters of the Hindu clerks of the Public Works Department, the survivors of whom escaped only with the clothes in which they stood up

Next we heard about the unfortunate Indian Grenadier Battalion allotted to India and on their way out of Pakistan by troop train. Their train was derailed somewhere near Kohat and the troops were attacked by an overwhelming number of Pathans as they tried to extricate themselves from the wreckage. They seemed to have suffered some ninety casualties before beating off the enemy. The Commanding Officer, George Shipway, recognised among the enemy bodies those of some Pathan soldiers of his previous regiment.

We learnt too of the disappearance of the British second in command of the Guides Cavalry, a regiment with whom we had been great friends. They, being stationed somewhere down in India and ordered to become part of the Pakistan Army, sent him ahead by train with a couple of men to make arrangements for their arrival in their new station. After leaving their old station they were never seen nor heard of again.

There could now be no possible question of we British Officers leaving the Battalion in Pakistan and coming home, as we had been perfectly entitled to do since 15 August which was Independence Day; my concern was first to get it safely down to Bangalore in the depths of India where it could sit on its collective behind, eating its rations and drawing its pay under the command of my excellent Subedar-Major, until some Indian King's Commissioned Officers arrived.

At about this time a little arrangement was made between myself and Lt Col Moore, the Commandant of the South Waziristan Scouts, which now seems quite incredible. He had a dozen or so British Officers to whom his wild crowd of a few thousand huge lean Pathans were absolutely and completely loyal, as our Gurkhas were to us. We arranged quite quietly between ourselves that in the event of a full scale civil war accompanied by a general massacre of the British, a thing which my senior civilian friends in Delhi and Lahore thought to be by no means improbable, we would by means of our own transport and every civilian lorry we could seize, take my Battalion down to the Indian Border supported by his Scouts, who would then be left to make their ways peacefully home through the country of their own co-religionists, or loot India just as they chose. We would then make our way to the Nepalese border, presumably fighting for petrol when necessity demanded, where I would say good-bye to those Gurkhas who wished to go home; then with a volunteer force of Gurkhas we would make our way to the nearest airfield or port, collecting any odd British we might find en route, and then evacuate ourselves, leaving our Gurkha force to amuse themselves in India in the fashion of their ancestors. A wild scheme suited to a wild country at a wild time.

XVIII

Speeding the parting guest

Trouble now started nearer home. We had always been at peace with the Wana locals; Gurkhas are quiet little men who never pick quarrels, but the former seemed anxious to drive us back behind the wire and we were not prepared to have our movements restricted.

First of all, an inoffensive sweeper was held up at the point of the knife when on his way to sweep up a camp picket some half mile away and later two unarmed Gurkha garden orderlies were likewise threatened, a nuisance that only stopped after we had hidden a couple of men with a Bren Gun among the cabbages; a little while afterwards our men were stoned while playing football and the time obviously would soon come when there would be bloodshed.

Rumours increased, railway and postal services were becoming increasingly irregular and one day we gleaned from our air mail copy of *The Daily Telegraph* that between ten and fifteen thousand Mohammedans had been massacred in Amritsar. Things seemed to be hotting up and it was with a feeling of relief that we eventually got our orders to move to Bangalore immediately.

It seemed, however, that these orders might have come just a little late, for Major Johnny Raw, the very experienced Political Agent, had already impressed upon the military authorities that the attitude of those bad boys of the Frontier, the powerful Mahsud tribe through whose territory we must pass, was beginning to give cause for grave anxiety; he further advised that the despatch by road of any but Mohammedan troops would be very risky especially through the Shahur Tangi and since all our lorries were worn out and liable to break down. It was not for me to question orders: orders are to be obeyed, but I wondered what those from higher authority had really been.

It was one of the main functions of the Political Officers on the Frontier to keep themselves abreast of what the tribes were thinking and doing and to inform the Army accordingly and I had never known their advice to be quite so blatantly disregarded before.

The District Commander, General Roger le Fleming, was a charming person and a good soldier but he was far away in Razmak; surely he was being kept informed of the political situation here? Was he perhaps sick or had he already retired and been replaced by some incompetent? Wireless communication in the hands of Indian Signals had become terrible and there never had been a telephone. Was up-to-date information getting through? Was it too far fetched to think that our own Brigade staff might be intercepting or altering messages to and from him?

As for our own Brigadier, John Booth, a pleasant and excellent soldier from County Wexford who was a fluent Pushtu speaker, what of him? Could it be that he was an unsuspected sufferer from Pathanitis, an even more deadly disease than the well known Arabitis. Could it be affecting his judgment? Did he refuse to entertain doubts of the integrity of his Pakistani staff? It would, of course, be optimistic to expect to get much sense out of Northern Command at the moment. Douglas Gracey, late of the 1st Gurkhas was now Commander-in-Chief of the Pakistan Army, General Roy Bucher that, or about to be that, of the new Indian Army; they seemed to be spending most of their time, with varied success, in restraining their armies from fighting one another.

Our last few days were spent in packing up our stores and in circumventing the machinations of the Brigade Staff who kept

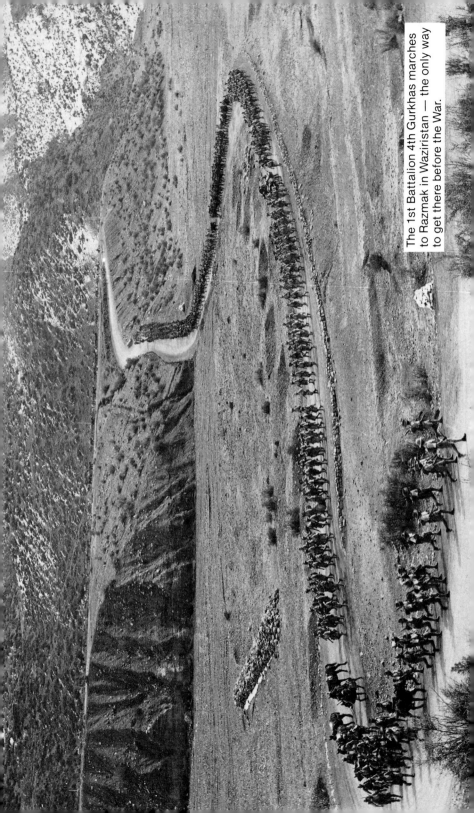

The 1st Battalion 4th Gurkhas marches to Razmak in Waziristan — the only way to get there before the War.

Waziristan Tribesmen — sometimes friendly,

infiltrating our lines, intent on the patriotic task of relieving us of equipment useful to Pakistan. Frantic messages from people such as our boot repairers would be received saying that the Staff Captain had sneaked in and was trying to take away all their leather and tools!

Now came a message that the Battalion of the Frontier Force Regiment in Manzai had received a warning order that they might proceed on operations against large numbers of Pathans who were crossing the Indus intent on raiding into the plains. We were to relieve them in Manzai, and if necessary go and assist them on the Indus later. This was not quite the news we wanted, but it would at any rate take us one step nearer Bangalore. A further blow was the information that there would now be only enough transport to ferry down half the battalion at a time.

As I drove out of Wana with the first half of the battalion I had plenty of material for reflection. When my friend Johnny Raw who kept his paid informers among the tribes and whose business it was to know what was going on in their minds and to predict their actions, had said that our despatch was very risky, it was to infer that there was grave risk of our being wiped out.

Every officer with sufficient frontier experience remembered that ensuring an uninterrupted journey for a convoy over this route in face of serious Mahsud opposition had needed a force of about a Division, 13,000 men complete with artillery, tanks and RAF support. Here was I going down with about four hundred men and a lot of stores in lorries with the route protected not by a Division of troops but by three armoured cars in unreliable hands and the South Waziristan Scouts, themselves all Pathans armed chiefly with rifles, and no artillery or RAF support. A further shortcoming was that my small wireless sets were insufficiently powerful to communicate from one end of the lorry column to the other, much less keep in touch with Wana or Manzai.

I never found out from what height came the order to send us down right now, nor the cogency of the considerations which made necessary this order (one might say gamble). I thought and still think that our Brigadier had misjudged things, due to the possibility that his own staff was witholding vital information from him, but why had he paid no attention to Johnny Raw?

What with one thing and another, it needed no great military genius to realise that if the Mahsuds were out for trouble we would soon be having a busy day, and, sitting in my jeep half way up the column pistol on knee, searching the hills with my field glasses, I awaited a sudden crash of rifle fire from in front, or behind, or at close range. If we were attacked before we came to the Shahur, it might be possible to get out of the lorries, turn them round, and cover them back; if attacked in the Shahur itself, the only plan would be to drive on until a lorry got immobilised and blocked the road, then jump out and seize the high ground above us. Every man in the column knew his orders and all we could do now was to sit in our vehicles and hope for the best.

On we drove, the Wana Mobile Column, two companies of troops in lorries, turning for home after a few miles and leaving us with armoured cars and, presumably, some Scouts on the hills above us. I did not, however, expect much to happen for the remainder of the twenty-four miles to Sarwekai; the Scouts might temporarily halt us while they chased a few enemy away, but the next twenty miles between Sarwekai and Jandola, both big Scout posts, might be packed with incident.

A few miles after Sarwekai, we came to the tiny little mud fort of Splitoi, exactly like something out of a novel by P C Wren, which guards one end of the notorious natural feature, the Shahur Tangi.

The Shahur Tangi is a very deep and narrow gorge about three miles long through which the little Shahur River forces its boulder strewn way. Never more than a hundred yards wide, it is at one end so narrow that two laden camels cannot pass one another and after heavy rain in the high hills the water rises rapidly from a few inches to as much as sixty feet of raging torrent. The sides rise sheer in great rock cliffs to the mountains above and the whole configuration of the ground lends itself to the laying of ambushes at which the Mahsuds are so adept. Into the cliffs is cut a single track motor road which, being unfenced and with sheer cliffs up one side and down the other, calls for a certain care in driving.

This place was the scene of a fierce little action in April 1937, when a convoy of about fifty lorries was stopped. In the fighting the troops lost twenty-seven killed, including seven British Officers, and forty-seven wounded; the graves of the Officers, most of whom had been down for a language examination, lie in a sad little row in the rocky sand-swept cemetery at Manzai. A revealing story is that of the humble non-combatant, some-body's servant, who, begging the Mahsuds to spare his life on account of his never having looked down the sights of a rifle in his life, had his right eye laughingly removed on the point of a dagger in case he might think of changing his mind.

The Shahur has the most evil reputation of any gorge on the frontier and, looked at closely, it was not difficult to understand why. Some of the bends were so tight that the view of even a lorry in front was blocked by a great buttress of perpendicular rock face and anything might be happening up or down the column without any of the participants being immediately aware of it. Furthermore, the sound of all these lorry engines in low gear would effectively drown the sounds of distant rifle shots.

Winding our way through the gorge and reaching Chagmalai, another little mud fort at the Eastern end of the Pass, I stopped the front bit of the column to wait for the remainder to close up; along they slowly came, vanishing and re-appearing round the corners until the last armoured car at the tail drove up and it was safe to proceed; we were now out of the really bad bit and approaching Jandola, beyond which lay the beginning of the flat stoney plain in which lay Manzai; once clear of the hills, the odds would no longer be so heavily in favour of the Mahsuds.

Driving through the gate of Manzai, I felt that I had been

misjudging my superiors; they had been proved right, and I was wrong, and provided all our luck held, we should be rejoined by the remainder of the Battalion in a couple of days when the transport had got back to lift them; this optimism turned out to be quite unfounded.

With the advantage of hindsight, I still have no idea why we were not attacked.

It was on the third day after our own arrival, when we expected to hear that they would be leaving Wana in the morning, that we got a long cipher message by wireless which took literally hours to decode as Pakistani signals operators were by no means accurate in transmission. Finding that it made gibberish and having to send it back not once but twice for retransmission, we eventually elucidated that the whole Battalion was to move immediately by air to reinforce a division whose number and location was not stated, and that while we ourselves emplaned at Tank, some twenty-five miles away by road, the rear half of the Battalion would emplane at Wana and meet us at our destination. While adjusting myself to the implications of this new arrangement, I felt rather puzzled as, having suggested a few days before that we might fly out to avoid the dangerous road journey, I had been told that Wana was too high for laden Dakotas to take off and that there were none available anyway. What could this mean?

Late that night another very mangled cipher message came through saying that the rear half of the Battalion would come by road to Manzai, but neither confirming nor cancelling the order about a further air move to join the unspecified division. This called for no action except the continuation of splitting up our kit into aeroplane loads in the morning, so I resumed my broken slumbers to be roused again before dawn with yet a third message saying that the two Companies in Wana would be flying after all and that we would all be flying to Chaklala near Rawal Pindi to join the 7th Division, as serious communal trouble had broken out all over the Punjab where all available troops were now required. Poor Robertson, my Adjutant, was getting no sleep at all for at breakfast time yet another was handed in; this was not, however, to implement the last one as I expected, for I had hoped to be told something about baggage scales and the future of all our heavy kit; it merely said that A and B Companies would be coming by road, but gave no indication as to when. Had our Brigade Headquarters gone quite mad?

There comes a time when it is obviously unprofitable to speculate further and I had about reached that stage when an Orderly came to tell me that there was a convoy approaching the gate. With a sigh of relief that my Battalion looked like being once more united, I strolled over to see them come in and was considerably surprised to see a huge green Pakistani flag mounted over the roof of every lorry; the lorries were full, not of Gurkhas but of Pakistani details going off on transfer.

There were several King's Commissioned Pakistani Officers with them, but they had no news for me. They also failed to report to me, as OC Manzai, the vital information, impossible later to verify or disprove, that the convoy had been stopped and searched by Mahsuds and only allowed to proceed after the latter had satisfied themselves that there were no Hindu troops on board. They may well have been ashamed of themselves — they certainly should have been if this were true — but in any case the significance of the big Pakistani flags was not lost on us.

Two more cipher messages having come through, both too badly transmitted to be intelligible, I decided that the only thing to do was to go back to Wana myself and find out what really was going to happen to us, so, getting a lorry off our friends the Scouts, I set off through the Pass once more. It looked more dangerous and forbidding than ever, but since no one knew we were coming, no one shot at us.

Poor Gibson, commanding the rear party in Wana, had been having a dreadful time. Every night after dark they had loaded up their lorries in silence and secrecy, prepared for a dawn move, and every morning the orders had been cancelled. The Brigadier, to my surprise, said that as far as he knew we were still bound for Bangalore, the RAF were doing a reconnaissance of the Wana landing ground, and I might next see Gibson, David Cotton, Malcolm Smith and the two companies at Rawal Pindi, Lahore, Delhi or even waiting for me at Bangalore. My re-iteration that I thoroughly distrusted his staff did not please him; he had chosen it.

I drove back to Manzai next day arriving just in time to be met by a cipher signal which had outstripped me and which told me to send a Frontier Force Company, which had just arrived in Manzai, up to Wana. They had packed up their lorries and driven off when another signal arrived which we were lucky to decipher by the time they had gone fifteen miles and which ordered them back.

Two days later I had an important visitor, an educated Pathan who spoke English and turned out to be the Assistant Political Agent; he informed me that a body of hostile Wazirs had taken up a position astride the road at a place not far from Wana and that a large party of Mahsuds had closed and were holding the Shahur Tangi! This information was too serious to risk delay by bad signalling, so I sent it immediately in clear to Wana Brigade.

That night at 2 am I was woken by a message to say that my companies were about to be despatched by road. This seriously worried me; the risk did not appear to be sufficiently calculated and, to be frank, was sheer foolhardiness. The Assistant Political Agent might have been wrong or the gangs might have cleared off, but I did not think either was likely. Wana Brigade had acknowledged my message but had it been shown to the Brigadier? It all looked very odd. In any case, I could not get in touch with him verbally at all and a wireless message could only repeat what I had previously said; if the first one had been withheld from him, this latter could only share the same fate. It was now too late to do anything except wait.

It is now necessary to survey the scene at Wana. At 2 am Gibson had been aroused and told to pack up and move off his force at 7 am. The bustle of packing up would, of course, be seen and heard by anyone hiding in the dark outside the camp, but would not give the latter time to get down to the Mahsud country and put them on the alert. What Gibson was not to know was that a civilian truck belonging to the Public Works Department had spent the night parked at a sufficient distance outside the wire for its engine not to be heard, and had been driven off directly their move had become apparent. The motives of its occupants are not hard to guess.

I had worked out the tactical organisation of this column with some considerable care. There is no way of organising a lorry column so that it can pass unscathed through a defile held on both sides by the enemy, but there is a choice of ways by which it may be given at least a chance of fighting back. Discarding the organisation employed in the original disaster of 1937 and with, Heaven knows, ample experience of the various methods employed in North Waziristan, I gave the following instructions.

The force at the disposal of Gibson was composed of two rifle companies and three armoured cars, the latter manned by Pathans of a famous Cavalry Regiment. With them was a number of other lorries carrying tentage, stores, rations and elements from HQ Company such as clerks, mule holders, armourers, tailors, etc. Added to the column at the last moment were five lorry-loads of Sikhs of the Indian Artillery who in direct contravention of every order pertaining to the Frontier, had been disarmed by their Pakistani superiors before being despatched. This was quite disgraceful; one would have imagined that the Brigadier himself or at least his British Brigade Major would have come to see the convoy off in these very particular circumstances, but this they had apparently not done. Poor Gibson did not know what to do, the convoy could not be delayed while he went and complained and to whom was he to complain? Everyone was presumably in bed. I myself would have refused to take unarmed Sikhs but Gibson was too junior to question Brigade Orders.

It has always been a joke among regimental officers of every civilised army to declare when things go wrong that 'the staff must be on the enemy side'. This time the staff really were on the enemy side and it was no joke. My orders to the column were based on the certainty that they would be attacked and stopped, although I could hardly tell them that.

All went well until the column had gone a few miles, when it was forced to wait for a very vital and sinister half hour for the rear armoured car which reported that it had broken down. With the advantage of hindsight this was obviously a put up job. A little later the column was met by Colonel Chambers, the new Commandant of the Scouts, for my friend had apparently retired on pension and was now in England, who imported the information that large bodies of enemy had been seen making their way towards Sarwekai and the Shahur Tangi. However, he ordered Gibson not to go back to Wana but to drive on. This latter order I have never understood. I should have told him to turn round and go back.

On entering the Shahur, David Cotton's Company came under fire which was continued the whole way along the Pass, but kept grimly driving on as I had instructed them, firing back out of their lorries at the Mahsuds in the rocks high above. They were more than lucky to get through with only three men wounded, since the Quartermaster Jemadar's lorry had its front tyre burst by a bullet but managed to carry on at full speed on the rim and thus avoided blocking the road; David Cotton was rather surprised at the behaviour of the leading armoured car which, instead of taking up a position where it would be passed and then firing on the enemy, just toured on in front as if nothing had happened.

Reaching the tiny fort of Chagmalai at the opposite end of the narrow bit of the Pass, this leading company, together with some lorries containing stores and odd men, could see no one behind them, so David Cotton, hearing heavy firing, debussed and started to counter-attack back along the way he had come; Colonel Chambers then appeared with some of his Scouts and, ordering David to take up a defensive position at

Chagmalai, himself then assaulted both sides of the Pass with some more Scout reinforcements from Jandola.

We will now pass on to the rear company under Malcolm Smith. A couple of miles short of Splitoi, which was at the Wana end of the Pass, they had come under heavy fire from a large body of tribesmen in position on the rocks on either side of them. The leading truck was hit and left the road, whereupon the company halted, leapt out and started to fire back. Major Majendie of the Scouts who was coming along behind and had room to manoeuvre, then attacked and drove the enemy out of their positions with the loss of one of his Jemadars killed and a Scout wounded. Majendie first ordered Smith to return to Sarwekai and then, extricating Gibson, told him to turn round his lorries and follow Smith as quickly as he could.

Meanwhile, in the centre of the convoy there was serious trouble. A lorry behind David's company was very slow and held up four lorries behind it, who soon realised that there was no one following along behind them. Going along as fast as the leading lorry would permit in the hope of catching up with the rifle company in front, they were unlucky enough to have the leading driver shot dead, his lorry slewing round and blocking the road. The enemy firing immediately redoubled, some men being hit as they tried to scramble out, others firing back from the sides of the lorries or the open road, there being a precipice down one side and a cliff up the other.

Then came a whirlwind knife rush on to the little knots of non-combatants, mule holders and unarmed Sikh gunners who were overwhelmed after a short fight. A Pakistani Naik (Corporal) then jumped out of the armoured car which had been standing close beside, not firing and giving no assistance and, telling the Mahsuds to hold six wounded Gurkhas from the rear-most lorry down on the road, shot them with his tommy gun one after the other as they lay struggling. A seventh man broke away as his companions were being stripped preparatory to being shot and, joining up with another rifleman, hid in the rocks among the cliffs from whence they engaged the Mahsuds looting the trucks, killing two or three each. They then hid until dark when they proceeded to walk the eighteen miles to Manzai over strange and hostile country; they said that the Mahsuds had lost about ten killed and wounded in this little action.

Having overcome all resistance, the Mahsuds moved off down the road with all the loot they could carry, to the relief of an elderly Sikh Subedar of the RASC who had been sitting quietly in his lorry the whole time, seeing and hearing everything but remaining unspotted. The few wounded survivors who had been able to hide then moved further away and it was as well that they did so, as another large body of Mahsuds appeared and proceeded to knife any bodies which showed signs of life.

Meanwhile down in Manzai we, of course, knew nothing of this. All the information we had was that our two rear companies were being despatched at presumably first light into the most notorious death trap on the whole Frontier, already held by a large number of Mahsuds and with Wazirs astride the road near Wana for the obvious purpose of stopping any troops who turned round and tried to get back.

I got little sleep that night, lying awake and hoping that this order was just another of those lunatic messages we had been receiving.

As the morning wore on I could not stop myself from frequent visits to the Northern perimeter wall just in case I might spot a tell tale cloud of dust on the horizon before the sentries did.

At about 11 am a Gurkha office orderly brought me a message. As he came marching over to me I prayed as I have never prayed before that this was a cancellation of its predecessor; it could hardly be much else. I grabbed it. It was from the Scouts in Jandola.

'Heavy firing in the Shahur. Will keep you informed.'

My first impulse was to go to their assistance but all our lorries had gone, there was no other transport in Manzai, not even mules to carry our mortars and reserve ammunition, and the Shahur was 18 miles away. All I would in effect achieve if we went on our feet would be to be rushed in the dark by over-whelming numbers of the enemy on ground of their own choosing and have from three to four hundred deaths on my conscience.

I signalled back to Col. Chambers for the loan of all his Scout lorries.

As I waited for an answer another thought struck me. Only by an Act of God could we ever see those two companies again for although their ammunition, food and water was calculated to last them several days in anticipation of just such an eventuality, they would have no cover from enemy fire. Out on the bare hillside, possibly in little groups, a target for snipers by day and by night, they would in due course be decimated after which the enemy would consider the time ripe for the final knife rush.

It then seemed inevitable that the enemy, their tails well up, their numbers even further augmented by success would attack Manzai. There would certainly be those among them who realised that the place would be difficult to defend by night as it has been built for a larger garrison, and who would know that it was full of valuable stores, rations, forage, tentage, petrol and the like, all well worth looting.

My next task would be to find out how many fighting men there were in the place and organise them. This was a narrow-gauge railhead and there were numbers of men coming and going from leave, courses and the like. I need not worry about their religion as everyone knew that Mahsuds attacked quite indiscriminately.

My projected plans for attacking, after being carried there by Scout lorry, were stopped by a message from Colonel Chambers who said that he would call on us if he got in trouble himself, but meanwhile he was doing all he could to get Gurkhas out of, not into, the Shahur Tangi.

About mid-day the Pathan Assistant Political Agent entered the Tangi with a Khassadar escort and brought out three dead Gurkhas, four dead Sikhs and thirteeen wounded Sikhs. By mid-afternoon the Scouts were in temporary control of the Tangi and firing had ceased, enabling them to bring out four more wounded and eleven dead.

The position at nightfall was hardly reassuring. David Cotton with two hundred and eleven men was besieged in the tiny Fort of Chagmalai, designed to hold only its original small Scout garrison, the only available space being a little courtyard a hundred feet long by eighty feet broad. On all sides were enemy, a very large body of whom were astride the road between him and Jandola. Gibson and Smith with an equal number were cut off in the much larger Fort of Sarwekai, again surrounded by enemy, a large force of whom were between them and Tangi, and another force had interposed itself between Manzai and Jandola with the intention of stopping me were I to try and get back. All of us were out of communication with each other.

Next morning the position had, if anything, worsened. The enemy forces so far from dispersing had been augmented during the night, for news travels fast. They were now several thousand strong, while women could be seen bringing up supplies on camels; parties could also be spotted building stone breastworks on the cliffs overlooking the road. It looked as if they meant to stay until the troops ran out of food and water. Three more bodies were brought in during the day and news was received from Jandola that a naked Gurkha had walked in there at dawn. He had been wounded and, while unconscious, stripped and left for dead; recovering consciousness later, he had gone down to the river for a drink and then hidden among the rocks; after dark, not knowing where the enemy were or that B Company was at Chagmalai, he walked the eight miles down the road to Jandola, passing straight through the middle of the enemy positions!

I was now in the infuriating position of being able to do nothing; my Battalion was besieged in three places many miles apart and it would take a huge force to extricate them. I had, however, expected something of the kind to happen and had ensured that each company was amply supplied. Colonel

Chambers, who was responsible for the Shahur area, had no illusions either, and his first act was to point out to Gibson and Cotton, with whom he alone could get in touch, that to give battle at this stage would stir up a hornet's nest in the entire country which, since no reinforcements were available, would prove a very serious matter for every garrison in Waziristan. His Scouts, however, were all fellow Pathans of the Mahsuds and, therefore, able to take liberties denied to men of any other race, and he might be able to get us out by unorthodox methods.

By the third day the enemy were, if anything, getting bolder and had during the night cut the barbed wire entanglement at Chagmalai in an attempt to loot the lorries for which there was no room inside the wall. At Manzai inaction was becoming very tedious, especially as we were quite out of communication except to Wana through the erratic Manzai wireless, and they had nothing to tell us. About two days later the Brigadier came down in a Scout armoured lorry dressed up in baggy grey Pathan trousers and waving turban, like a Scout, and obviously feeling very embarrassed. He had little to say but gave us the first laugh which we had indulged in for sometime.

Chambers was now sitting in Jandola awaiting his opportunity, and the Mahsuds had now cooled down sufficiently to allow free passage to the Scouts who were running in supplies in armoured lorries. The Assistant Political Agent, himself a Pathan, called a 'jirgah' or tribal meeting in the valley about half a mile north of the road; it was he who had a big say in the distribution or witholding of the money which the government lavished on the tribes to keep them quiet, and he was thus a man of very considerable importance. While this meeting was in progress eleven empty Scout lorries slipped down to Chagmalai and B Company, who had previously been warned to leave everything behind except their arms and ammunition, quickly embussed and drove off at full speed. It was some minutes before the enemy realised what was happening and, although making frantic efforts to regain their position, only a few succeeded in bringing accurate fire to bear on the lorries as they negotiated three sharp hairpin bends leading to the top of the Pass. Several lorries were hit without, however, any casualties, and once at the top a Scout escort in lorries met them and brought them down to Manzai.

Colonel Chambers who came with them was equally optimistic about bringing out A Company in the near future but to me the chance of pulling off the same trick again seemed rather remote. There was no particular need for speed, A Company had plenty of food and ammunition, Sarwekai was a big Fort and with Gibby was Captain Oldrini one of the Scouts who, of course, could speak Pushtu, the local language. Chambers had been to see Gibby and I could now check up the extent of the damage we had received.

The whole force has suffered twenty-five killed and twenty-six wounded, of which eleven and seven respectively were Gurkhas, most of the remainder being the unarmed Sikhs; a number of lorries had been burnt and a quantity of kit looted; much of our equipment had been riddled with bullets including our officers Mess armchairs.

Along with B Company came the armoured car containing the treacherous Corporal disguised as a Scout and concealing a dagger. He was, of course, promptly arrested and I hoped that he would be quietly shot while resisting. He, however, gave no opportunity, and at a subsequent date I sent him down to District Headquarters with a host of witnesses from different races and arms of the service, all with concrete evidence. To my amazement and fury the Court found him not guilty and let him off scot free. I wished I had hanged him out of hand in the first place and damn the consequences.

I heard a long time later that the Cavalry Regiment to whom these armoured cars belonged had been through a rather unpleasant experience. Being destined for the Pakistan Army, they had left their Sikh and Dogra squadrons to join some other regiment and had then come up from Central India by train. On the way they asked their British Colonel if a crowd of some hundred Mohammedan women and children refugees whom they saw from the train windows might join them but he, knowing that he might have to fight his way through to Pakistan and that there was no room in the train anyway, not unnaturally refused. As the train steamed out of the station they saw a Hindu mob massacring the women and children.

A few days later the unexpected order came for the Battalion to move to Bangalore where it would be rejoined by A Company when it had been extricated. I did not like leaving A Company but had no real justification for lodging a protest. The next step was to be Tank, some ten miles away as the crow flies, but far longer by road; the railway from Manzai to Tank was, unfortunately, out of the question as it had been breached by flood.

While pondering over the move, a Pathan came to my office and desired to see me alone. He stated that he was a spy with information of great importance. It was obviously undesirable to send for a Pushtu speaker, so I had great difficulty in making out what he wanted. The latter was, of course, money, but his information seemed well worth it and I paid up. He said that a considerable force of mixed Pathans, including Bhittanis whose land marched with that of the Mahsuds, were lying up in the very broken ground half way between Manzai and Tank with the intention of attacking my convoy. I had already expected this and since this was outside the Scout area and I could no longer rely on the armoured cars, the matter called for some thought. I made what I hoped to be the best arrangements, but in the event during our move we did not see a single enemy or fire a shot. They must have been watching us and had thought better of it.

On arrival at Tank we were busy fortifying our camp around the railway station when a cloud of dust from the road along which we had just come disclosed the arrival of another convoy. They looked like Scout lorries and my relief was tremendous when out of them piled Gibson and Smith with their troops. It had been raining fairly heavily during the past week up in the hills and Chambers had shrewdly suspected that the Mahsuds would eventually tire of getting wet out on the bare hillsides. Waiting for definite information that large numbers of them had, indeed, got fed up and gone home, many having come from long distances, he seized the opportunity during a particularly violent rainstorm of darting in as he had done before, and evacuating everybody.

There was, however, another far more important factor, the Act of God that had drawn vast numbers of Mahsuds away from us. That was the Kashmir trouble which was now starting to boil up. The locals, attracted both by the prospects of slaughtering the infidel and of unbridled looting were finding us an unrewarding waste of effort which could be put to better use. So they had left us.

Kashmir had from time immemorial been the property of the Mohammedan power until captured from them by the Sikhs in 1819. After the British-Sikh war it was handed over to us in 1846 as part of the indemnity and then handed over to the Hindu Rajah of Jammu in exchange for £750,000 as a reward for his consistently loyal attitude towards us.

In 1947 directly after the partition of Pakistan and India the Hindu Government of Kashmir pursued a policy of systematic persecution of its Mohammedan subjects, such as the massacre at Bagh in Poonch on the 26 August of Mohammedan civilians by the State Troops because they had contravened an order in regard to the observance of 'Pakistan Day' on 15 August. This massacre was followed by the infiltration of Akali Sikhs and of so-called heroes of the INA whose activities on behalf of the Japanese during the war are best glossed over.

Another authenticated atrocity occurred on the Jammu/Kathua road where two crowded convoys of Mohammedan evacuees who had been promised safe conduct to Pakistan were massacred by armed bands, their Sikh escorts joining in the slaughter. The position of the Mohammedan population in the power of this unholy triumvirate can well be imagined, and some five hundred thousand fled from their homes to seek refuge elsewhere.

Indian mountain batteries could come into action absolutely anywhere.

The Waziristan Views were magnificent.

It is not surprising that the remaining Mohammedans quickly got in touch with their co-religionists, the Frontier tribes, who sprang to arms and crossed the Indus at many points on their way to Kashmir; nine hundred Mahsuds left us and walked down to Tank where they actually boarded lorries and thousands of other Pathans went by different routes. It is thus entirely due to the Kashmir situation that any of us got out of Waziristan alive, but this I only found out later.

XIX

Uneasy journey

Our next move was to be by narrow gauge railway from Tank to Mari-Indus on the banks of the Indus River where there was a large transit camp at the railhead of the broad gauge. Once on the broad gauge we would sit in the same train while it travelled through Lahore and eventually took us to Bangalore which it could be expected to reach in four or five days if we were lucky. We were not, of course, abreast of the difficulties of railway travel at that particular time.

Mindful of the adventures of the unfortunate Indian Grenadier Battalion, we took a few precautions. It had reached our ears that trains had a remarkable tendency to stop in the middle of ambushes when they could as easily go on. So the first move was to detail British Officers with tommy guns to sit in the engine cab and guard's van and ensure that the Pakistani train staffs fulfilled their duties to our full satisfaction. Then, again, we connected up all the coaches by field telephone.

There but remained for Derek Royals, our Mortar Officer, to mount a section of mortars in an empty goods wagon, sandbagged in and ready for instant action, and there was little more that we could do by way of preliminary arrangements. Armed sentries in every compartment by day and night are a normal procedure in India where rifle thieves are only too eager to thrust a brown arm through a window and silently remove everything within reach.

Again our numbers were too great to enable us to travel

together, so once more the Battalion was split into two halves.

Just before departure I received a signal that about fifteen hundred enemy were in position astride the Pezu Pass, the one really difficult place on the route, but there seemed little I could do about it until we got within range of them.

At each little wayside station I made enquiries as to what lay ahead, but the replies were all cheerfully non-committal. At Pezu station itself we were amused by the Station Master who informed us with refreshing candour that the enemy would take no interest in us once they realised that we were Gurkhas, it was those ... Sikhs that the country was after!

We did see small parties of tribesmen sitting on the tops of the hills which indicated that we should not be molested; if they had been out for trouble, we should have seen nobody except in the final stages and then dagger in hand at close quarters. After emerging from the Pass, the train was escorted by two companies of Pakistani lorried infantry who formed an advance guard along the road which ran beside the line. We soon realised why they were there as, standing among the crops and outside every village for mile upon mile on either side, were all the male local inhabitants, brandishing sporting guns, spears, swords and ancient muskets, all waiting for unarmed refugees or even Sikh troops, but not prepared to try conclusions with us.

On two occasions the train stopped while the Pakistani troops removed boulders from the line and ordered back the watching crowd of armed men to a respectful distance. These Pakistani troops were commanded by a British Officer who said he was having a very good time; his men were recruited from this very district and every night were feted in one or another village. In his spare time he was shown the very best of duck and partridge shooting, while the men played hockey against the village teams. He was, however, rather embarrassed at having to shoot some of his hosts of a few nights before whom he had stopped in the act of murdering a train load of Hindu refugees; everyone, however, realised that orders were orders, and he did not seem to have lost any popularity over the business.

On arrival at Mari-Indus the camp staff seemed surprised to see so many of us, as they had heard that we had received four hundred casualties, which goes to show the folly of paying too much attention to second or third hand information. There was a definite air of despondency about the place, as very few trains were running and none had come in for several days. The place was packed with troops, mostly Hindu, from every branch of the service.

They all seemed rather miserable, as the only smooth and level place where they could stroll about or play games was along the river; this, however, was denied them because of sniping from the rough ground on the opposite bank only about five hundred yards away. Our clothes all badly needed washing, the water looked warm and inviting for a swim and, since we could put down heavy mortar fire on to any point on the opposite bank within a matter of seconds, I decided that the camp, for the duration of our stay, must go back to normal.

For any non-swimmer the swimming parades were nearly as dangerous as the chance of an enemy bullet, since, with upwards of a thousand men plunging about, splashing each other, laughing and shouting, it would be very difficult to spot anyone who got into difficulties and sank beneath the surface.

Across the river lay the village of Kala-Bagh, a most picturesque place with its square towers and solid looking reddish mud brick houses rising in tiers up the steep hill, the whole surmounted by a large mosque on a pinnacle of rock. Indian towns and villages which are off the beaten track nearly always provide something of interest and, although its reflection mirrored in the still surface of the great river was probably far more attractive than the reality, I decided that there would be little risk in boating over and having a look round.

The inhabitants, all Punjabi Mussulmen, gave us a most enthusiastic welcome. Never before had they seen so many Europeans; there were, I think, four of us. Troops normally only spent a night in transit at Mari-Indus, and Kala Bagh was difficult of access and strictly out of bounds. The village turned out to be at least four times as big as we expected as the hill was honeycombed with passages cut out of the solid rock, whole streets being roofed in as protection from the fierce summer sun and caves enlarged into houses of which rooms were divided off by curtains. We were conducted through a maze of galleries into the house of the headman to join him in a cup of tea, small boys being cuffed and gaping townsfolk thrust back into side passages to allow us unimpeded progress.

Hard kitchen chairs were produced, a small table brought forward and covered with a spotless cotton tablecloth and tray after tray of sticky sweet Indian cakes handed to us by a crowd of young men standing around the walls and anticipating our every movement. The green tea, poured out of a samovar in frontier fashion, was drunk out of thick glasses and heavily sweetened.

The normal conversational courtesies having been observed and reference having been made to the state of the crops and the sharp rise in prices, this talk inevitably turned to local happenings. The sniping had not been done by the local Punjabi-Mussulmen but by scallywags from the Pathan villages higher up in the hills, for this was on the border of Pathan country. These Pathans had even staged a large scale raid on Kala-Bagh itself with the object of massacring all the Hindus most of whom, however, they had been able to save. I could not refrain from asking, 'Were there any Sikhs and did you also rescue them?' An old grey beard permitted himself a slight smile, 'Yes and no. There was a family of them but they were killed immediately.' The surviving Hindus had been sent to a place of greater safety across the river and I decided to institute enquiries about them on my return. The time was now getting late and, stopping to purchase a few silks at, of course, the proper price and not what we should have been asked in a more civilised area, we returned to our boat escorted by half the village.

Next day we found the Hindu refugees under military guard in a large wall enclosure not far from the transit camp. One of them talked perfect English and was a man of obvious culture; his story was this:

205

Just outside Kala-Bagh was a Hindu-owned coal mine of which he was the manager. Most of the technical staff being Hindus, they had on the outbreak of the disturbances decided to sleep in Kala-Bagh where there was a number of Hindu shopkeepers and where the Mohammedans had always been perfectly friendly. All went well until one night when without warning a horde of several hundred Pathans burst into the town and, battering down the doors of the Hindu houses, proceeded to massacre the unfortunate inhabitants. Thirty-two had been killed, regardless of age or sex, some had been sheltered by friendly Mohammedans and others had escaped in the darkness.

When dawn came they had all been collected by the local Mohammedan magistrate, what remained of their houses and their contents had been shuttered up and sealed and they had been sent under police guard to the magistrate on the Mari-Indus side of the river. The latter had put them under guard in his courtyard but, having no ready facilities for dealing with them and possibly wearying of this additional responsibility and trouble, had after forty-eight hours sent them back to their homes in Kala-Bagh. They had immediately appealed to the first magistrates who put them under Punjabi military guard in a big white walled-in temple on the river bank but here they had again been attacked that very night and several more killed and wounded despite the resistance given by the guard who had killed several attackers.

The village was obviously unsafe for them, so once more they had been escorted back across the river to the Mari-Indus side and placed in the courtyard. This, however, was too much for magistrate B who seemed to have washed his hands of them in disgust, as he had not been seen for five days. As we talked we walked round. They were all in a shocking state having, as yet, received no medical attention whatsoever; their only food was some sacks of grain which the mine manager had managed to buy at an exorbitant price, but they had no method of grinding and no means of cooking it.

This courtyard was the property of the mine and had been

206

used as a store; it had piped water but no sanitary arrangements.

I immediately sent for our doctor, furious that the camp doctor should have done nothing. Ours was a very keen young Madrassi who, to his disgust had spent the entire war in a large hospital in Northern India in some subordinate capacity and here at last was his chance of showing his mettle. As he started examining half amputated limbs and assorted knife, bullet, shot and axe wounds, I noticed that the elderly, the women and the children had suffered more than the more active, a matter which upon reflection should cause little surprise. For some reason, among the far worse horrors, I remember an old, old man who was quite paralysed through having been clubbed up and down the spine, and a small boy of eight or nine whose back was criss-crossed with cuts as the result of having been held down and beaten with the blade of a dagger.

We did what we could during our short stay, but on my last inspection I found the place empty. No trains had left the station, so we could only assume that the unfortunate Hindus had been whisked off across the river yet once more. There was nothing I could do; we were just off and the civil authorities were hiding from me. I had no transport to send the refugees anywhere and no place to which to send them; I was especially sorry for the cool, brave little manager, and I wondered if even now their bodies were in the river.

One morning a few days after we had arrived a whole Sikh Battalion with its troops' families drove up in lorries. Their CO, the only British Officer, said that they had driven through in the night from Dera-Ismail Khan where they had been stationed and where they had received a warning order to be prepared to move down to India shortly. The circumstances of his move may startle devotees of strict obedience to orders. Realising that even the most secret movement order would probably reach the Pathans before it reached him, he decided to take a chance, his will to live being strong, and his sense of duty to his battalion being stronger than any fear of official displeasure. Keeping his lorries loaded up, he quietly opened his perimeter gate one night and drove off, without seeking permission from or informing Brigade Headquarters, District Headquarters or even the Officer-in-Charge, Dera-Ismail Khan. Driving all night through hostile Pathan territory, including the enemy on the Pezu Pass, he arrived without incident except the accouchment of a Sikh woman in the back of a lorry.

We had seen enough of Mari-Indus when one morning an empty troop train drove in and with it a signal for us to entrain and proceed as far as Lahore.

Lahore is a lovely spot in winter and the thought of spending the first night for two years unencircled by barbed wire was very appealing. How nice to be able to walk about outside the camp without the risk of being sniped, how nice to be able to hail a taxi and drive to a smart hotel for a drink. More than anything, I looked forward to snatching an hour or two in the Punjab Club sitting out on the green lawn with my friends, away from bugle calls, words of command and orderlies with messages. In Lahore we should still, of course, be in Pakistan, but in a part of Pakistan that was no more a foreign country to a Fourth Gurkha than was India.

Meanwhile, we must make the wounded as comfortable as possible and not relax any special precautions for at least another twenty-four hours. We were to go through the Western Punjab from where the old Indian Army recruited the bulk of its Mohammedan troops, but who knew what influences had been brought to bear upon this martial race in the last few months? Without their British military and civilian officers they could very swiftly turn into a most dangerous foe. It was also now reported that gangs of Pathans were roaming about the Punjab, heading towards Kashmir, and to them the derailment of a train and subsequent scramble for loot among the wreckages, especially rifles, would be all in the day's work. We were not quite through yet, thought we, as we climbed in. As, however, the train rattled on without any untoward occurrence, we gradually relaxed.

We were travelling through very sparsely populated country

which looked much as usual. We only met one other train all day, and that shot past lurching and swaying, vastly overladen with people clutching their boxes, bundles, baskets and babies, crammed one against the other on the roof, swarming over the engine, the buffers and the running boards, standing on the window sills, clinging anywhere they could find a handhold.

Just as it grew dark the desert gave way to sparse cultivation and as the landscape became more civilised one occasionally saw the odd village in flames against which were outlined shadowy darting figures, bent, presumably, upon massacre or escape. It looked very macabre.

Feuds, flames and stark unbridled ferocity are part and parcel of the Frontier Independent Territory where lay our proper soldiering, but not of the friendly, peaceful Punjabi countryside. We were coming to the district where ten years ago everyone used to greet my girl friend and myself as we rode in the evenings, and where, turning for home, we watched the fast flying flocks of loquacious parakeets whiz like comets across that pale blue sky and laughed at the important naked little boys driving the great grunting buffaloes home to be milked. There suddenly out of the carriage window was what looked like the actual mosque to which we one day drove in the car, and where they made us take off our shoes and put on felt slippers, smart embroidered ones for me but inferior ones for her because she was only a woman, and she would always tease me about it.

At some little silent station, silent because the shouting Hindu soda water vendors or purveyors of betel nuts or sticky sweets were probably now dead, James Castle, my second in command was handed a military signal by the Station Master which directed us to detrain not at Lahore but at Amritsar across the Indian border. Had not some newspaper said that between ten and fifteen thousand muslims had been massacred here? Well, no doubt we should soon find out.

XX

Amritsar 1947

Even if one has some control over their timings, troop trains always succeed in arriving at their destinations at impossible hours of the morning and ours, true to form, drew into Amritsar station at 4 am. The Battalion was left to try and slumber on, while sentries and patrols climbed out and took up their normal positions round the train, and Derek Royals collected his Tommy Gunner escort, did a quick reconnaissance and started the cooks on to lighting fires on the platform and boiling up the morning cup of tea. I roused myself and strolled along to the coach serving as a hospital to have a look at the wounded, where I was greeted by the keen and highly efficient young Madrassi doctor.

There seemed to be rather a strange smell, unpleasant even for an Indian railway station, borne on the wings of the gentle breeze which sprang up with the dawn. The first feeble rays of rising sun revealed that we were not quite alone; on the platform, just beyond where the cooks were standing over their cooking fires, sprawled the corpses of five slaughtered Mohammedans.

We were tucking into a little breakfast when some officers and men from our own Second Battalion drove up, all armed to the teeth, which very much surprised us. They intimated, with nasty grins, that we were no longer destined for the fleshpots of Bangalore but were staying here where we would find our time fully occupied. As I tried to adjust myself to this new and totally unexpected situation the Brigadier appeared, welcomed us rather more profusely than mere politeness demanded, said he was very glad that the Battalion was so strong, intimated that we would find conditions far worse than war and asked me to come along to Brigade Headquarters.

The missionary ladies who ran the girls school which we were given as billets were understandably startled at having nearly a thousand Gurkha troops suddenly wished on them, and were more apprehensive as to what might happen to their beautiful lawns than relieved that they could now count on being safe from the blood thirsty mobs who had been howling round their walls and engaging in witch hunts through their compounds.

The general situation as outlined by the Brigadier was that there had been a general massacre of the Mohammedan population of Amritsar, which now could be said to be very nearly over, not because of the Sikhs and Hindus having calmed down but because it was becoming increasingly difficult to find any more Mohammedans to slaughter. There were, on the other hand, vast numbers of Mohammedan refugees from further East who had to be escorted across the border to safety, while equal numbers of Sikh and Hindu refugees were coming through from West Punjab and the Frontier Province to be settled, in theory anyway, on the land vacated by the Mohammedans. This colossal migration, unparalleled in history, was made no easier by the reaction of the population of East Punjab, here largely Sikh, who had been taking every opportunity given to them to attack the Mohammedans wherever they found them, sparing neither man, woman nor child. The Brigade was here to protect these Mohammedan convoys as they passed through and induce the indigenous population to quieten down. Meanwhile, all military personnel must go fully armed, all vehicles must carry a light machine gun, as rifle fire had been found inadequate for protection and British Officers must be especially careful of their own personal safety.

A tour of the city and suburbs revealed that rumours had not been exaggerated. While the fury and the slaughter had abated, it was too recent for the place to start returning to anything like normal life. All shops were shut, very few women were about and, as yet, little attempt had been made to clean up. The predominantly Mohammedan areas gave the impression not so much of having been looted and burned but of having been reduced to powder by aerial bombardment. Whole streets were blocked by piles of rubble, alleys had disappeared, great steel girders lay twisted up at odd angles, large brick houses had not a wall standing. In the nearby suburbs which I drove through there lay the occasional freshly murdered corpse.

Quickly tiring of ruins and smell, we drove round the Civil Lines. At the Post Office we were welcomed by a charming old Hindu postmaster who explained most apologetically that work was at a standstill since all his Mohammedan staff who had not run away had been killed and, in any case, no mails had come in for a considerable time. He did not advise us to post letters as he had no means of sending them anywhere but hoped to be again at our service at some future date when communications had been restored.

Our first role was railway protection. The main line, the only one now in use, ran through about a mile and a half of suburbs on each side of the passenger station which was prolonged by goods sheds, warehouses, marshalling yards, workshops and all the layout to be expected at the biggest commercial centre of the Punjab. The whole length of the track from where it left the open country was flanked on both sides by an irregular line of hovels and houses of all shapes, sizes and heights, they in turn being overlooked by high roofs rising from the labyrinths of bazaars behind. Apart from this sniper's paradise, the problem was made difficult by two foot-bridges and the road bridge carrying the Grand Trunk Road, all three of which had proved excellent stances from which to lob grenades into open goods wagons filled with refugees passing below. In addition, there were two level crossings and some open spaces through which large mobs might rush and attack the slowly moving carriages.

This all resolved itself into a perfectly straightforward

problem of getting the timings of West-bound trains, and none but refugee trains were running and they only once or twice a day. What did complicate the matter beyond all measure was a gigantic floating population of about thirty thousand Sikh and Hindu refugees who were living on the railway track waiting for something to turn up.

The daily routine for the whole Battalion was as loathsome as it was monotonous. Everyone having got into position and reported all quiet, I would set off on my tour. Threading my way in a Jeep through the streets of the Civil bazaar, past choked sewers and accumulated filth, I used to reach the beginning of the sector, the most easterly level crossing. This, flanked on one side by a large open space and on the other by a park was where the main bulk of the crowd had chosen to live until they could find rail accommodation to take them somewhere else. Here they stood, and sat, and lay and died, devoid of any arrangements for food or for medical attention, or for shelter or for sanitation. Some had been there as long as three weeks.

Directly one of our Officers appeared he would be surrounded by a dense mass of humanity asking if he had any instructions for them; where they were to get land, work, food, medicine, lodging, anything? What was going to happen to them? One tried to curb one's imagination and avoid looking at the clouds of smoke floating up above the park from the dozen or so huge bonfires, on which glowed strange and sinister shapes.

All had very similar stories. They had rescued what they could of their pitiful possessions before their homes had been seized or burnt. They, the lucky ones, had eventually got on to a train bringing them across the border to this strange country which few had seen before and here they had been told by dubious civil organisations that they would be parcelled out with the land evacuated by the Mohammedans. Their wanderings had taken them a long time during which members of their families, firstly the very old and the very young, had died. Those with more initiative, finding nothing being done for them beside the railway line at Amritsar, had pushed on as far as Jullundur,

213

Ludhiana and Amballa where they had heard that things were better, only to return disillusioned. Many had already spent all their money in buying food at exorbitant rates. Had this crowd been composed of the degenerate sweepings of the cities one could perhaps have taken a more detached view, but they were mainly the hard-working, honest Punjabi peasantry, whose natural charm and dignity one so much admired and from whose ranks were recruited the Army. Among them were a sprinkling of pensioned and demobilised soldiers, some disabled, some with decorations for bravery. Was this to be their reward?

Among these thousands we were able to rescue exactly one, the ancient white bearded Sikh Master Tailor of the Guides Infantry whom we one day spotted among the crowd. Having spent his entire life as a loyal servant of the Guides, he had been forced to leave them when they became part of the Pakistan Army, and since we had in the same way lost the services of our own excellent and faithful Mohammedan Master Tailor, we enrolled this old Sikh grandfather in his place.

While inspecting the picquet at the level crossing the whistle of an approaching train would sometimes be heard, a signal that the picquet, my escort and I must hurl ourselves into the fray. It being obvious that the wheels of the train could do as much harm as any possible enemy gang, we would leave all else and force our way through the crowd, cajoling, shouting at and thrusting back the thousands who were sitting with all their baggage on the actual track, too tired and dispirited to make any voluntary move. As a west-bound train of Mohammedans slowly crawled past the mass of Sikhs and Hindus there were no signs of animosity on either side. All they did was to stare miserably at one another. East bound trains were impossible to deal with. At the first glimpse of the engine as it rounded the bend the whole crowd would scramble to its feet and surge towards it then, despite the fact that not a square foot of train was visible for passengers, a few hundred more would climb on the roof or cling round the buffers to be transported to no one knew where, leaving for the few minutes a seething chaos in which parents vainly sought their children, and families collected up their scattered belongings.

My inspection over, I would brush off the myriads of bloated flies that crawled lazily about me and, puffing hard at a cigarette and being careful where I put my feet, would pick my way back to the jeep glad to inhale lungfuls of fresh air as we drove away. Paying a quick visit to the footbridge which presented no particular problem, I would steel myself for the Grand Trunk Road Bridge, the main artery between the two halves of Amritsar.

Closing this bridge before the approach of a train was simplicity itself; opening it after anything up to an hour later, during which time the train had been expected any minute, was difficult; vehicles as they drove up made no attempt to pull to the left but blocked up the entire width of the road for hundreds of yards on either side. The withdrawal of the the two lines of fixed bayonetted troops at the bridge ends was the signal for two solid streams of tightly packed tongas, bicycles, barrows, buffalo carts, private cars and laden donkeys to charge each other, becoming hopelessly interlocked in a matter of moments. Only Indian police could sort out this mess, but where were the Police? We had at a very early stage located and visited all the various Amritsar Police Stations and barracks, only to discover that the fifty per cent Mohammedan component had been murdered, while their Sikh and Hindu fellows were so disorganised, demoralized and under-strength as to have disintegrated as a force.

The next port of call was the Passenger Station. The station yard presented a scene not unlike the level crossing, being entirely filled with refugees, but here at least someone had made an attempt towards sanitation. A portion of the pavement on which lime was infrequently sprinkled being set aside for the purposes of nature. Apart from the stench, this was not a favourite place for officers to hang about as, shortly before our arrival, there had been an incident. A British Officer on duty at the station, seeing a jeep drive up containing what appeared to be four uniformed police, strolled out to see what they wanted. He soon found out, as he was shot down at a few feet range by the occupants who had then accelerated away before the sentries just inside the station could catch more than a glimpse of them.

Inside the station, which was cordoned off by barbed wire, all was quiet. Here I would waste much breath cursing the little Indian RTO on the rare occasions when he let me find him. Since ours had been the last troop movement, he could hardly be said to be overworked and had been given the job of finding out the approximate timings of refugee trains from the station staff and informing us over the telephone. This he would never do properly, his favourite gambit being to announce that an expected train was practically upon us, resulting in a wild scramble into position, closing of the bridges, and a long wait for a non-existent train. As a variant of this he would declare that no more trains were running that day, wait until we had marched back to our school and then telephone to say that a train full of Mohammedans was only a few miles away. I was then faced with the choice of halting the train out in the country where it might be attacked, or letting it run the cordon of the unguarded bridges and city snipers.

There remained but one more area to visit, the fringe of the Northern suburbs. Passing along beside the sidings and marshalling yards, not a shed nor a wagon without their full quota of desperate humanity, we came to the Headquarters of the furthest away rifle company, that of Ken Saxton, situated in a house between road and railway and overlooking a vast dusty expanse used for tipping rubbish.

Here the LMG sections and mortar detachments, sitting alert beside their weapons on the low flat roofs, all had handkerchiefs tied over their noses; when Gurkhas bother to do this the smell must be pretty bad. This had been a Mohammedan quarter and now a gang of sweepers, their turbans wound round their faces, spent their day dragging up an endless succession of decomposing corpses on the end of long lengths of fencing wire, which they then proceeded to burn on a dozen or so fires dotted about that area.

It is loosely said that one can become accustomed to anything, but none of us, British or Gurkha alike, showed any signs of becoming accustomed to this.

We had not been long in Amritsar when Brigadier Salomons suddenly got orders that he would be replaced by a new Brigadier from Delhi, a Sikh, and that he himself was to take over an administrative job elsewhere. This seemed part of the policy and British Officers who had volunteered to stay on and see India through her initial troubles were optimistic in thinking that they would be left in their own commands. A similar case in Pakistan had caused a little local stir. The Brigade Commander of either Bannu or Kohat, having volunteered to stay on, was sitting one morning in his office when a young Pakistani Officer with his wife arrived to take over his bungalow, announcing that he himself was assuming the rank and the command, while the British Brigadier would be a sort of second in command, with the rank of Colonel.

Hardly had Brigadier Salomons got his marching orders when he got a signal intimating the early arrival by air of Lady Mountbatten and staff on an inspection, and that she would require a guard. Although this guard was the only way in which the military were to be involved, it was plain to Salomons that the local Deputy Commissioner would not have a clue as to what to do, and I was asked by him to find out what needed doing and then get the DC to do it.

Lord Mountbatten had resigned from the position of Viceroy on the assumption of Independence by the new India and by Pakistan. He had, however, accepted the appointment of Governor General of India but not of Pakistan, a decision which gave great offence to the latter country, savouring as it did of taking sides. We were now in India, and what should have concerned the Civil Authorities was that the wife of the Governor General must be housed and treated in a manner calculated to maintain the prestige of her office in Armitsar and the Eastern Punjab.

The DC was eventually run to earth and, since these officials knew that British Officers visited their offices only to urge more work upon them, he took a little finding. I did not expect to meet anyone of the calibre of the last DC I had known in Amritsar, Penderil Moon, a fellow of All Souls, nor did I. He was naturally polite, like all his race, but it proved impossible to discover what, if any, instructions he had so far received.

This interview got us nowhere, but the arrangements had to be made quickly. However secret the daily programme might be, Lady Mountbatten and her staff still had to eat and sleep, and since I was providing the guard, I obviously had to know where to send it. Where would they be staying? He could not say. Where had he in mind for them? He would find somewhere. I was not yet seriously alarmed; we had a good forty-eight hours before the planes touched down and, with the enormous manpower that India provides, most astounding performances can be achieved; the machinery must, however, be set in motion, and that immediately.

I started running over a list of things that must be done, suggesting that there might be some little point that he had not fully appreciated in the short time at his disposal.

Firstly, he must provide a house; this should be simplicity itself, since every Government Department maintains a house in every Civil Lines to accommodate its inspecting officers, all furnished and with a resident caretaker.

The next essentials were a staff of trained servants, food, fuel and all the rest of it. Leaving the domestic arrangements, I passed on to the necessary briefing of the police he would have to produce, and as fast as I outlined the arrangements I kept on thinking of others: reliable cars, chauffeurs, provision of sufficient petrol, messengers who knew where important people lived. The DC, however, looked as if he had heard enough. I closed the interview and left not exactly full of confidence, promising to return in the cool of the evening to see how things were getting on.

Returning rather before the time I had said, I just caught him scuttling off somewhere and was gravely informed that all arrangements had been completed. This sounded too good to be true which, of course, was the case. The proposed accommodation turned out to be somewhere called the Amritsar Hotel. I had never heard of an Amritsar Hotel, unless it was a place situated in the bazaar quarter of Amritsar and, as far as I can remember, out of bounds to British troops. It did not sound at all suitable.

'What about the Public Works Department Inspection Bungalow?' 'No, that is too small.' 'Why not the Canal Department Rest House?' 'No, that is too far away.' 'Then why not the Judicial Department Circuit House?' 'That is being lived in by the wife of a High Court Judge, a refugee from Pakistan; there are ladies in all the bungalows and they will not move.'

The Amritsar Hotel it had to be, so there I repaired for a look round. I at last found the place: a low dirty white building, sprawling in a dusty refuse-littered compound and simply seething with people. Pushing through the mob and stepping over the body of someone asleep on the floor of the entrance hall, I approached a figure sitting in a broken down cane chair who stopped scratching himself to inform me that all rooms were occupied. This seemed self evident, and he further divulged that the hotel was now the headquarters of a Congress relief organisation.

Being conducted to the leader, a feminine acolyte of Mr Gandhi and explaining that the building was being requisitioned by the Deputy Commissioner for a few days for Lady Mountbatten, I received a purely non-committal answer. The lady was obviously unprepared to budge. I watched her ruminating a little, presumably on the subsequent reaction of the Mahatma. I thought it judicious to remark that Lady Mountbatten was coming in connection with relief work, which rather put her on the spot since our conversation was in public. Giving way, she graciously promised to relinquish four out of the eleven bedrooms, while the dining room and the lounge could be shared by all. This seemed about the best I could achieve without powers of authority and, scandalous as the whole business was to my old fashioned ways of thinking, I could only accept that this was the new way of doing things.

Were anything to happen, I should no doubt be the scapegoat, but what an extraordinary set-up with no Police screening, no CID and no passes. Domestic arrangements could hardly be worse. A filthy hotel, dirty servants, a terrible cook, inadequate furniture, no modern sanitation, no privacy. What a dreadful reception for any woman.

The party arrived and, with the briefest pause for refreshments, started off on a whirlwind inspection. This went on for four whole days during which time every revolting sight must have been seen, every nauseating smell smelt; she must have had nerves of steel. I am not in a position to know what was or could have been achieved, but the refugees were at least given positive assurances that the highest in the land were deeply sympathetic with them in their troubles. As the time came for me to watch the aeroplane disappearing over the tops of the trees I was filled with admiration for what had been a very courageous effort.

I too was glad that someone of importance could pass on information of what was going on in Amritsar. We, no doubt, had a Divisional Commander somewhere, but neither he nor his staff came anywhere near us. I later had the same complaint from our Depot Commander at Bakloh whose superior Commander refused to answer letters or get in touch in any way and seemed to have ceased to exist. The explanation was, of course, the universal disorganisation with which the very new and very young Indian Commanders were, as yet, unable to cope; one can sympathise with them.

XXI

Farewell, Punjab

So far I had little time at my disposal to see what was going on outside my immediate vicinity, so I took the opportunity after everyone had settled down to their duties to visit our Second Battalion who were in camp near the Beas bridge some nineteen miles down the Grand Trunk Road.

Apart from the desire to get a little fresh air, I wanted to find out their actual work which we might shortly find ourselves doing, as they were engaged in convoy protection duties. The prospects of fresh air even out there seemed slightly dubious, as their CO had warned me to bring along my respirator, and he as an ex-POW in Japanese hands might be expected to have become inured to stench. It was as usual necessary to move armed and tactically, since there had been rather too many desertions of State Forces troops who had stolen lorries and light automatics and who were known to be making a good thing out of escorting rich refugees to the border and were not above ambushing single vehicles for loot.

I had known this road well in the dear old days. As a subaltern in Jullundur I used to keep a horse in Lahore, and on Saturday afternoons was in the habit of driving in the eighty odd miles, dancing until two in the morning, getting up at five to hunt, lunching at Faletti's Hotel to the strains of the Police Band and somehow driving back on Sunday evening. Long and straight it was sheltered in most places from the sun by a double row of trees and one motored along in the sharp air, watching the glowing green bee-eaters sitting in pairs on the telegraph wires and listening to the whistling of the grey partridges among the crops on either side.

Today, however, even though we were very soon forced to put on our gas masks, we saw enough through their eye-pieces to confine our attention severely to the ribbon of tarmac. Once we had got clear of the city the countryside was one vast charnel-house; at intervals of a few yards along each side of the main road and out in the neighbouring fields lay some stinking atrocity; men, women, children, oxen and buffaloes lay singly and in little groups where death had taken them in the preceding weeks. Vultures waddled about pecking and tearing aimlessly here and there, too gorged to fly, village dogs snarled and growled but could not be bothered to fight over grisly heaps of rags from which limbs stuck out grotesquely. Along here was our Second Battalion area.

The Second Battalion told us that convoys composed of about twenty thousand refugees with one thousand bullock carts were being marshalled a few marches beyond the bridge and were passing through twice a week; while en route they had to be guarded day and night from armed gangs of Sikhs and Hindus who were constantly trying to attack them; very many of the refugees were already in the last stage of exhaustion and, together with the very old, the very young and the sick, added to the quota of bodies which were left lying in the camping areas every morning when the convoys moved off and which had dropped along the roadside by day. Where they fell they died and where they died they rotted.

The troops were having a bad time as they had been marching nineteen miles a day in the dust and the heat four times a week for the past several weeks, while every night there was nothing else but to sleep within smell of the corpses of the night before last, and last week, and the week before that. The job, too, was unrewarding; the marching troops were quite insufficient to guard the whole length of the long unwieldy convoys which, as may be imagined, spread themselves across the entire width of the road and up and down it for miles, while the dozen or so Battalion Jeeps found themselves driving along in bottom gear jammed in among the convoy. From the time of hearing distant screams five minutes might elapse before the nearest troops could get to the scene only to find a fresh bunch of victims sprawled, hacked and twitching in the dust; only on rare occasions did Sikhs or Hindus show themselves as they ran away through the tall crops in which they had been hiding awaiting their chance, and then the nearest Gurkha Jeep driver would turn his vehicle off the road and go bounding at full speed across the rough fields, the Bren Gunner in the seat beside him firing as they went.

Railway protection seemed unpleasant enough but this road convoy protection for which our turn would come in due course might prove even worse.

Back at our Brigade Headquarters, 'morning prayers' (our daily order groups) were in the best battle tradition; the place, too, had the right atmosphere, for one day a tank driver maintaining his tank only a few yards away was suddenly shot by a sniper. The Battalions not engaged in refugee protection were busy guarding the new border, in many cases a purely arbitrary line across the map which was not easy to pick out on the ground, and were very nearly at war with their opposite numbers. At Waga by the canal bridge where the Grand Trunk Road now crosses the border the opposing troops had little to do but sit in slit trenches wearing their steel helmets and shake their fists at one another, but out in the country, where the peasantry were not slow to take advantage of the situation and were making nightly cattle raids into each other's villages, things were different. The happy yells of the raiders mixed with the imprecations of the raided would soon attract the attention of the opposing military patrols, who, hastening to the scene to restore order, would bump into each other in the dark, shots would be exchanged, reinforcements called up and daylight would disclose every sign of a brisk little battle.

One day I decided to cross the border and have a decent meal at the Punjab Club. Passing through the Indian front line and driving for about fifty yards with what appeared to be every weapon of both sides pointing unpleasantly near us, my Jeep was stopped by a road block of very cheerful and polite Pakistani troops from the 10th Baluch Regiment who said that they were still commanded by a Colonel Baker, an old acquaintance of mine, and that I had better go and take lunch off him.

Directly we crossed the border I noticed a difference, beside the road were not fields of stinking corpses but huge mass graves into which, so I heard later, the bodies had been shovelled by Pakistani bulldozers. Just to the North of the road was a whole forest of little tin bivouacs consisting of two sheets of corrugated iron bolted together at the top, hardly commodious but at least offering some protection from the wind and rain, a provision which was totally lacking on the Indian side.

Dropping my driver and escort with a Battalion of the 8th Gurkhas who were still on the Pakistani side of the border, I made for the club which I found packed with resident Europeans, many of whose jobs had vanished but who had been retained for refugee work and who had given up their houses and sent their wives home.

Most of the civilians had undergone unpleasant experiences. Grey, formerly in the Gurkha Parachute Bn. with me, now the Amritsar Manager of the Imperial Tobacco Company, had been cycling to his office after breakfast one morning when, rounding a corner, he had nearly run into a large Sikh methodically slicing a Mohammedan youth to pieces with a sword.

General Arnold, a retired Sapper, out from home to help with refugee relief, had been dozing in his carriage at a station outside Delhi, when he suddenly saw a figure take a flying leap from the next compartment over the heads of the crowd on the platform who thereupon started chasing him: he was very surprised to hear that it was not a pick-pocket but a Mohammedan and sorry to see him being killed a few fields away. One of the canal engineers, driving up a canal road with an 8th Gurkha escort had been furious to see a crowd of men tipping the contents of a couple of large bullock carts into his precious canal and, hastening up to remonstrate, had been horrified to find that they were laughing and tipping out the bodies of slaughtered and mutilated women and children. So it was with all of them, each had been witness of some nasty scene which he was unable to forget.

It was very nice to gossip at the bar. I was told in a secretive whisper by a total stranger that he had just had a letter from General Lockhart in Rawal Pindi who had said that the 4th Gurkhas had been wiped out in the Shahur while coming down from Wana, nor would he pay any heed to my plaintive interjections that this was not the case and that I was the CO.

I also heard from a more reliable source that as a direct result of our little trouble, the 1st Gurkhas had been escorted down from Landi Kotal in the Khyber Pass by all the troops available in Peshawar and by His Excellency The Governor, Sir George Cunningham, himself.

Settling down to read the daily papers which I had not seen for a few weeks my eye was immediately caught by a paragraph in the current edition of the *Civil and Military Gazette*, the paper on which Kipling had worked, which complained bitterly of the gross excesses of the troops on the Indian side of the border who spent their time pillaging refugees and had, in this case, on a train between Amritsar and Waga looted them of eight hundred sewing machines and three thousand silver watches. This was really too much, so, after lunch, I went down to the erstwhile Residency, now the Public Relations Office, where it did not take long to discover that this report had been officially released to the newspaper on the evidence of one excited refugee without any attempt at corroboration whatsoever. I was just warming to my work of giving the Officer-in-Charge (some newspaper man in the uniform of full Colonel) a little homily on the crass iniquity and gross stupidity of issuing untrue stories calculated to inflame communal passions and make still harder the jobs of people who were trying to get the place back to normal, when in walked a smartly dressed Pakistani, so I had the pleasure of repeating my words to the Minister!

Next I called in at dear old Government House to pay my respects to Sir Francis Mudie, the British official appointed by the Pakistan Government as Governor of the Western Punjab.

Some of the old Mohammedan servants were there, but the place seemed very strange without the Hindus. The Sikh orderly who could walk on his hands had been replaced by a Punjabi-Mussulman who gave me a very smart salute with his left arm — he had left his right at El Alamein; the fat, courtly old Ram Badal, the chief of the tent pitchers who looked like a Hollywood Rajah; Ganpat, the chauffeur, and the rest had all gone off to the new India and were now God knew where; the tower of strength, Akhtar Hussein, the ADCs stenographer who knew the whole Table of Procedure by memory, was very down in the mouth; it seemed that he had invested his life savings in real estate in Amritsar and had now lost the lot and would be murdered if he returned to make enquiries.

The Personal Staff were engaged not on ceremonial nor on entertainment but on refugee work. They were suprised that the place should have been so badly furnished in our day, and taking me round pointed out that there were no curtains in this room no carpet in that, terribly worn out cretonnes in a third and so on; it was obvious that the previous Superintendent, a Hindu, had spirited away, perhaps stolen, most of the nicer things during the hot weather when the late Governor, Sir Evan Jenkin, and his staff were in Simla.

Returning to Amritsar, I was within the next few weeks visited first by General Sir Roy Bucher, then or a little later Commander-in-Chief, who was extremely appreciative and helpful; our next visitor was Lieutenant General Sir Dudley Russell who was not quite so cheerful; I did not know what he was doing there either, but later was told why he had little to be cheerful about. It seemed when our old friends the Mahsuds and South Waziristan Wazirs, together with some Mohmands and Swatis from the Malakand had entered Kashmir to assist their co-religionists, they started by massacring a few nuns in a convent and then moved on to Srinagar, the capital. The

Maharajah of Kashmir had then abdicated and asked for military assistance from India to prevent a further massacre. It fell to General Russell to organise a brilliant air lift which deposited Indian troops in Srinagar from where they spread out as far as they were able over Kashmir. This seizure of Mohammedan Pakistan by Hindu troops sent by Mr Nehru's Government was altogether too much for Mr Jinnah of Pakistan but the latter had no troops to spare and had to be dissuaded from weakening his main front down in the plains where lay the main threat to the whole of Pakistan.

This seizure of half Mohammedan Kashmir by India may be compared with advantage to the situation in Hyderabad in South India where a Mohammedan ruled a state whose subjects where mainly Hindu. Refusing to be bullied by India who insisted that he give up his state and sack his British Prime Minister (Tony Davy, an old friend of my ADC days), the Nawab despatched his little Mohammedan army in a gallant effort to stop the invading might of India, to have it annihilated by tanks and aircraft.

One wondered what would happen once this blood bath and the Kashmir question were over and finished with. Was the withdrawal of British power the signal for the new Governments of the country to revert permanently to the laws of the jungle? What would be the eventual influence on their countries of some of these good Officers and very decent fellows who had lived with us and been trained by us, of which my Sikh Brigadier was an excellent example? Would they pass on Western ideas or would they eventually be swamped? How about some of those educated and accomplished ladies of whom Dinah Jinnah was so soignée and delightful a specimen, Dinah who before the war had just returned from being brought up and educated in England and finished in France and who was determined to do her level best for her country?

One felt that social standards would be maintained among the upper classes and that many European ideas had come to stay for good. Have not the Romans left Britain over fifteen hundred

227

years ago but are we not still clinging to their legal system and many of their customs?

I was then and am now quite unqualified to forecast the political futures of either India or Pakistan.

It was, however, December 1947, I was still in Amritsar and as the weeks passed I got more and more sick of the sights, the smells, the bloated, crawling flies, the all-pervading atmosphere of hopelessness and misery to which there seemed to be no end. On my infrequent visits to Lahore I would be infuriated by the air mail copies of the British daily papers which reported the self-congratulatory speeches on their handling of India by Government Ministers who must have either been very ignorant or very dishonest.

When one reflects that the biggest mass migration in the history of the world was preceded not by months of planning by trained and adequate military staff; nor advised by senior members of the Indian Civil Service who, even if they had already retired, would have been pleased to return and round off their life's work; when one realises that this mass migration was preceded by the sudden exodus, not only of British key men in all departments, but of their British subordinates and staffs for whom Indian replacements were virtually non-existent; when one is very forcibly made conscious that in place of co-operation between two countries in the interest of all their people, there was nothing but suspicion, violence and diplomatic deadlock, then one ceases to wonder at anything that one saw. Even if one does not say 'I could have told you so' one does not cease to blame those guilty men who allowed this to come about.

What was there now to keep me? I felt very tired; my spine never stopped aching; my Battalion was no longer in any danger of being cut off and decimated; my keen young second in command was longing for the privilege of being able to command for just a week or two pending the arrival of an Indian CO and Officers; I had done what I could to ensure that seven of my eight Officers achieved their ambition of getting regular commissions and joining Her Majesty's Gurkhas in Malaya, which, in fact, they did, only one preferring to come home to the University; there was nothing more I could do for anyone by staying.

I must now go and search for a new home, a new life, new friends.

Looking back, it can be argued that the life of a British Officer of the Indian Army would not have suited everyone but it is very sad that no one else can ever sample it. It may sound pompous to suggest that the loss is mutual. I hope we gave good value.